SOMETHING
WICKED
WAITS

J.E. JACK

To Porkchop, your passing has left a huge hole in my life, but I'm grateful that you had a chance to read this before you left.

And to Ray Bradbury, whom I never met but whose stories sparked the creative fire of my own.

ACKNOWLEDGEMENTS

I've never included an acknowledgement page with my books before, but this book would not have been possible without the help and guidance of two people. When I first got the idea for this book, I reached out to all that I knew who might have any information regarding carnivals. Alieta Sampley with "The Thrillville," answered and initially helped me with this project by pointing me in the right direction. And if you ever need to go experience a great carnival, be sure to get with Alieta and her crew at www.thethrillville.com.

Also, as always, my wife and editor, Marcel. Without her, none of my books would be possible.

CONTENTS

1

— • —

"I understand," the man said. "Are you sure? We've been coming to your town for a few years now and you've always had a spot open for us before. Is everything all right?"

A few moments went by as the man listened. The sweat on his forehead beaded up, which wasn't entirely due to the heat of the mid-summer day, as the frown on his face opened up to reply, "I appreciate you offering a spot next year, but we really need the full route this summer if you're gonna see us next year."

"I see," the man said after a few more moments, then he hung up the receiver and left the phone booth to join his wife at a nearby table.

"Everything okay?" she asked, but she could tell from the way he moved that things weren't. They had traveled together for so long and stayed in such close quarters that they could read each other like a book.

"No, things aren't good. That's the second town that's cut us from setting up. We have a couple more spots coming up, but if things continue on this way and they also cancel, I'm not sure how we're gonna pay everyone and keep people fed."

"Are they giving us back our deposit money?" she asked.

"Yeah, but that's not the point. If we don't generate enough cash this summer, we won't have the money to secure locations next year...and the deposits we get back from the towns that canceled will only go so far. It'll barely cover the gas for all the trucks to get there. You know that."

"I know, but if they give our deposits back, at least we have that."

"Well, of course, honey," the man snapped, "but, like I said, that's not the point. The point is that the deposit won't cover our costs and we need more money."

As soon as the words left his mouth, he regretted them. His wife was only trying to help, and taking out his frustrations on her wasn't going to accomplish anything.

"I'm sorry. I didn't mean to come across like that. I'm just worried," he said.

The weight of the world seemed to rest heavily on his shoulders, so much so that they slumped. He inherited the traveling show from his father, who had been dead for eight years, God rest his soul. There were tough times in the past and he had, on occasion, wondered why in the world his family had ended up doing the traveling show circuit. The stress of constantly being on the road in order to make ends meet, coupled with making enough money to keep it going the following year didn't help. His father passed away young at 58, and he couldn't help but wonder if the show was what put the final nail in his coffin.

The man looked at his wife and he could feel the anxiety and shame of the family business creep up—not shame about the business itself. When things were good, it was a lot of fun and it had been the only life he knew since he was a kid. But when it wasn't good, he felt that he should have never brought his wife, or anyone else, into it, not to mention his kids. It didn't happen a lot but when it did, it was miserable. The mere thought of affecting his kids made his feelings of anxiety much worse.

"It'll be okay, Bill," his wife said. "We've managed so far."

They'd been married for 15 years. They married young and what she said had always been true. They had managed so far, but there was a first time for everything. Like the rube who had never won a thing in his life, walking away from a game booth with a giant stuffed animal named "Binky" for his girlfriend—yep, there was a first time for everything.

Bill met Dani, his wife, when he became fed up with the carnival life after an argument (that he couldn't even remember anymore) between him and his father. He decided to try his hand at going to a junior college in upstate New York back in '78, but it didn't take long for Bill to realize that the academia life wasn't for him, either. He did, however, walk away with one good thing from the whole endeavor. To Bill, it was the best thing that had ever happened to him (when he wasn't momentarily frustrated); he had won the attention of a certain young lady who gazed at him now. When he heard of his dad having trouble keeping the show running, he felt compelled to return right away. He came back, and Dani refused to stay behind. Why Dani followed him, he didn't know, but he always liked to joke "my luck, her curse," which always got a few laughs from those he told it to—that is, except for Dani.

They married not long after, much to the frustration of her parents, who didn't want to see their daughter "run away with the circus," which Bill always thought was funny, because they had never been affiliated in any way with a circus. It was a traveling carnival, but he didn't expect a couple of suckers to understand, though he would never call them that in front of Dani.

He sat down on the bench next to his wife. "I guess I could always become a truck driver and haul other stuff besides rides," he said.

"Oh stop. It's not that bad. We still have the other towns on the route," she replied.

"But what if more cancel? I mean...I've almost never heard of this happening even once...but twice? It's un-heard of."

"Honey, they won't...and besides, if they do, we can pick a town and rent a lot," she replied.

"Maybe. I know we've done it before, but something about all this just feels "off." And...that's not something I really want to do. That's always in the grey area when it comes to the insurance, both for us and whoever we rent the lot from," he said thoughtfully.

"It'll be all right, Bill," she said again.

He looked at her and smiled. 15 years later and he was still in love with her. She always knew what to say to help him calm down when he was worried or frustrated. Even if it wasn't utterly profound—just the normal words that you say out of concern for another—it always worked coming from her.

"All right, well, we have a couple more nights here in Charleston. Let's hope we get some good news," he said.

They were currently in Charleston, Illinois. It was a small town in the central-eastern part of the state, whose claim to fame was home to the parents of Abraham Lincoln, more than a 150 years prior. The two towns that had canceled abruptly were Bloomington, Indiana and Shelbyville, just outside of Louisville, Kentucky; the carnival had been slotted to set up shop in those towns a little later in the summer. The next spot on the route was Harrisburg, Illinois.

Every traveling season, they generally took the same routes, bouncing around from town to town like a pinball—one to the next, usually hitting the same towns or others close by on the same general route each year. Traveling season started mid-spring and continued to mid-fall, roughly a little longer than half of the year. Things changed a little from time to time, obviously. For instance, last year, instead of going to Harrisburg, they detoured to the small village of Stonemill, not too far from Harrisburg, in southern Illinois. So that wasn't the issue. The issue was towns canceling at the last minute, and that worried Bill. They didn't usually do that. He couldn't help but think that maybe some fireball show had come in and stolen his business. He hated those fly-by-night, shady operations that preyed on reputable outfits, as well as their customers. They made a bad name for all traveling carnivals since locals don't know the difference.

What his wife said was right. They would survive. They always had, but it didn't make it easier. Her words would echo in his mind over the next couple of days, "It'll be all right, Bill."

They weren't the biggest traveling carnival, but they weren't a small outfit, either. They had about 40 people, a few large rides (including a Ferris wheel), and several food and game booths. And just like everything else in the world, it took money to run. Sure, the company had reserves but not enough to go a season without going headfirst into bankruptcy. People had to be paid, and the loans that they took out to buy those rides like the Ferris wheel, had to be paid, as well.

With that phone business done, they took the opportunity for a small break to rest a moment and talk about nothing important. Being on the road was rough. Some days felt like they were 38 hours long because when it came to the show, there was always something to be done or overseen in order to have a successful event. So, little moments like this one—just sitting with his wife and talking about nothing—were a treat. But no treat lasts forever, and it was time to get back to work.

Bill stood up first and offered his hand to Dani, who took it to stand. They both walked back toward their carnival, which took them by the entrance where the ticket booths were located.

"I still don't see why we haul that car around," Dani said.

"Huh? Oh, that," Bill replied as he looked at what she referenced. It was an old '58 Buick Special, two-toned in color with turquoise that ran along the bottom and white that ran along the top. His dad had had that car ever since Bill could remember, and although it looked like a million dollars on the outside, it didn't run. It sat on a trailer right near the entrance.

"I don't know. My dad always placed it there. Said some ballyhoo doesn't need to be spoken in order to get people interested in attending," Bill said.

"People don't care about that car. I mean...it looks nice, but it has nothing to do with bringing people to the show. I never understood why your dad was adamant about keeping it and placing it right there at every event, front and center," Dani said.

"I'm not sure. I guess it kind of became our symbol. It's our show because you see our car out front," Bill replied.

"Don't you think the billboards and advertisements tell people it's our show?" Dani asked.

"Well, yeah...but how many people really pay attention to who is behind the show...other than other carnies?" Bill replied. "Besides, Dad and I always had the conversation about fixing it up one day."

"We should just sell it," Dani replied. "Be one less thing to haul around."

"I can't do that. Besides, if we ever win the lottery, I will have the time and money to fix it up with Jason and Laura," Bill said, half-jokingly.

"You don't play the lottery and I don't think our kids are interested, even if you did win," Dani said, as her lips parted in a dazzling smile.

"They just don't know they'd be interested yet...speaking of which...where are our kids?" Bill replied.

"I'm not sure where Jason is, but I saw Laura earlier helping with the funnel cake booth," Dani replied.

"Isn't she a little young to do that?" Bill asked.

"She's 12—more than old enough to help out," Dani said.

"I know, I know...it's just hard to believe she's almost a teenager. It seems like just yesterday she was five. Time goes by so fast," Bill said.

"Well, if you spent more time with her, you might not be surprised at her age," Dani said.

That cut like a knife, though Bill knew she didn't say it to be mean. It was a fact and no matter how he felt about it, facts were facts. Running the show took a lot of work and he didn't always have quality time with the kids. Jason, being 14, now spent more time shadowing him but he was in that awkward stage. Thankfully, Bill didn't see the rebellious streak that he had displayed with his own parents in Jason—at least not yet. The whole family spent more time together in the off-season when they weren't on the road, but that only lasted a few months, then it was back at it again. The whole show was like a big family, and everyone wanted or needed him at different times—practically 24/7. Unfortunately, that didn't leave much time for his kids, or for himself, for that matter.

"Well, jokes aside, I can't get rid of that car. I don't know...every time I see it, it reminds me of my dad, so selling it is out of the question, unless, of course, we don't make any money this summer," Bill said, as the peculiarity of it all sneaked back into his mind. "On that note, I need to go talk to George and Brad and see if they have any ideas. Maybe they have some contacts that can help."

George Bronson and Brad Williams were the other two that headed up the show. George and his family oversaw the concession stands, while Brad and his family oversaw the gaming and other miscellaneous booths. Bill's responsibility was de facto leader of the outfit because he oversaw everything to do with the rides; since his dad ran the show before him, it naturally fell to him once he passed. Of course, the show had other temporary, seasonal sign-ons that would ply their trade for the season and share a set percentage of whatever they took in with the show. Bill remembered when he was growing up, a lot of those sign-ons were the crazy sideshows such as a man-eating chicken, or the bearded lady tents, but those kinds of acts dried up over time. Some of these sideshows remained, like Lady Zara's Fortune Telling, a genuine mitt show, otherwise known as a palm reader, that signed up almost every year to participate in the season.

Bill walked past the ticket booths and on to the midway, and although he had seen it for what felt like a million times, he still couldn't shake the excitement of seeing the carnival on full display. The lights, the sounds, the excitement—it was all there. That was why he truly never left. It was in his bones...and blood. It was more than that, though. After his father passed, he loved it even more because, although they didn't always see eye to eye, having things like that broken-down car out front and taking in the scene along the midway helped him to hold on to memories and connections. Some people had scrapbooks and photos. He may have had some photos, but Bill's scrapbook was the carnival.

He continued and walked to the backyard, a place that was reserved for sleeping quarters and management, to find George and Brad. They had a trailer that acted as a sort of command center that they called the HQ. On hot days, it was a welcome relief to walk through that door and into the arms of blessed cool air pumped out by the air conditioner. Thankfully, the insulation blocked out most of the noise from outside, but they could still hear the dim sound of power generators that kept the lights on and the air conditioner running.

"Hey Bill," George said upon seeing Bill enter the room. "Think we should send out the 24-hour man?"

"I'm not sure. Let's give it a day," Bill replied.

"Why? We usually send them out around this time...two days left before we pack up," Brad commented from his desk against the wall on the far side of the small room on wheels.

George and Brad not only had a stake in the carnival, but they also worked with Bill's dad before Bill took over. They were both at least 20 years Bill's senior, but for whatever reason, they followed his lead. George had a full head of brilliant white hair and Brad had short, salt and pepper hair that reminded Bill of a military haircut. They were sort of "night and day" from each other. George had a beer gut, probably from being over concessions, and Brad remained on the muscular side, since he used to be the main bruiser that kept everyone in line.

That was one another thing that Bill was thankful for—there were a lot of traveling shows out there that had questionable practices and unsavory people but his dad, with the help of Brad in the latter years, always kept a tight ship, meaning it was a well-organized business and a safe and entertaining place for families. George and Brad had the same idea. Everyone who worked for the show knew what they were there for—to entertain and to make money, but that money had better come honestly, with no outright and unwinnable gaffs at the game booths. Sure, there was slight bending of rules here and there, but outright thievery, dishonesty, and general troublemaking was not tolerated. If someone didn't fall in line with that, then they were quickly notified that they were no longer welcome to stay for the rest of the season. If a seasonal worker did stay for more than a couple seasons, they were part of the family, and it was a loyal one at that. It was the one thing that set them apart and one of the reasons Bill couldn't understand the last-minute cancellations; they put on a good and safe show where the odds of winning were fairer than other shows.

"I don't know. I just have this funny feeling and want to hold off a day before we send him," Bill said.

"What kind of feeling?" George asked, looking back up at Bill from the green record book he was working in.

"We got a cancellation," Bill replied.

"Another one?" George asked.

George and Brad looked at one another quickly and then back at Bill, who nodded. These types of cancellations didn't happen very often and neither man could remember the last time it had. George took the end of his pencil, licked it, and went back to work in the records book.

"Well, it's just one more town. We can make do without it if the rest work out."

"I'm not so sure, George; it was an impression I got when I spoke to the town representative. Nothing that I said seemed to matter. It was like talking to a brick wall. They were nice, but still acted like I wasn't part of the conversation," Bill said.

"Well, you can't win them all. Maybe we can extend a day or two, work some deals with the locals and then go to the following town early," Brad said.

"Maybe," Bill said, but he still had a funny feeling he couldn't shake.

2

It turned out that Bill's hunch had been right. The next day, just before he sent the 24-hour man out to find the next location and put out signs to direct the carnival convoy to it, his beeper buzzed on his belt. He looked at the number. He recognized it as the number of the contact in the next town, which wasn't unusual. Sometimes, there were last-minute adjustments, but the number caused a chill to run up his spine.

He shook his shoulders to get rid of the goosebumps and walked over to the pay phone that he used the day before. It was one of those booths with a blue hood that protected the phone from the elements but didn't do much for the customer beside provide shade if the sun was almost setting in the west. There was an angled shelf below the phone where an attached phone book was supposed to be, but it was missing in action. It looked as if someone had ripped it completely from the cable, as the end looked stretched and frayed. Its condition hinted at grief and sadness, but Bill didn't have time to dwell on how the state of the phone booth made him feel. He dug a coin out of the pocket of his faded and worn blue jeans, fumbled with it, almost losing it before he fed it to the phone and dialed the number.

The connection was not great, but Bill could hear it ringing through the crackled line. He wasn't sure anyone was going to answer and was about to hang up because he didn't want to lose the quarter for the call to go to an answering machine. When he reached to put his finger on the cradle to disconnect, he heard a voice answer, "Chamber of Commerce, Harrisburg. How may I help you?"

Bill didn't have his files in front of him, but he remembered that the contact was Mr. Mackey, who, although he worked for the Chamber of Commerce, also wore a different hat part-time. He was a member of the fair board and worked with carnivals, as well as the county commissioners, to organize and facilitate shows. Bill had dealt with him a time or two before, organizing the show in years past, so he asked the operator for him.

"One moment..." the voice indicated before clicking a button, and immediately Bill heard elevator music drift through the connection. It would have been something nice to listen to, but since the connection seemed to be bad, he heard crackles and the music sounded as if it was a warped record on a turntable. It sped up, slowed down, sped up, slowed down. The tempo came across as so unnatural that it would have given anyone who had heard it a disconcerted feeling.

Mr. Mackey came on the line and Bill could tell by the greeting that this would not be an advantageous call. Mr. Mackey wasn't what Bill would call a friend, but after several years of working together, it wasn't like Mr. Mackey didn't know how much he needed the business.

"Bill...I have some bad news," Mr. Mackey said.

"I've been getting a lot of that lately. What's yours?" Bill replied.

"I'm sorry to hear that, but we have to cancel this year's show," Mackey said. "I know it's tough to hear, but the damnedest thing happened yesterday. A summer storm popped up out of nowhere, rolled through, and heavily damaged the area where you were slotted to set up. We cannot safely have you at that location now, and there are no other available spots in town."

"Seriously?" Bill asked, dumbfounded. He felt his knees were about to buckle at the absurdity of the past week. His right hand on the phone receiver and his left hand grasping the corner of the phone booth were both quite literally white-knuckling from squeezing so hard.

"I know, it has to be a big wrench in your plans, but don't worry, we'll be ready for you next year," Mackey said, his voice jovial, but it came across more like "I'm sorry, bud, but I still have to drive this knife into your chest."

Bill's mind reeled. He had never heard of a show being dropped like his was this summer. Even the worst show out there, which was full of convicts and questionable morals, still had places to go. Bill's show was out of options.

"Do you know anyone that can take us? I've had a few cancellations, Mackey. I don't know if we can survive if we don't find an alternative," Bill replied.

"I'm sorry. I'll ask around and see what's out there. If I find anyone that has a spot for you, I'll send them your way."

"Thanks, I really appreciate that," Bill said while stifling his emotions, then hung up the phone. This time, his wife wasn't at the nearby bench, and he had never felt so lonely in his life, save for the first few hours on his way to New York to start college many years before.

He'd have to get with the fixer and sometimes patch man, Jimmy Longford, to see if he could sweet talk the locals into letting them stay a couple of extra days. Jimmy could typically be counted on to smooth over jams and "fix" things with local authorities. A kind of schmoozer that gave people free tickets in order to avoid minor trouble, or offer money to avoid real trouble and to keep people off their backs. Bill hated to think of it as bribery but that's how the some of the backwoods towns and cities worked. It wasn't a good idea to stay in one place too long. One, interest waned after about a week and people would quit coming, so the opportunity to make money became less with each passing day. And, the longer they stayed in one place, the more it brought the kind of people you didn't want to show up—the kind that start fights or look for insurance claims. If you keep on the move, you generally avoid those undesirable situations, but if you stay around, people get creative because your mere presence is a reminder that prods them into action, eventually.

It took him 20 minutes, but he found Jimmy near his RV, sitting out front in a lawn chair, having a beer with his lunch. When he saw Bill walking up, he yelled "Hey, boss. Whatcha need?" with his mouth full, then quickly took a swig from his beer can to wash it down.

"Don't have too many of those," Bill said, pointing at the beer. "We still have a long day ahead of us."

"You know me, Bill. This won't slow me down none. But you didn't walk all the way over here for that. What can I do you for?" Jimmy asked.

"I need you to see if we can stick around for a bit longer here."

"What's wrong? Next spot have a problem?" Jimmy asked.

Bill wanted to tell him the situation, but at the same time, he didn't want the word to get out. Then he would have a whole bunch of people worried. That kind of uncertainty was like cancer. It spread and festered if you didn't take care of it quickly. Much better to not let it start to begin with.

"No problem, but a conflict with the route for the next spot. We just need to stay here a couple extra days if we can," Bill said.

"You got it, boss," he said, and guzzled down the rest of the can before standing up to go grease whatever hands needed to be greased. Normally, dealing with location representatives was his and Dani's job, but over the past couple of years, Jimmy had really shown a talent for making things happen that wouldn't have happened had he not been involved. He hated to say it, but Jimmy was better at wheeling and dealing than he was, so instead of being intimidated by his talent, Bill encouraged Jimmy for the benefit of the show.

Coming back into the main area, he saw Jason, his son, reading the midway with his head down, looking for change, dollars or any other sort of valuables that had been dropped on the ground, oblivious to everything around him. Bill walked over and surprised him with a hug from behind and yelled, "Gotcha!"

"Dad! What are you doing?" Jason said, his body squirming to be let go.

Bill let go after a moment and looked at his son. "Scared ya, didn't I?"

"No...well, maybe a little. But Dad...don't do that. It's embarrassing," Jason said.

"For who? Everyone here knows us. Why would you be embarrassed?" Bill asked.

"Not everyone," Jason said.

"Who...townspeople? Who cares what they think? They think we are all a bit loony tunes and don't like our kind anyway," Bill replied. "Aren't you supposed to be helping Tom with some of his rides?"

Tom Starling was Bill's right-hand man when it came to the ride component of the show. He wasn't sociable, and

Bill suspected that had something to do with his cleft lip scar. Tom had been with them since before Jason was even born. He started out as a ride jock, then worked his way up to managing all the rides, including setup, breakdown, maintenance, etc. He was good at it too, as he was very efficient at keeping things moving...but horrible at keeping two cents in his pocket. He was always broke. Bill trusted him, though.

"Yeah, but he gave me a little break, so I thought I might be able to find some cash or something," Jason said.

Bill couldn't fault him; it was a pastime for everyone that worked the circuit. You'd be surprised at what gets left behind by or falls out of the pockets of carnival-goers. Last year, Jason found a crisp 20-dollar bill, just lying in the dirt. Since then, he was hooked on keeping his eyes on the ground during free time, and well, all the time during a show. The unspoken rule for the folks that worked for Bill, including his son, was if you found it and no one was there to claim it, finders keepers, but if you saw it drop from someone, you'd best let them know they dropped it. Bill wasn't exactly a religious man, but he wanted to do right by whatever was out there. His dad had been the same way, and he hoped he would pass on this trait to both of his kids.

"All right, son. Have you seen your sister?" Bill asked.

"I think she's at the funnel cake booth," Jason responded.

Even though Bill had a thousand things running through his mind, the comment from Dani continued to ring loud and clear. "Well, if you spent more time with her, you might not be surprised at her age..." He knew he needed to make more of an effort to spend time with her. She wasn't getting any younger, and the apathetic teen years were right around the corner. He could see the booth clearly when he made the corner onto the main thoroughfare that split the carnival in two. Usually, the concession stands were first followed by game booths and shows, followed by the rides, with the Ferris Wheel at the back, like a mountain overlooking the village below. It was the best way to get people to experience the whole show by having them see everything else by the time they arrived at the rides, which is what really brought the crowds in the first place.

The booth didn't sell only funnel cakes, though that was the main selling point, as it was advertised in a banner over the window. The booth itself had the patriotic colors of red, white, and blue. It gave off a clean and open look with windows on all sides. Bill didn't even like funnel cakes, but the smell was tempting, even after all the years he'd been exposed to them. When he got closer, he saw Laura was at the window, taking orders. He didn't want to disturb her, but then she saw him and squealed, "Dad!"

Bill waved at her and waited in line, which only had one person besides him. When the person in front of him left, he walked up to the window.

"What will it be?" Laura asked, very professional, with a toothy smile.

"Oh...um...I will have a moment of your time, if it's not too expensive," Bill said playfully, returning his own smile.

"That will be five dollars," Laura said, then quickly added "Just kidding," letting out a little giggle.

And in a dash, she disappeared from the window and quickly reappeared from around the corner and at his side with her arms around him.

"Hey, kiddo," Bill said, then looked back into the booth and yelled, "Hey Brenda, I'll have her back in a moment."

Brenda, who was George Bronson's daughter, was around 40 and waved a hand in acknowledgment. "Take your time, but don't take away my best worker for too long."

To Bill, Laura's smile seemed to grow a little wider at the compliment.

"You staying out of trouble?" Bill asked.

"Dad, come on," Laura said, as she rolled her eyes. "With so many eyes on me since I'm your kid, I don't think I will ever get into trouble without you knowing."

And that part was true. The carnival was akin to a small village, in that everyone took part in taking care of one another, whether or not it was wanted, especially the kids. The world was a tough place full of not-so-nice people. Most carnies understood this because they had, at some point in their lives, had dealings with bad people, which caused them to pinball into the carnival life. Hence, the reason that pretty much most, if not all of them, looked out for the kids that traveled with the show. There weren't a lot of kids that were with the show full time, as most of the current workers were older or didn't have kids. Those who did usually traveled without them, or at most, would bring them on for a couple weeks here and there. Bill's kids were always on the route with them and most times, they didn't have other kids their age to hang out with. When Bill was growing up, it was the same—they all looked after their own. Wherever his parents traveled, he was there, and with so many eyes on him, there was nothing he could get away with it. His dad always found out whatever it was he wanted him not to know. So, he understood where she was coming from.

"That's the joys of being the boss's kid, I guess," Bill said.

"You don't understand how annoying it is," Laura replied.

"If only she knew," Bill thought to himself. "I think I have an idea, but can't change things now, can we?"

"So, what do you want? You don't usually come see me in the middle of the day," Laura remarked.

"I saw your brother earlier and thought of you, so I wanted to make sure you were okay— that's all," Bill said.

"Oh...okay...well...thanks, but I really need to get back and help Brenda. She is showing me how to get people to add more stuff to their orders!" she said excitedly with a grin that would have given the Devil a run for his money.

He watched her run and thought about her future. For that matter, he thought about Jason's, as well. Would they continue in the business? They made good grades and adapted well. Since they were on the road so much, the kids were home-schooled half the time. He had to give Dani most of the credit for doing such an excellent job of sharpening their brains.

Something caught his eye further down the midway, near the section for gaming booths. He saw one of the relatively new carnival workers, a guy by the name of Peter Thorston. A tall, blond kid, early twenties, with long, stringy hair and a neck tattoo of a rose. He had apparently rolled in from out west somewhere a couple of years ago. He didn't really know where he went during the off season and honestly, he didn't care, as Bill didn't really like the guy. Despite this fact, Brad swore by him and said that he was good at barking people into whatever game booth he was running, so he kept him on the past couple years. In the world of the traveling show, two years' employment basically still made him a temp. He was a trouper, for sure, but he'd have to be with the show a couple more seasons before he was really considered a permanent fixture. His status was a step above a townie, who was basically a day laborer, because at least he was here regularly and working. The show would protect him if there was trouble from outsiders, but he wasn't truly part of the "family" yet. In Bill's experience, people like Peter showed up for a couple of years, then moved on. Whatever the case was with the guy, Bill didn't like the current look in Peter's eye. He was staring way too hard at a mark in front of him—a young couple, maybe mid-twenties, pushing a stroller. Nope, Bill did not like the look at all. It reminded him of a mountain lion stalking its prey. Bill walked toward him.

Since the show had been here most of the week and it was midday, it wasn't particularly crowded at the moment. It wasn't empty either, so there were many eyes that could witness whatever Peter was contemplating. He walked faster as he saw Peter act like he was yelling at someone behind him, then bumped into the man with the stroller. He then turned around, grabbed hold of the man's arm and apologized profusely. "I'm so sorry, man...I didn't see ya there," and stepped back. The couple shrugged it off. No harm, no foul. Then Peter disappeared into a booth.

Bill didn't see it, per se, but he knew that Peter had just pickpocketed that couple. He glanced around to see if anyone else noticed, but no one appeared to have. He picked up the pace and turned into the same booth that he saw Peter stroll into, which happened to be the air gun booth. There were a couple kids there plinking away, and he saw Peter talking with Mark McGee, a middle-aged man with a thick, red beard who had come from Chicago and started working with them a few years ago.

"Peter," Bill said.

"Yeah?" Peter replied.

"Can I have a word with you behind the booth, please?" Bill asked.

"Well, I'm kind of busy. Brad wanted me to..." Peter started.

"It wasn't a request; you and I need to have a talk." Bill could feel the anger building, and he knew his face was turning red. He could feel it. He could also plainly see that Peter was about to become ornery and Bill didn't want to cause a scene where customers could see. However, he would if he had to, even if it meant grabbing one of the air guns and clubbing Peter over the head. This was a civilized outfit, but Bill knew that sometimes a person had to be uncivilized in order to maintain a civilized environment.

Mark looked at Bill, then back to Peter and spoke up, "You better speak to the man, Peter. You don't know your place."

"I know my place. I belong here just as much as everyone else. I work my ass off for the little thanks I get in return," Peter snapped back at Mark.

Bill's hands clenched into fists as he stepped closer to Peter. "You are coming with me. We are about to have a come to Jesus meeting here in a minute, and we'll know exactly where your place will be."

Peter looked at Bill, and from the look of it, knew that he meant business. He looked at Mark for help, who only shook his head and went to help the kids reload the air rifles.

"Come with me," Bill said and turned without waiting to see if Peter followed. All Bill could think about was the Hell there would be to pay if he didn't. He walked to the small alleyway between booths and turned around, part of him thankful that Peter was at least smart enough to follow.

"I saw what you did, Peter," Bill said.

"I don't know what you're talking about, man," Peter said.

"First off, you will address me as sir, boss, Mr. Donovan, or just plain ol' Bill...heck, you can even call me "el jefe" if you like, but don't call me "man" like we're best buds. I saw what you did, and I don't keep a company like that. It causes trouble," Bill said.

"But I..." Peter began,

"Don't lie to me," Bill said.

"I didn't take nothin'," Peter said.

"I said don't lie to me," Bill reminded him.

"I didn't..." Peter began again, but before he could complete the sentence, Bill punched him in the face. This totally caught Peter off guard, as he was not expecting it. Peter was taller than Bill, and definitely younger, but Bill had been around the block a few times, so knew how to get rough and how to use his weight. Bill followed up the punch by grabbing Peter's arm and, using his body to spin him to the ground, where he crouched over him. Bill then patted him down and found the wallet that Peter took from the young couple. Once he found the wallet, he stood up and stepped back from Peter. He then threw the wallet so it landed right by Peter's face.

"I'm giving you two options. You can either return that wallet—and I might give you one more chance—or you can keep it and pack your shit," Bill said.

"You assaulted me...I could..." Peter tried to speak but was interrupted again.

"You could go to the police? You'd turn me into the police? Well, I have news for you. I don't think that's your driver's license in that wallet there. Just what do you think they'll do when I point that out? Here's the thing, Peter, in case you haven't figured it out. We're a family here and we protect each other. I run a tight ship because of that. It's one thing to change the odds to a game to win more than the rube...but outright thievery? People don't like our kind, anyway. We're outsiders everywhere we go and all we have is each other. You potentially ruining our reputation and my relationship at this location could really screw us next year...and all for what? For you to selfishly have an extra 20 bucks?" Bill said. He was hot, and he was doing everything he could to keep from shouting, but once he got on a roll, it was like a steam engine that had the valve fully open. He had to vent.

Peter lay there, looking up at Bill. "So, I'm giving you one more chance. You gonna give it back and tell them you found it or are you packing your bags? We don't have room for someone that doesn't put family first," Bill said.

Peter mumbled something, but Bill couldn't quite hear him.

"What?" Bill asked pointedly.

"I'll give it back."

"That's a good choice Peter...a very good choice." Bill offered his hand to help Peter to his feet. Peter reluctantly took it and stood up, then bent over to pick up the wallet. "Give it back and then get back to work. I won't give you another chance," Bill said, and left the alley. To Bill, the matter was over, so he left to focus on more pressing issues, like keeping the show running. He didn't give Peter any more thought, but that would change if he later discovered that he hadn't returned the wallet. Had Bill looked back as he was leaving, he would have seen the pure hatred reflected on Peter's face.

3

B ill walked into the manager's trailer, grabbed a water bottle from the small refrigerator, and sat down
wearily on one of the unoccupied open chairs. George
Bronson was there, tallying up food inventory in his green
record book, with a pencil. Brad Williams was nowhere to
be found.

"You know where Brad is?" Bill asked.

"He was here an hour ago. Said something about the
horse race game being down, so he was gonna go work on
it," George said. "Why? What's up?"

The horse race game pitted townsfolk, or players, against
one another. When the game started, all the horses were
lined up overhead, on one side of the machine. Up to
10 players had seats in front of their own personal lane,
in which they rolled balls, aiming for different holes at
the end of the lane. Each hole had a different number of
moves, which would reflect on the horse overhead. So,
the player that rolled the fastest and was the first to sink
the balls into the correct holes won the horse race. Bill

imagined it would take Brad a while to get that machine working again if it went down.

"Nah. It's nothing. I had to come to an understanding with one of the barkers that runs one of his booths," Bill said.

George looked at Bill's hand where the knuckles were bright red, and replied, "Uh huh... well, I hope he understood. Need some ice?"

"What?" Bill asked and then looked down at his own hand. "Oh no, it doesn't hurt, but we do have other problems."

George put the pencil down, clasped his hands, and waited for Bill to elaborate. Bill should have come here straight away after the last phone call, but seeing his kids was worth the momentary delay.

"The next spot canceled on us. I got Jimmy working with the locals to see if we can extend here a couple of days, but I'm not hopeful. We need to see if we can find any open parking lot between here and Missouri that will let us set up," Bill said.

George let out a sigh that doubled as a long whistle. "I don't think I've ever heard of a route getting canceled like this one has. It's like people suddenly don't want our money...or want us to make money for that matter."

At that moment, they heard someone stomp up the steps and open the door. Brad came in, his shirt wet from sweat.

"Brad, you're getting too old to be out there turning a wrench on a larry machine. Have one of your boys look into it," George said.

"If I did that, they would just make it worse," Brad replied.

"Oh, come on now...they can't break it any worse," George replied. "If it's broke, it's broke. All you're gonna do is harm yourself in this heat."

"I may be no spring chicken, but I still got a few good years left," Brad said, then looked at Bill. "Mind passing me one of those waters?"

Bill leaned back in his seat, reached over to open the refrigerator, and retrieved a water bottle to hand off to Brad. Brad continued to tell them about the larry machine, which, in carnie speak meant it was a broken machine.

"I looked at it and thought I'd figured it out, but after I worked on it some, I just can't get it to work. I may have to reach out to the manufacturer," Brad rambled before he twisted the cap off the water bottle and guzzled half of it down in an almost audible gulp before he finished. "Woooeeee! I needed that. What are you guys doing?"

Bill filled him in on what he had just told George, then they all sat there going round and round, brainstorming ideas. George ran his hand through his white hair a few times. Bill rubbed the whiskers on his chin and pursed his lips as they talked about the pros and cons and what ifs. It was always good to have a plan...and then a plan B, C, D, E, and F, if you could afford it.

At the end of it all, nothing had truly been decided except for what Bill had mentioned at the beginning of the conversation. They would try to extend here a couple of days to see if they could stretch until the next spot, and if that location canceled for whatever reason, beat the bushes for other spots that they could set up the show.

"By the way, Brad, now that we're done talking about this other stuff, I want to talk to you about Peter Thorston," Bill said.

"I heard. You found him with a wallet that wasn't his and he returned it," Brad replied.

"Oh, so he did return it. Good," Bill said. "I know we aren't choirboys here...and it's one thing to bend the rules a little to make some money. I know our people do that...but it's another to do things that will bring heat to the rest of us."

"Bill, you don't have to say anything more. I'm in agreement with what you did and...how you did it," Brad said, looking down at Bill's knuckles. "You'll not find me complaining."

"Good. Just wanted to make sure," Bill replied.

"Well, I'm going to have Dani call around and see if we can get some empty parking lots on standby if we end up not staying here. We still have two more days, but you never know...and with this summer going the way it's going...Let's not get comfortable," Bill said.

George couldn't help but chuckle. "When are we ever comfortable, Bill?"

"We never are, so don't start now," Bill smiled back, then left the trailer to go find his wife. At this time of day, she was probably at their personal trailer going over the accounts, which consisted of allocating funds for gas, paychecks, and other miscellaneous expenses. She liked to do this in their trailer instead of the one reserved for management where Bill had just come from. She found it distracting, with all the comings and goings, and she needed a quiet environment to go through the numbers. Bill couldn't blame her. He did, too, and sometimes it got a little loud in the HQ trailer.

"Hey, babe. What brings you back so soon?" Dani said quickly as she looked up from her desk.

"After you're done with that, would you look for some parking areas we can set up for the next week? We still have a couple of days, but we need to find something," Bill said.

A little frown crept up on Dani's face. "Another called, huh?"

"Yeah...but hey, I saw Laura today, and she was excited. Learning all about the upsell from Brenda," Bill said.

"Oh really. I bet she was happy to be doing that..." Dani replied and waited a few moments before adding, "Are you okay?"

"Yeah. I can't control things and I'm frustrated. You would think you would get used to it after all the years we've been at it, but this summer has been especially challenging," Bill said.

"Going over the numbers here and we're doing okay. We won't come out ahead, but we won't lose our shirts, as long as we keep the rest of the route," Dani said. "At least the bills will be covered."

Bill really wanted to reach into the cabinet for the bottle of Jim Beam that he kept there. He wasn't much of a drinker but every once in a while, when times were tough, he'd reach in there for a little "liquid feel good." He knew if he did this time, though, he wouldn't stop at one drink. The way he felt right now, he would have killed the entire bottle and that would not help at the moment. He sighed and sat down beside Dani.

"How are you doing?" he asked.

"I'm okay. Worried about you, though," she replied, looking at him.

"I'll be okay as long as I have you," he said and smiled. She had a twinkle in her eye and leaned over to give Bill a kiss, which he returned. The kiss was unexpected, but the feeling of warmth gave Bill momentary refuge and stoked a fire in his body. They continued to make out, enjoying the moment. Being on the road, they didn't have much "alone time" from the mere nature of the lifestyle, being so busy all the time. But every once in a while, they would sneak some in and to Bill, this looked like one of those times. He was about to suggest they head back to the bedroom when the door flew open, and Jason ran in. The building fire that stirred in his body immediately extinguished.

"Hey Mo...What are you guys doing? Ugh...gross!" he exclaimed. He was more embarrassed than anything, having caught them going hot and heavy.

Dani immediately blushed, and Bill thought to himself, "Well, so much for that" and replied to Jason, not the least bit embarrassed, "We're married, so it's okay. What do you need?"

"I...uh...I..."

"Spit it out," Bill said.

"I came to see if Mom knew where you were, but you're here so...anyway...I think there's trouble brewing near the gaming booths," Jason said.

Bill looked at his watch and noticed the time. It was now going into early evening and Bill felt like he hadn't done anything. Where did the time go? But he didn't have time to dwell on it. If there was trouble, he needed to go see what was going on.

"Okay, go get Brad and have him meet me over there. What did you see?" Bill asked.

"A few townies...and they don't look like they're here for fun," Jason said quickly.

Normal people would call the cops in this situation, but Bill knew from experience that calling the cops never worked out well for the carnies. They were easy to blame for whatever reason the local cops felt like giving. They were the more convenient scapegoat, no matter who initiated the conflict. That's why carnies took care of their own troubles and problems.

Bill left quickly, almost running to where Jason had said he last saw the group. He hoped Jimmy was around and maybe he had already defused the situation. Or Brad...or anyone...When he came into view, he saw no one had and the situation was broiling. It was a group of young jocks, probably from the local high school football team. They were more than likely teenagers who were bored and wanted to cause trouble. It didn't happen often, but when it did, it never ended well.

They stopped in front of the booth where Peter was working. Bill heard one of the group say, "There he is. That's the guy that stole from me yesterday."

Bill's heart sank a little because he knew that Peter probably did just what they were accusing him of, but unfortunately, since Peter worked for the show and as long as he had, Bill had to look out for him. Peter's face took on a deer-in-the-headlights look as the small group of accusers pointed him out, but quickly regained composure. Working for the carnival, a person had to be quick, so at least Peter had picked that up. The other families, innocent bystanders, and patrons of the show knew when they saw trouble and backed away from the commotion. "I better get this under control quick," Bill thought to himself.

"Are you sure?" one of the other teens asked the accuser.

"Of course I am. I was coming out of the 24/7 diner down on Main Street when this loser bumped into me. I didn't think nothing of it until I got home, and my wallet was gone...and the only person I had contact with was this guy. Of course, when I went back, he was nowhere to be found. But I came here with my little sister yesterday and spotted him."

By now, Bill saw other troupers quietly picking up items, such as pipes and heavy sticks that were like axe handles, to help if things escalated into a fight. The gang of teens didn't see any of this, but Bill did. The feeling in the air was electric, and it wasn't because of the flashing neon lights or the buzzing sounds of nearby games.

"That's right, you sleaze. You heard me. I want my wallet back and I want my money," the accuser, who was wearing a letterman's jacket, said.

"I don't know what you're talking about, man," Peter said. "I've never seen you in my life before. Get outta here."

"I'm not leaving without my wallet," the kid wearing the letterman jacket said.

"I'm warning you. Get out of here," Peter said, "Or there's gonna be serious trouble...for you."

"Bring it, punk. I'll beat the ever-living crap out of you. I see someone already punched you once today," the kid said.

"Look around you," Peter began and nodded to the other carnies who were nearby, standing ready.

"I don't care. I want my wallet and if these other people attack me, my dad's a lawyer and I guess I'll own a circus," the kid said in a cocky manner.

Bill broke in at that point and pulled out a side of him he didn't use too often—the showman. "A circus? Why...this isn't a circus, son. It's a place of wonder and beauty built to excite! A circus?! A circus is just a bunch of clowns and animals." Bill said this all while moving his hands with a flourish at all the rides and games around. "We are here to astound you! And give you joys like you've never known elsewhere. Now tell me—did you say that you lost your wallet?"

The sudden appearance of Bill took the kid in the letterman jacket aback, but then he remembered his friends, and at the mention of losing his wallet, he also remembered why he was there in the first place.

"Yeah, that asshole right there stole it!" the kid said.

"Oh, I'm sure there's some misunderstanding. I'm sorry that you're missing your wallet. I have an idea! How much did you have in your wallet?" Bill asked.

"He sto...huh...what?" the kid asked.

"How much was in your wallet?" Bill asked again, in his showman's voice that had a tone of leading excitement.

"I had about 30 bucks," the kids said.

"Ah...I have an idea. How would you like to play a game? I got one for you," Bill said as he saw the milk bottle toss behind the group of teenagers in front of him.

"And..." Bill said as he walked over to the booth. He pulled out four 20s from his pocket and placed them on the counter. "If you win, you'll get these four 20s and...you'll get a book of tickets so you and your friends can ride all the rides free for this evening. Since you lost your money, I hate to see you have that happen to you. What do you say?"

"But he stole it?" the kid said, which came out more as a question than a statement. He was not as full of vinegar as he had been a couple of minutes before.

"I'm sure it was a misunderstanding and besides, it might not have been him. I'm giving you the chance to more than double your money here and have a great night on the house...you know, for your troubles."

The kid wearing the letterman jacket was visibly torn; he was mad about having his wallet stolen but he really only had 20 bucks in there and the wallet was a five-dollar Velcro deal he could pick up anywhere. If he won, he would have more than enough to buy another. Bill saw that the kid wanted to be angry, but his eyes kept shifting to the greenbacks on the counter. The kid looked around one last time to see that his friends were eyeing the rides, so he agreed. "Okay, fine."

Bill looked around to see that the situation had been defused to the point that the troupers began to relax and put their pipes and other weapons away. "Step right up, step right up!" Bill said. He looked at the man behind the counter. It was Sam Millford. He'd been on the circuit with them a long time. Bill gave a knowing nod, and Sam nodded back to show he comprehended. Sam then reached below the counter, brought out six milk bottles, and went over to the stand to replace the milk bottles that were already set up with these new ones. The milk bottle toss was a game where the player had three chances to knock over the bottles, which were set up like a pyramid. Of course, the game was rigged a little—the bottom bottles were slightly heavier, making it more difficult to tip them over. A player could still win if they knew where to throw the ball, so Bill didn't really consider it cheating. But with the nod that Bill gave to Sam, Sam replaced the weighted bottles with regular bottles, which would ensure a win pretty much anytime someone threw it, as long as the ball hit one of the bottles.

Bill picked up the money and flourished to the crowd, waving it in the air and then placing it back down on the counter with his index finger stuck right in the middle of the stack of four 20s. "Come see the young man with a cannon for an arm folks! Watch him knock over these bottles and win the prize!"

Might as well stroke the kid's ego while he was at it, Bill thought to himself. The last thing he and the show needed was any issues with the locals that would cause them to be run out of town.

By this time, the crowd that had previously vacated the area because of possible trouble brewing, returned like moths to a flame. There was something going on here and they wanted to watch. Bill's eyes scanned the area from the kid to the gathering crowd. He saw Jimmy step up with another gentleman, but since the light was fading, he couldn't see who it was. The only thing going through Bill's mind was, "hurry up kid, and get this over with. I really have other things to do and don't need this distraction." But as he saw the crowd grow, he saw the potential of increasing the odds they would spend more money after seeing this excitement...so maybe it wasn't a bad distraction after all.

The kid with the letterman jacket stepped up to the counter, with his athletic build and his friends backing him. There was no way he was going to lose this, and he knew it. The kid took on a predatory grin and grabbed the three baseballs.

The kid was taking it all in—basking in the glory of the moment. It was the kind of basking that would have been cute on a four-year-old, but not so much on a 16 or 17-year-old and only added to the obnoxious behavior that he had exhibited so far.

"Come on Frank, knock 'em down!" one of his friends called excitedly, but also impatiently. They wanted to hurry and get on the rides.

The kid, or rather, Frank, hefted the baseball in his hand and took aim. Bill watched it all in stride. Thank God it would be over momentarily, and they could all go on about their business. Then something strange happened. The kid wound up and threw the ball like a professional baseball pitcher. Even if the bottles had been weighted, a throw like that likely would have knocked them all down. The ball rocketed forward and right into the pyramid of bottles, and everyone knew—just knew—that the bottles would tumble right over...except they didn't. Bill couldn't believe it. He watched that ball slam right into the center and the bottles didn't budge, not even a little. It was as if the ball had smacked into a brick wall.

The crowd gasped in surprise. Bill looked at the ball that had rolled back to the front of the booth, then at Sam, who only shrugged his shoulders, but his face had the same look of astonishment that Bill was sure reflected on his own. He had to play it off, though, so no one would suspect anything. Bill said, "Tough break, kid...but you have two more chances...two more chances to knock those bottles over. Come one, come all. Come see Frank destroy these bottles!"

The crowd grew and Frank looked at the remaining balls in his hand, at the bottles, then at Bill. "This game is rigged. Those bottles should have fallen."

"I can most assure you it's not. Give it another try," Bill coaxed. In fact, if anything, it was rigged for the kid to win. He should have, but he didn't. Something that Bill couldn't explain was going on, and Bill felt it. He'd seen many strange things over the years, but this was different. If anyone ever asked him about it later, he wouldn't be able to articulate it, but he knew—somehow, he just knew—that no matter what the kid did, he would not knock over any of those bottles. The show was on, and the audience was watching. There was no backing down and just giving the kid the money, just to have them all move along. They were stuck in this charade now.

Not wasting any time, the kid readied another ball. Bill, meanwhile, was almost praying to himself, "please knock over the bottles, please knock over the bottles..."

The second ball struck even harder at the center of the pyramid and the same thing happened. The powerful throw didn't move the bottles even a fraction of an inch; they didn't even teeter. Bill felt sick. This isn't turning out at all like he had expected it to.

The kid was angry now. "This place is full of cheats."

The crowd, who had seen the throws, murmured among themselves. If this kid didn't knock over the balls on this last throw, everyone would walk away with the mindset that this carnival was a sham. People talk. They wouldn't be able to explain how the bottles stayed upright, but even if they could, they would walk away with one thing in their minds: how the carnival cheated this kid and made him look like a fool.

"One more. Go ahead and knock those bottles down," Bill said, somehow maintaining the showman's façade.

The kid just looked at Bill. There was a quiet fury on his face. The kind that was dangerous. If the kid had a knife, Bill was sure he would use it on someone.

Frank stepped up to throw his last ball. Bill begged quietly to God, Mother Mary, Jesus (and whoever else was listening) that the kid would knock the bottles over with his last ball. But even as he prayed out of desperation, he knew what the answer was going to be.

To Bill, time slowed down as the kid threw. He saw the ball leave his fingers. He could see the crowd and the kid's buddies' excitement rise with the throw. 80 bucks was on the line and that was nothing to sneeze at. The ball barreled through the air and into the bottles—and again, for the third and final time, there was absolutely no effect.

It was as if someone knocked the wind out of the entire crowd. The excitement and the spiraling uneasiness of what the crowd, including Bill, had witnessed, didn't match with what should have happened. Everyone became silent. The only things that could be heard were the "dings" and "zaps" from the nearby electronic games, and distant screams from the rides. At this booth, however, you could have heard a pin drop.

Then, from the throat of the kid with a pitcher's arm that should have won the game but didn't, came a litany of curse words and accusations. The crowd's murmur returned and crescendoed. Bill heard thunder in the distance that should have been drowned out by the noise in front of him. A low rumble as clear as day. Bill briefly lost himself but quickly realized that something needed to be said or done. All eyes—from Frank, the jacket-wearing, foul-mouthed kid with the bad attitude, to the crowd, to Jimmy and the person who had walked up with him, to even Sam behind the counter (who knew firsthand that the kid should have won)—were on Bill because they were all stunned.

Bill's focus came back and although he had missed most of the kid's stream of profanity, he realized that the kid was looking at him, expecting an answer. "Oh...uh..." then the showman took over. "Why, I'm flabbergasted, kid! I don't think I've ever seen someone fool that many people—me included—with such a throw. I've heard of trick pitches, but I've never actually seen one in real life! That ball looked like it was going a mile a minute but it must have been an illusion. Bet you strike out a lot of hitters with that type of skill and control! Have you played baseball all your life? For that, you win what I promised, because I'm seriously impressed!

Bill then looked around. "Isn't it astounding, folks! Let's give him a round of applause. What a show he put on!"

Bill knew what he said sounded lame, but with a little voice inflection and money-waving in front of the kid's face to disrupt his thoughts, he hoped it was enough to avoid trouble. He prayed that the kid, with the crowd clapping for him, would take the bait and just leave.

"I don't want your damn money. You cheated me," the kid screamed. "And for that, you're gonna pay. We're gonna wreck this place and there ain't nothing you're gonna be able to do about it. When my dad hears about this, he'll sue the shit out of you."

The tension that had subsided earlier was now back with a vengeance. The crowd, after seeing the kid lose and anticipating more trouble, had dissipated and started to scatter down the lane. A couple of bystanders remained to observe, as if they were watching a train wreck they couldn't turn away from.

"I did not cheat you, son," Bill began, but it went nowhere, as if it wasn't heard at all. The kid and his gang looked like they were about to start a fight. Sam reached under the counter and had one of the weighted bottles in his hand; he was ready to use it as a weapon if need be.

"Hold it there, Frankie," came a voice, which caused the gang to freeze. The voice came from the figure that was with Jimmy. They had both stepped forward to stand between Bill and the group of angry teenagers.

"Sheriff Bellview," Frank replied, stunned for a moment, then went on a rant. "Sheriff, these people cheated me. They need to be arrested."

Bill looked at the man. He wasn't wearing a uniform. He was wearing jeans, boots, and a button-up shirt—professional, but not a uniform. On his belt was a silver-toned, five-pointed star, right beside a large, holstered revolver.

"Now hold on here, Frankie. I know your father and I heard what you said. Now you know he wouldn't approve," Sheriff Bellview said in a friendly manner.

"But...these..." Frank started.

"I don't want to hear it. You take the money this man offered...and the book of tickets...and enjoy your evening like you know you're supposed to," the sheriff said.

"Well, my dad's gonna hear about this!" Frank almost shouted.

"I'm sure he will," the sheriff replied.

With that, Frank grabbed the money from Bill and walked away with his friends trailing. By this time, the small crowd had completely disappeared, leaving only Bill near the milk bottle booth, along with Jimmy and Sheriff Bellview.

"Sheriff, I sure am glad you were here. That could have gotten out of hand," Bill said.

"Save it," the sheriff said, any pretense of friendliness gone.

"You shouldn't have made the kid look like a fool. That only made it worse. I came here on behalf of the local organizers after Jimmy here asked to extend. I was going to approve it but after seeing that...along with the reports I'm getting of increased shoplifting in town...I can't prove it's your people doing it, but...I think it's best that you just pack up and move along to the next town. Understand?" the sheriff said it in a way that no one could not have misunderstood.

Bill wanted to say something—anything. He was on the verge of begging, but he hadn't stooped that low yet. Even if he had, he doubted Sheriff Bellview would budge.

Jimmy stepped in. "Ah, Sheriff, come on, we aren't bad people. How about we give your family a free night with refreshments to boot? How's that sound?"

"Sounds to me like a bribe," the sheriff replied. "Pack your things and leave when it's time."

The sheriff walked away, and Jimmy stood there, watching him go, a little shell-shocked by what had just occurred. "What just happened?" Jimmy said, turning to Bill. "He was in a good mood. He was talking about how great the show was and how much money the town was making...then snap...night and day. Now he wants us to leave...I don't get it. I'm sorry, boss. I did my best."

"It's okay, Jimmy. Go see if you can help Dani. Call around to see if there are any parking lots we can rent. I think that's the only choice we have, now" Bill said.

"You got it, boss," Jimmy said and walked away.

Bill watched him go, and he, too, was dumbfounded by what took place. Those bottles were the damnedest things. Sam spoke up when Bill turned toward the counter. "I know those bottles are the regular bottles. I don't know what happened. Maybe it was like you said...that kid faked those throws, but that was some grade A acting."

"Hand me one of those balls, Sam?" Bill asked.

Sam bent over and picked up one of the balls that the kid had thrown and handed it off to Bill. His mind was still trying to make sense of what he had seen, and he had to do one more thing to confirm something. He didn't know in his hearts of hearts exactly what he was confirming, but he was confirming something, all right—something he couldn't explain, not even to himself. Bill took the ball in his hand and squeezed it. Feeling the thread along his thumb, he tossed the ball lightly at the milk bottles. A light, underhanded throw—if the bottles had been weighted, they wouldn't have fallen but if they weren't weighted—well, at least one would go down. He watched it sail through the air until it connected with the standing pyramid of milk bottles. And just like Bill expected, they all toppled over.

4

Bill didn't say anything. There was nothing to say. He was short on words and long on what a rube might call the heebie-jeebies. Another thing that had Bill perplexed besides the milk bottle toss was the thunder he had heard. He looked around and there wasn't a cloud in the sky. He looked down and then back to Sam, who seemed a bit awestruck, as well, because he pulled out a cigarette and lit up, taking a drag before offering Bill the pack. Bill had quit smoking three years prior, for no reason in particular other than the fact that his kids were growing older. He wanted to be around longer than his old man had been for him. That didn't mean he didn't want to light one from time to time. He almost broke, but he waved it off.

"I don't know what happened," Sam said, as if discussing some quantum theory of mathematics that didn't make sense, the smoke creeping out as he spoke. "They should have been knocked over."

A part of Bill wanted to discuss it, but another part wanted to run far away and hide. But why he felt that way, he didn't know. "Well, it's too late to do anything about it now, Sam. You did what you could, and you did a good job. Thanks," Bill said.

"Oh, thank you," Sam replied.

Bill always made it a point to praise the work of those who actually worked. Bill couldn't pay them much to begin with, and encouraging people and making them feel important didn't cost anything. But, it wasn't just that; he truly cared about his people—keeping them safe and out of danger from outsiders, as well as insiders, which reminded him...Peter.

Bill went looking for Peter next, but he wasn't at the booth where the kid had confronted him. In fact, as soon as the attention was off Peter, Bill hadn't see him at all. He must have ducked out, and who could blame him? "Out of sight, out of mind," as the old adage goes, but Bill still had a bone to pick with him. If he stole from that kid in town, he would have to go.

From there, Bill expanded his search and also fell into his habit of doing general spot-checks of different things—booths, people, whatever else came across his attention. He did this daily to make sure that he was accessible to his folks and to fix any problems that needed to be resolved. He had made it a point of doing this for so long that now, it was second nature and most of the time, he didn't realize he was actively doing it.

He inadvertently ended up on the row where all the extra booths, shows and exhibits were located on the lot. They weren't necessarily employees of the carnival. They were mostly freelancers that traveled with the carnival and set up shop, paying the carnival a percentage of whatever they made on the route. Some of them had been around long enough that they were an integral part of the outfit, whether they were paid by the carnival or not.

"Bill...Why don't you come out of the sun and sit over here?" Bill heard a woman's voice say. Of course, he knew whose voice it was. It was the voice of the all-seeing Madame Zara. She had been with them for as far back as he could remember, as a fortune teller. Bill didn't believe in that stuff, but he knew that local yokels, no matter where they went, ate that stuff up. When she talked to rubes, she always spoke in tones that came off as mystical, but to other carnies, it was like talking to anyone else. There were no theatrics here. She was an older woman with a dark tan and flowing, white hair. Her real name wasn't Zara, though; it was Kathy Kosnowski. How she ended up on the route reading mitts, Bill didn't know, and he never thought to ask.

"How are you doing, Kathy?" Bill asked as he walked over and sat down next to her.

"Doing well. What's going on with you? Any problems?" Kathy asked.

"What? What makes you think I have any problems?" Bill asked.

"Because I know all," she said jokingly and then added, "And people talk. They can sense something is wrong. Well, those of us that have been here a while."

"I'm just looking for Peter. You know that young, tall, string bean of a blond that rides the gaming booths?" Bill asked.

Kathy nodded, indicating she knew who he meant. "I haven't seen him, Bill. Are you sure that's the only thing that troubles you?"

Bill hesitated and was about to get up, but then leaned back into the chair. He didn't want to stir trouble over nothing, but if people already suspected there was something wrong, then they would more than likely assume the worst. Sometimes a little information is better than no information at all. "Just the normal stuff of keeping the train moving, but spots are drying up. We are going to have to barnstorm it, find an empty lot and set up shop, then weather the storm until the route moves again...speaking of which, you didn't happen to hear thunder today, did you?"

Kathy looked up and around at the sky, but saw nothing that resembled a cloud. It was the same clear sky that Bill had seen before. "No, I haven't heard thunder. I just listened to the weather reporter on the radio, who claimed that it should be clear for the next week. But you know how weather people are—five percent chance of rain and 100 percent chance of being wrong."

"That's what I figured. I thought I heard some earlier, but I doubt it now. There was a lot going on at the time," Bill said, then stood up and stretched as he did so.

"Do you want me to read your fortune?" Kathy asked.

"No, I'm good," he replied.

"Oh, come on. What have you got to lose? I have no customers and if they see me reading someone, they might get interested."

"Okay, fine. What do you want me to do?"

"I know you think this is all an act and for the most part it is, but sometimes, the spark comes through," she replied.

"You tell that to all the marks...or just me?" Bill asked with a smile.

Kathy looked at him, a slight smirk emerging on her face. They were sitting in front of her tent, in two chairs beside a small table. Her act consisted of palm or tarot card reading, but if she could really take the mark for a ride, she would have them follow her into her tent to use the old, magical, crystal ball that had been handed down through the ages...at least that's what she told her customers. In reality, she bought the thing from a musty, dusty magic shop in New Orleans that catered toward voodoo and occult items, about 15 years ago.

Kathy reached into her bag, brought out a tarot deck and placed it on the small table between them.

"Okay, you know the drill. Pick three cards and they will represent your past, present, and future," Kathy said.

The cards were black with gold trim—very fancy-looking. Following Kathy's instructions, Bill reached over to pick up the deck, shuffled and placed it back down on the table. He picked three cards and laid them face down.

Bill was wasting time at this point and was only mildly interested. So far, it didn't seem that anyone noticed the tarot reading, so it wouldn't act as a marketing tool to draw in more interest, as she had hoped. As he put down the last card, a queasy sensation came over him, and a trickle of sweat ran down his forehead. He went from being mildly interested to not being interested at all, then was reminded of the more important tasks that needed tending.

"Kathy, I think I'm going to take a rain check. I suddenly don't feel well and I really need to get back to make sure we have a spot to stay in," Bill said and stood up.

"Are you sure? You've already drawn. Maybe this will give you an answer," Kathy replied.

Bill, for whatever reason, wanted nothing to do with an answer. He felt a hot flash, almost like a rash developing, but somehow he knew it was related to the odd, recent events, along with the tarot cards laying in front of him.

"Yeah, I'm sure, but thanks anyway." Bill walked away abruptly, almost rudely, and as he walked away, he felt better. "I'm going crazy," he thought. But he wasn't. He finally chalked it up to the stress of trying to keep too many proverbial plates spinning on poles to keep them from crashing to the ground. He was just overtaxed and tired. That's all.

Kathy watched him leave and if anyone had been watching, they would have seen a concerned, almost questioning, look reflected on her face. She then turned her gaze to the unfinished reading with the three cards face down. "Oh well, time to clean up," she thought to herself as she reached over to scoop all the cards together. However, before she did, a gust of wind blew in, causing all the cards, even those still stacked, to scatter. They didn't go far, and Kathy quickly jumped up to gather them. When she had finished gathering them, she turned around and noticed that the wind had left one card face down on the table; it was the card that showed the future. She pursed her lips. She knew she shouldn't look at the card, but curiosity pulled at her until she caved and reached to flip it over. When she did, she jumped back and gasped. The card displayed a large "13" across the top, along with a flag carried by a skeleton. It was otherwise known as the "Death card."

Kathy quickly stacked all the cards, including the Death card, and counted to make sure she had them all. Once she confirmed she did, she then gave herself a reading—something she hadn't done in years; this surprised her, now that she thought of it. Taking the deck of 78 cards, she shuffled them for some time to make sure that whatever energy was in the cards was all hers and not left over from Bill's reading. She cut the deck and shuffled some more. She knew of more elaborate readings, but she decided to just go with the same reading that she used with Bill, the three-card draw. She cut the deck one more time, just to make sure, then drew three cards and placed them in a row, face down.

Kathy looked down and a peculiar feeling came over her. It wasn't fear, per se, but it wasn't far from it. It was like a shadow of fear—a trepidation. It took an effort on her part to reach over, flip the cards, and follow through with the reading.

Like ripping off a Band-Aid, she thought it would be best to waste no time. She quickly flipped all the cards face up. She reeled back as if someone had slapped her in the face. All three cards facing her were the same—the card of Death. She didn't understand how that was possible. The deck was only supposed to have one Death card in the stack. She looked up and around to see if anyone else was nearby. Besides the usual traffic, there was no one close enough to play a trick on her.

Kathy looked back down at the table, back to the three cards of Death but when she did, two of the cards were no longer the same. Instead, the only remaining Death card lay in the middle. To its left was the "The 10 of Swords" card, which showed a dead body on the ground; the body was impaled by 10 swords, which looked like small crosses coming out of its back. On the right was now "The Tower" card, which depicted a disturbing image of a tower engulfed in fire and two figures plummeting from the top. As she looked at the two new cards, she heard a commotion not far from her tent, which caused her to jump. She was so focused on the table and wasn't expecting an interruption. She looked up, alarmed, but realized it was two families that were greeting each other—nothing sinister—but when she looked back down at the cards, the remaining Death card was now replaced with the "The Hanged Man" card, one that shows a man suspended, upside down, by one foot and his other leg forming a figure "4."

Kathy Kosnowski had been part of the travel circuit for years, ever since her first husband passed away when she was 30; that had been 32 years ago. She didn't have kids, and she found that the travel life suited her. She had been taught to read tarot cards by her grandmother, who had come from the old world, when she was a kid. Her husband didn't like it. He was very controlling, the norm for marriages at that time. What wasn't normal, however, is that he was physically abusive, and hid it well. They could show up to church on a Sunday morning and no one would question that they had a picture-perfect marriage. After his passing, she found the traveling show, which opened up a world of possibilities for her. She felt free for the first time in years, and the traveling troupe became like her family, watching out for her.

She had seen many things since the time she started this new life of hers. Some of those things had been scary but this—what she just experienced—brought up old memories and a dread she hadn't felt since she was married, all those years ago. She knew she wasn't crazy, but she couldn't explain how the cards had changed, and that terrified her because she was supposedly the expert in readings. The swirling of emotions and the sense of dread caused her to feel nauseous, and her legs to feel like lead weights.

"Can I have a reading?" came a voice that brought her back to reality. Kathy looked up to see a young man, mid-20s, standing about 10 feet away in the lane, looking at her.

"I'm sorry. I'm closed for today," she said as she stood up, gathered her cards, and folded the chairs. She didn't wait to see if the young man heard her, nor did she wait for a response as she moved everything inside the tent. She stuck a makeshift "closed" sign over the tent's opening and went inside, closing the flap behind her.

5

B ill left Kathy's tent and walked around some more, unsuccessfully looking for Peter, then headed toward the back lot. A couple of hours had passed and he wondered if they had made any progress regarding a spot to go to after they left this town.

He stopped by his trailer first, expecting to see Dani, but she wasn't there. He then went over to the management trailer and walked in. It was a full house; Dani, George, Brad, and Jimmy were there, discussing different options.

Brad looked up. "Where've you been?"

"I was looking for Peter. He's caused us a lot of trouble," Bill replied.

"Jimmy told me all about it. Sounded to me like some punk kid from town," Brad said.

"He was a punk kid, all right, but there is no doubt in my mind that there was something to his accusations. I'm sure Jimmy told you that whole fiasco ruined our chances for sticking around a couple more days," Bill said.

"Yeah, he did," Brad said. "I'll talk to Peter."

"You better before I do," Bill replied. "I'm about to send him packing. He's been nothing but trouble."

"Yeah, yeah...I understand, but he's the least of our worries right now," Brad said.

"We've been looking for spots all afternoon and calling around from that pay phone...and no one has anything available. It's nuts. I've never seen anything like it," George said.

"It's true, Bill; it's like we've been blackballed or something. Every single place we've called, there is no interest in the slightest...no conversation...just flat-out 'no'," Dani said.

"Have you tried sweetening the pot by giving them more money?" Bill asked.

"No, you don't understand. We can't even get to that point. They say 'no' and hang up," Dani replied.

"Yeah, boss. I've turned over every stone I can think of. I even reached out to my cousin's husband, who owns a little convenience shop with a large dirt parking lot, and even he said 'no.' I mean...we aren't particularly close, but he wanted no part. Wasn't even interested in the conversation... and that guy is always looking for a deal," Jimmy said.

"We may have to go back to winter's quarters and call it a bust," Brad said, scratching his ear.

"Winter's quarters" was where they holed up in the off season. It was a base of operations of sorts near Louisville, Kentucky. Normally, around late October-early November would mark the end of the travel season. From there, they would return to winter's quarters, where they would settle in, park, store all the equipment, and plan the next year's route. This was also the time they would repair or replace broken equipment, so everything would be fresh and ready to go come March, when they would be on the road again.

"If we do that, then I'm going to have to sell some rides or face bankruptcy, Brad," Bill said matter-of-factly, then continued, "I'd rather not do that because that will set us all back. If we don't have the rides to bring the draw, then we're all going to suffer."

"What other options do we have?" George asked.

"I don't know," Bill sighed.

"I guess we'll keep looking and come up with more leads. But I think we'd better go somewhere that has more pay phones to call from. That one we've been using right outside is so hard to hear anyone on," Dani said. "I think I saw a line of them at that grocery store on the way into town."

The room felt stifling to Bill. Although the air conditioner was running at full speed, sometimes in the middle of a hot summer day, with the sun beating down on the exterior of the travel trailer (which was lacking in insulation), the air conditioner barely kept up with the heat. Most times, it only made it manageable and just slightly better than being outside. The sun was setting now, and the temperature was comfortable for everyone else. Bill couldn't help but feel a little claustrophobic. He felt like he was on a one-way, dead-end street, with no exits or options...and the more he thought about it, the more distraught he felt.

"I gotta go for a walk," Bill said.

"Are you okay?" Dani asked, concerned.

"Yeah, I just need some air and time to think. I have to think about what options we'll be forced to take if those leads go nowhere...I'm okay, though," he said and put on his best smile. Even though she could usually read him like a book, there were some times that she couldn't. This was one of the latter, and for that, Bill was thankful. He didn't want to worry her or anyone else. He didn't feel fine. In fact, he felt quite the opposite, but he knew that if he took time and went for a walk to clear his head, that would help...somewhat.

Bill Donovan was a man with a problem, and he knew it. He avoided walking through the midway. If he did, the small things that needed to be fixed or other issues that needed to be addressed would keep him from being able to focus and would quickly overwhelm him. In life, at least for Bill, he found that sometimes, the best thing he could do was nothing—just go for a walk to clear his head. He'd think about random things until his subconscious came through with the answer. Sometimes it did and sometimes it didn't. His mom was the one who taught him that trick and Lord knows she did a lot of walking during her days to deal with the stress of the traveling show. Unfortunately, she passed away about five years after his dad did. She had no more interest in continuing on the route after he was gone, so semi-retired at winter's quarters. He hoped that wherever they were, they were together and happy.

An hour later, he still had no answer. Bill had walked all around the area and nothing came to him. The light of the sun was now gone and all that lit up the evening were the sparkling neon lights of the carnival rides. He looked up into the sky and couldn't see the moon; it must have been in the new moon phase. It was up there, of course—he just couldn't see it. Bill felt like whatever was going on, it was like that moon. He couldn't see it, but he knew it was there. But unlike having concrete knowledge of the moon and its different phases, he could just sense that something big was looming over them. It was out there and that was that. He had no solid evidence, other than the fact that too many strange things were happening at once.

He walked back to the trailer and went back in. It looked the same as it had before. George was in his usual space. Brad and Jimmy were gone, but Dani was still there. She looked defeated; her shoulders slumped. When Bill came in, she gave him a tired smile and Bill knew that the efforts to find another spot were unsuccessful.

"Are you okay?" Bill asked.

She shrugged her shoulders. "Yes, just stressed, like you. Nothing worked out. We must have spent five bucks in quarters calling all the possible leads we had...and nothing...just nothing."

Now it was his turn to tell her it would be all right, even though he didn't feel it. Oftentimes, it was better to be brave and not acknowledge your true feelings. Sometimes, people needed to feel a sense of strength, even if Bill didn't feel strong at the moment. Words, even if they were just a "show" of words, could change a situation from bad to better or from bad to worse, depending on how you used them. In this case, of course, he was trying to make it better, at least for his wife. Also, with George in the room, he didn't want word to get around that he was losing hope. It was a fine line he had been walking all week, telling people about the cancellations without it making things worse. It reminded him of a tightrope walker crossing from one skyscraper to another. The stakes were high, and Bill felt a strong wind blowing, but he had to stay on that rope—the only difference being that Bill never asked to be on the rope.

Bill asked Dani to take a walk with him, so they could get some fresh air (and also talk outside of George's earshot). They held hands and strolled around the backyard for a bit. He offered words of comfort, although he didn't feel very comforted himself. "Honey, we're gonna keep trying. And...like you said before, things will be all right...one way or another. Maybe tomorrow, after a good night's rest, we'll come up with some fresh ideas and have better luck."

"Yeah, maybe you're right," she replied. They sat down in some fold-up chairs in front of their personal trailer, just taking in the sights and sounds, and she put her head on his shoulder. They sat like this for a bit, then Dani decided to return to the HQ trailer to see if anyone else had any news. Bill said he was going to do a final walk-through for the night and see if there were any fires he could help extinguish.

The night air was warm, but not as warm as the day had been or as stifling as the inside of the trailer was. It was pleasant out. The sounds of the carnival were music to his ears, and it sounded wonderful—the roaring of the rides, the laughter and yells of families having a good time. It was magic. He hated the thought of possibly losing it all and now regretted having stretched himself to buy a couple of new rides over the past two seasons. He had recently gotten a brand new Scrambler to replace the old one that was beyond repair. Since business had been steadily growing the past few years, there was no reason to think it wouldn't be the same this summer. So, he took out a hefty loan. He had also bought a Gravitron. Both this and the Scrambler move in a circular pattern, but the Scrambler has more moving parts. Even so, it's a simple machine. It consists of a central axis with three spokes that jut from it, each with their own mini axes that contain four, geometrically balanced seats. When the central axis spins, the outer ones spin, as well, creating a centrifugal force for riders in the seats. They're flung to the outer reaches, then whipped back through the center, just to get flung out again. It gives the riders the illusion of going fast when they aren't going very fast at all.

The Gravitron is an enclosed, circular platform ride with padded panels lining its interior walls, one for each rider. The occupants lean against the panels and as the ride quickly spins, they're pinned to the wall and lifted off their feet due to centrifugal force, until it stops. It's been said that what you feel while riding is equivalent to 3G, not far off from the gravitational force that astronauts experience when going to space.

The Gravitron cost more than he wanted to spend, but no one could have expected the kind of summer they were experiencing...and, it wasn't until this week that this summer's circuit took a turn for the worse. No one would have expected it in a million years. Bill kicked himself for putting them all in this situation. He almost always erred on the side of caution, but the one time he splurged a little...well...wouldn't you know that this would happen.

They had to pack up tomorrow and go...somewhere. He prayed a miracle would come through. That a surprise would happen at the last minute that would save the day, but he knew it was foolish to hope for such things. His dad always told him, "Hope is a nice thing, but it doesn't pay the bills," meaning that it was careless to rely on hope without working toward whatever you were hoping for.

He walked near the front of the midway, where the entrance and ticket booths were located. He saw the broken down, yet beautiful, car sitting there on the show trailer, and it reminded him of his life at the moment. It looked like things were going well from the outside—sure, he was running a carnival, but on the inside, he was in debt and if things didn't change, he'd be as broke as that broken down, beautiful car. "So stupid," he thought to himself. His wife was right. Why did he bring that car and insist on parking it out front at each location? No one cared. The public barely looked at it as they passed to go inside. The only one that seemed to care about that damn car was him, and he wasted a ton of money just carting it around. He sighed in disgust. He should have listened to his wife and stopped hauling it years ago. After looking at the car, he looked over to the ticket booth and saw Rita, another long-timer, in one of them, so walked over to say "hello."

He opened the back and walked in; the lady sitting in the small booth, not expecting visitors, jumped and looked back. "Jesus, Bill, you scared me."

"I'm sorry, Rita, I was just coming to see how things were coming along, as far as sales," Bill asked.

Rita had dyed red hair that hid her grey (but not very well), went a little heavy on the makeup, and was always smacking on gum. "Oh, you know, it's the last night so we're doing all right. People getting it in while they still can."

A family came up and stood at the window.

"What'll it be, hon?" Rita asked the father.

"Four wristbands, please," came the reply.

In a reply that came as routine, she told them the price, then had the parents reach through the small opening of the window to secure the wristbands. She then handed over two for their kids, who were maybe seven or eight, and big enough to ride rides, but not quite big enough to reach their hands into the window.

"Next!" Rita yelled, as the family walked away.

Bill looked out and saw the lines. It wasn't as big as the first night, but it wasn't too shabby, either. If only they could have stayed a few extra days; it wouldn't necessarily see them out of the woods, but it would have helped.

Bill bid Rita a good evening and left her alone. He then he felt a buzzing on his belt; it was his beeper. He'd only had it a couple of years and it was still sort of new to him. He looked at the callback number but didn't recognize it. With his beeper in hand, he checked his pocket for change. Having none, he stopped by Rita's booth again, but instead of opening the back, he quickly cut in front and went to the window.

"What'll be it be, hon...Bill, what are you doing?" Rita asked.

"Rita, you got a quarter? I need to go make a phone call," Bill said.

"That'll be 25 cents," Rita said, smiling, and opened the change drawer, withdrawing one single and shiny quarter. She placed it on the counter and slid it forward through the window.

Bill grabbed it. "Thanks! I owe you one."

Rita waved her hand through the air in an "it's nothing" gesture and yelled "next!" as Bill walked toward the phone booth outside the midway. It was the same lonely and mistreated phone whose better days were far behind that he'd used every day to try and secure the next spot. He checked the change return door first, as it was a habit that he had picked up over the years. People had a way of forgetting their change when a call didn't connect. Finding no change, he picked up the receiver and placed it in the crook of his neck. He brought out his beeper so he could read the number and dial it.

The sound through the handset was crackly, and Bill could barely hear the dial tone. He punched in the numbers, and it rang. It rang three times and a crystal-clear voice answered, "Good evening, this is Victor Bright. How may I help you?"

The clarity of the line surprised Bill more than anything, after a week of using the phone and listening to a bunch of static during conversations. For once, to have a clear line where he heard exactly what he was supposed to hear and nothing else caused him to look at the receiver in surprise before putting it back up to his ear. "Yes, this is Bill Donovan with Donovan's Delights Entertainment."

"Oh, yes! I just called not that long ago, and I must say, good sir, that I appreciate the quick response. I heard you were in a bit of a pickle, and well...I may have the means to help you. That is, if you decide to take me up on my offer," the voice said.

The hairs on the back of Bill's neck raised; he knew when someone was selling him something. He'd been selling all his life, but this voice and the timing made him uncomfortable.

"Who have you been talking to?" Bill asked. He didn't want to give too much away because if people knew they had you over a barrel...well...a deal doesn't always work out well for the desperate. The feeling reminded Bill of that deodorant slogan a few years back: "Never let 'em see you sweat!"

"Oh, come now, Mr. Donovan—I've heard talk. That's all. You need a place to set up. I have a place you can do that. I'm the mayor of Brownsville, a small town, you see, and it's our anniversary next week. Unfortunately, but fortunately for you, what we had planned fell through. And that leaves you with a golden opportunity to come and celebrate with us. You'd be the heroes of our town and we'd be indebted to you," the man said.

Bill's mind raced. This wasn't how getting a place to set up usually goes. Most of the time, a town's promoter or the county fair board reached out to set things in motion. Bill had never heard of a mayor reach out on behalf of a town, especially at night. He wondered which one of the two was more desperate, he or this Victor Bright guy.

"Where are you located?" Bill asked.

"Well, we're in southern Illinois, kind of between Marion and Carbondale. You've heard of those towns, I'm sure," Mr. Bright said.

Bill had heard of those towns; they were along the same route they had planned on going. Harrisburg, Illinois, the original spot they had planned, was only about 30 minutes away. Anyone in the area knew of Carbondale. It was a college town and home to Southern Illinois University, whose sports team chant was "Go Salukis!" since their mascot was the swift and agile dog.

"Yes, I have heard of those towns. So, what about setup? How long do would you like for us to stay?" Bill asked.

"Two weeks at least. Maybe longer if things go well," Mr. Bright replied.

The situation was music to Bill's ears, but he'd never seen a deal go quite like this before. The way this summer had been going, it was the first for many unseen things. Before Bill could ask about the specifics regarding money and percentages to make it worthwhile for them both, Mr. Bright spoke first. "And we have a bonus, since this is last minute, just for you to make an appearance and set up. Then my percentage of what the town will get will be nominal."

Bill felt like he was the butt of a joke. Everything was falling into place and almost too perfectly. Bill knew for a fact, though, that if it were someone playing a trick, he wouldn't be a friend to them after that. There are jokes and then there are jokes. This one fell into the latter category, meaning it would be mean-spirited and not worthy of friendship.

Mr. Bright gave out some numbers, both for the bonus and the percentage from sales. The numbers were both more than fair and honestly, anyone would have been pretty dumb to pass up the situation. Bill had to ask, "Are you pulling my leg?"

"Why, no Mr. Donovan. Why do you ask?"

"Well, those are pretty generous offers, sir, and I just want to make sure before I bring my people there. I'd hate to get there and find out that what you just told me and what you say after we arrive are two very different things," Bill said.

"I can understand your hesitancy, Mr. Donovan, but I assure you, what I say is my word and what I intend to keep. Is that okay with you?" Mr. Bright said.

"Sounds fine," Bill replied.

"I'll have the contract drawn up and you can sign it when you arrive," Mr. Bright said.

"We'll sent out our 24 hour...I mean...we'll send out a guy to map out a route tomorrow, while we pack up here. Once he knows the way, he can point us in the right direction," Bill said.

"Yeah, that's a good idea," said Mr. Bright, "because I hear there's some construction on I-57 around Mt. Vernon. May want to take a detour to save you some time and frustration getting caught up in bumper-to-bumper traffic. It should be good to get back on 57 around Benton, a little bit north of Marion."

"Thanks for the heads-up. I'll let everyone know. We've got plenty of maps, so we'll figure out the best way to go," replied Bill.

"Well, I tell you what—you know that truck stop off of I-57, just west of Marion on Route 13?" Mr. Bright asked. "I'll have one of my people waiting there for your guy, and then we'll lead him back to our town. Unfortunately, and I hate to admit this, our town doesn't show on any of the maps. Can you believe it? Oh, and I've tried to write those map book publishers, but they don't care about one small town in the middle of southern Illinois," Mr. Bright said.

"I don't think I've ever heard of that. I thought all the towns were listed. I mean...I've been to some pretty small villages, and they were on the map. Even Stonemill. We were there last year and even that was on the map," Bill said.

"Be that as it may, that's the situation and how it is. Brownsville doesn't show up on the map, but I can assure you that when you get here, you'll see the town in all its splendor," Mr. Bright said.

"All right, I will send my guy out immediately then...and Mr. Bright?" Bill asked.

"Yes?" Mr. Bright asked.

"I appreciate you reaching out and I look forward to meeting you," Bill said.

"Not as much as we look forward to meeting you," Mr. Bright said and the line disconnected. Mr. Bright must have hung up because the static was back, as if it had always been there. Bill hung up the receiver and heard the coin inside the machine drop, but instead of dropping into the internal compartment when a successful call connected, it dropped into the coin slot, as it does for unsuccessful attempts. Bill stuck his finger in the slot and retrieved his coin. "Must be my lucky day, after all," Bill thought to himself.

6

Bill returned to the management trailer triumphantly, with an extra bounce in his step. "We got a spot!" he blurted immediately when he ran into the room.

George and Dani were still there, and Brad and Jimmy had come back. They all looked back at him in surprise, then came a barrage of questions.

"Where?" George asked.

"How did you manage that?" Brad asked.

"Who did you contact?" Dani asked.

There were more questions, but they became lost in the excitement of the new development. Bill raised his hands to quiet everyone. When they did, he told them about the phone call and the offer.

"Really?" Brad asked. "That's one for the books. A town reaching out, just out of the blue."

"Strange thing, indeed," George agreed.

"Has anyone ever heard of Brownsville in southern Illinois?" Bill asked.

No one had.

"I haven't either," Bill said. "Well, we'll send you out tomorrow, Jimmy, to find the spot. It's about three or four hours southwest of here. Not far from Harrisburg or that little town we detoured to last year—Stonemill. Remember?"

"I remember that town. That's the one that had that crazy storm pop up out of nowhere," Jimmy said. "Oh, yeah...How could I forget? After we left, there was that huge pileup on the interstate and we got stuck in traffic for hours. We had to really hustle to get set up at the next town on time."

"Yep, that's the one. Anyway, if you travel on down 57, there's a truck stop west of Marion where the Brownsville town representative will meet you," Bill said.

"Sounds good. Do you know what time, or who I'm supposed to meet? Anything as far as what they're driving or what they look like?" Jimmy asked.

"You know, I didn't think to ask any of that," Bill replied.

It took Bill aback because it was one of those usual things that you asked. Who, what, when, where, and how...and he had asked none of these. In the end, he chalked it up to the huge relief of getting a spot clouding his mind and his judgment. "No, worries. Tomorrow will give you plenty of time to get there to establish what and where we need to be. It'll be fine," Bill said.

"If you say so, boss," Jimmy replied.

"Wait a minute? What county is that in?" George asked.

"That's an odd question. Why do you ask?" Bill replied.

"I don't know. I remember there was a county in southern Illinois that bad things seemed to happen in. I heard about all kinds of stuff when I was a boy, but it's been many years," George said.

"Let's take a look," Dani said, while reaching over to a cabinet to pull out the new 1995 Rand McNally Road Atlas. Its cover was adorned with a beautiful picture of a large mountain reflected in a lake. It was the kind of scene that would make anyone long for a road trip. She opened it up to find Illinois and then searched.

"Hmm. I can't seem to find Brownsville on the map," she said.

"Oh yeah—the town's mayor said you wouldn't, but he did say it was west of Marion, before you get to Carbondale," Bill said.

"Okay, I found Carbondale," Dani said with her finger tracing on the page, "And here's Marion. Strange...I see a Herrin, a township called Energy, and a few others...but no Brownsville. I've never heard of an atlas not showing all towns."

"Yeah, the mayor, Mr. Bright, said we wouldn't believe him. I'm sure there's some sort of explanation for it," Bill replied.

"Oh, here is it. Jackson is the name of one county and Williamson is the name of the other county, right next to it," Dani said.

George let out a sigh. "I want to say it was one of those counties. I don't know, Bill. Maybe we should pass this one up."

Bill couldn't believe it. They were saved, and George Bronson looked a gift horse in the mouth. It didn't make sense; he never really seemed to care, nor did he usually offer an opinion about anything, yet here he was, changing course.

"I don't think we have much choice, George, unless you have any better ideas," Bill replied.

"I don't."

"Then what's got you not wanting to do this one?" Bill asked.

"I'm not sure. Just feels off," George said.

"This whole summer has felt off," Bill replied and then continued, "It's either this spot or bankruptcy for the show. I have my doubts too, but we're kind of stuck."

"Yeah...I know, but..." George began.

Bill interrupted and said, "Well, how about we go and see what's there? Once we do, if things still feel off, we just keep driving. We won't set up. We'll just keep going."

"That works for me," Brad said.

"I guess so," George said, but his voice did not possess any strong conviction. He was still on the fence and Bill was pretty sure that no matter what he said wouldn't change that, so this had to be good enough. Good enough to at least get there and see.

"All right, it's decided. We will pack up tomorrow and then be on our way," Bill said.

Later that night, Bill had trouble sleeping. He dreamed he was an insect, and he was caught in a spider web. Try as he might, he couldn't get free. Just as the spider came to him and was about to sink its fangs in, he woke up. He'd get back to sleep, just to have the same dream. It must have happened at least three or four times and each time he woke up, he was slightly more disturbed. It had been a long and stressful week; he continued to be able to roll over and go back to sleep. In the morning, as what usually happens with dreams, he forgot all about them.

Bill couldn't understand why he was so tired. When he got out of bed, it was early. Pack-out days, coupled with the travel, were some of the longest days for a traveling carnival, since there were so many moving parts (no pun intended). They would have to dismantle the rides, pack them away safely, then get back on the road. It would take at least eight to ten hours...and that was with everyone steadily working, with no breaks. In the dead of summer, they tried to get up a couple hours before dawn so they could avoid having to do the grueling work in the hot sun. This never truly helped, because no matter how hard they worked or how well they planned, there was so much to be done that it would always carry them through the heat of the day.

Bill got on his feet, dressed, opened the door, and looked back at Dani, who was still asleep. He knew he should have woken her up and she would probably be mad at him, but she looked so comfortable. It was still dark outside, but he knew it wouldn't be long before a thin, neon blue line would appear on the horizon, which would quickly turn into an orange line, from which the day would only get brighter from there.

He met up with Jimmy, who helped out a bit for the first couple of hours, before heading on to find Brownsville. Every little bit helped and the more they could get done before he left meant that they would get on the road that much faster.

"Good morning, Jimmy," Bill said.

"Morning, boss. Sleep all right?" Jimmy asked.

Bill couldn't remember much of the night, but he knew it was restless and that he hadn't slept well. "Hmm, don't think I did. I believe I tossed and turned all night."

"Same. I didn't sleep well, either," Jimmy replied. "But I never sleep well right before we pack up. Mind is full of stuff to be worried about, ya know?"

"I can certainly understand that." Bill smiled as he looked at Jimmy. "Quite well, in fact."

"Want some coffee?" Jimmy asked, pulling out his tall, plaid Franklin thermos.

"Sure," Bill said, as Jimmy poured from the thermos into the little cup on its top.

"Aren't you going to have some?" Bill asked.

"Yeah, in a little bit, but mostly, I'll drink it later while I'm on the road," Jimmy said.

They walked around the midway, and the breakdown of the carnival was already in full swing. Booths and rides were in the process of being taken apart, one piece at a time. Vehicles and trailers were everywhere, along with people moving like ants—a steady flow of deliberate action.

Bill spent the morning essentially directing traffic and made sure those who needed help got it. Brad and George were doing similar duties for their areas. Most of the concession stands that George ran were the easiest components to break down and organize into the convoy, since most of them were trailers to begin with. Secure the items inside, shut the hatches and window coverings, hook them up to the truck, and "Voila!" you're done. Next, as far as time consumption, were the game tents and booths. And finally, the part of the carnival that took the longest and required the most help from everyone, were the rides.

Some rides were easy, as they were basically their own trailer, like the "dark rides." These are the ones with cars on a conveyor belt that take the riders into, say, a haunted mansion with screaming mechanical ghosts and other figures made of particle board, that leap out at the riders. For those rides, all that was required was to secure the different gags, take down the façade, which comprised all the colorful and ghoulish art, store it inside, then shut and lock the doors. But other rides, like the Scrambler, required more finesse, more people, and more muscle. Some rides had their own trailer, whereas others required a total breakdown and moving those items onto trailers, one piece at a time.

About halfway through the morning, Jimmy took off, along with his half-full thermos of coffee, which surprisingly was still hot. Bill could see steam rise as Jimmy poured himself a cup before he hit the road. "All right, Jimmy—remember, that truck stop right off the exit. We've been there before, but it's been a while," Bill said.

"Got it, boss, and I will page you when I find the place and get to the phone," Jimmy replied.

"Sounds good...and Jimmy?" Bill asked.

"Yeah, boss?"

"If something feels off or you see something concerning, let me know right away. Leave immediately, or whatever you have to do," Bill said.

"You think there is funny business going on?" Jimmy asked.

"I don't know, Jimmy. This summer's been full of shenanigans. I just don't want this to be another or to get you caught up in it. That's all," Bill said.

"You got it."

Jimmy took off in his dirty, red, 15-year-old truck, a 1980 GMC. It was the kind of truck that had a rumbling sound that could be heard coming or going long before or after it was seen.

"There he goes," Dani said, coming up beside Bill.

"Hey, hon, did you sleep well?" Bill asked.

"Why didn't you wake me up?" she asked.

"I don't know. I was planning on it, but then you looked so cute and like you needed the rest," Bill replied.

"While I appreciate that, today wasn't the day to do that. There's so much to be done," Dani said.

"I know. I mean...I know. But it's getting done, so it doesn't hurt. Right?" Bill replied.

"Well, being your wife, I don't want any of the others to think I'm not pulling my weight here," Dani said.

"I can most assuredly tell you they know you pull your weight—and mine, too, most of the time." Bill smiled, then said jokingly, "And besides, you're my wife and I think it'll be all right being that...uh, I'm kind of the boss."

Bill enjoyed the banter between his wife and himself. And although what he said was true, he was the boss and at the end of the day, he was responsible for everything that happened with Donovan's Delights Entertainment. He tried hard every day to never come across cocky to anyone, unless it was one of those situations that he had to—like when he had to let someone go. Which reminded him, he hadn't seen Peter at all this morning...or at all since that altercation with the town kids. He didn't dwell on it too much, because problems like Peter always showed up sooner or later. When that time came, he'd deal with it.

The day steadily moved on and the lot showed less and less visual evidence that a traveling carnival had been here. It still amazed Bill. After all these years, they could show up and make the equivalent of a small town for people to enjoy within two days, then disappear like they had never been there, only a week later. Though, there was always a slight feeling of sadness, too, that spoke to the more esoteric nature of life in the "here today, gone tomorrow" sense that everyone eventually experiences. The only thing that truly lasts are the memories and experiences made and even then, only for the lifetime of each individual.

Bill did one last walk-through, then went over to where the convoy was staged to get on the road. He saw Kathy, the mitt reader, sitting in the front seat of her small motorhome. The pull-behind trailer that carried everything she owned, was already hooked up to it. When she saw Bill, she waved him over.

"Hey, Kathy. How're you doing? All packed up?" Bill asked.

"Yes, I'm doing fine. The next town we're going to...I heard rumors they called you first. What's the name of the town, by the way?" she asked.

"A place called Brownsville, Illinois, about four or so hours southwest from here, between Marion and Carbondale. Why?" Bill asked.

"Well, I just feel like I need to tell you to be careful. Something doesn't feel right about all of this," Kathy said.

Bill had known Kathy a long time and, although she was perceptive at times, he wouldn't exactly set a clock by her. With that being said, a broken clock is correct two times a day and what she said did pique his curiosity.

"What makes you say that?" Bill asked.

The look on her face was unfamiliar to Bill. She had always been upfront and direct in all the years that he had known her, but to see this obvious hesitation was new. She looked like she wanted to say something and was in inner turmoil about whether or not to do so.

"Are you okay?" Bill asked.

She looked directly at him and responded, "No, I'm not. There is a black cloud ahead. I don't know what it is or when it will be here, but...I've never been so sure of anything in my life."

The relief on her face was evident as she spoke, as if she was glad to get it off her chest. "I'm not crazy, Bill. You know me. I'm not one to over-dramatize anything unless you're a mark."

"I never thought you were, Kathy," Bill said.

"Yeah...well...these feelings and thoughts are about to make me go crazy," she said with a chuckle that belied humor. It was more of a nervous tic. Kathy must have been flustered, because Bill had never seen her this way before.

"In fact," Kathy continued, "I'm scared and if you weren't family, I would be gone by now...and to be honest, I'm not sure how long I'll stick around."

Something had her spooked and the way she acted and spoke spooked Bill, as well. Before he let his imagination run wild, though, he would take a pragmatic "wait and see" approach, especially since she didn't know what there was to be worried about.

"Well..." Bill began, and waited a few moments to collect his thoughts before he continued. "I appreciate you letting me know. We're in a tight spot, but this next stop should be good. I tell you what—you stick around and if you see anything, you let me know right away, okay? We'll leave together. All of us. All right?"

Kathy nodded her head and said, "Thank you for listening to me."

"Anytime, Kathy...and I mean it. You're practically family. You see something, let me know."

Bill walked away from the encounter perplexed, as if he were still in a dream. He knew he wasn't, but if he had woken up next to Dani right then and there, it wouldn't have been surprising. He couldn't dwell on it, as he still had a responsibility that required his attention, but along with all the other oddities this summer had produced, it only added to the shadow that lingered at the edge of his mind. It was the kind of shadow that was always there and surprised him when he least expected it, or was distracted by something else entirely. When he was young, he went to stay for the summer with some of his cousins in Florida. It was in the middle of hurricane season and while he was there, a storm formed and approached where he was staying. This feeling was sort of like that—you couldn't see the storm, but you knew it was out there and it was headed your way.

A cold wind that didn't match with the temperature of the hot day hit Bill and caused him to shiver momentarily before he shrugged his shoulders to regain himself. "There I go getting lost again in my imagination," he thought to himself. As quickly as it had come, it was gone and Bill was right back to it, losing himself in work. 30 minutes later, the convoy of questionable vehicles—from semi-trucks hauling rides to beat-up cars, trucks and motorhomes—were taking the show on the road. So long, Charleston! Hello, Brownsville!

Bill sat down in the truck that hauled his family's travel trailer. It was an '85 Ford King Cab pickup that burned through oil more than he liked to admit. It had been giving him some problems for the last year, but with a little tinkering here and there, he had luckily been able to keep it running. They sure couldn't afford another truck right now.

Dani, already in the passenger seat, had been waiting for him to arrive. Bill looked in his rearview, then back to see Jason and Laura in the back seat. The trip hadn't begun yet, but they were already nose deep in books they had brought with them.

"Ready, kids?" Bill asked.

Jason shrugged his shoulders and Laura looked up from her book, a series about babysitting, and said, "Sure thing, Dad." Then went right back to reading.

"Oh, the joys of youth," Bill thought to himself. In fact, Bill couldn't remember the last time he picked up a book to read for pleasure. He had enjoyed them growing up. He believed his favorite was a book about Ivanhoe, or was it King Arthur? At any rate, the last time he really enjoyed them was when he was probably a little older than Jason was now. Looking at his kids, he realized that he now shared a view with his own dad of the countless times he would ask if they were ready to go, and Bill had his own nose stuck in a book. Things have a way of repeating themselves in the strangest of ways.

He looked back to the front, shifted the idling engine into drive, and stepped on the gas. Yup, Bill thought to himself, the more things change, the more they stay the same.

7

— o —

Traveling was an adventure, but it wasn't without its pitfalls. When a convoy had 20 plus vehicles, there was always something unexpected bound to happen, such as a blown tire or running out of gas. Thankfully, that sunny morning, they were moving right along, with no problems. The sky was bright and blue, and they had a spot to go to. The kids switched from reading to playing road games, like "Animal, plant, or mineral?" in which the guesser could ask 20 questions to figure out what the other player had in mind.

Dani worked on a crossword puzzle from the newspaper they had picked up at the last gas station they stopped at right outside of town that morning. Bill was listening to the CB; they were all on channel 15 and used that to communicate any issues, detours or to banter back and forth occasionally.

On this day, however, there wasn't much chatter. Being on the road took a toll after driving in a loose convoy for a while. Bill enjoyed the driving though, and he loved looking at the passing land as they traveled. From the road, they could see the small villages and towns along the way. Many times, when going from point A to point B, they didn't have a straight shot on the interstate, like this time, when they had to detour from I-57 for a while. They would have to take rural highways and other backroad byways to get to their final destination. Bill enjoyed those moments the most. They drove carefully through those small towns because they had to make sure that there was enough room for some of the bigger trucks to make turns. They also didn't want to make any trouble with the cops. For the most part, they rarely had run-ins, but some small towns had the kind of law enforcement officers that, just like anywhere else, wanted to make a name for themselves or had something to prove. But besides that hazard, it was an enjoyable experience and if you paid attention, like Bill did, you would see the nuances of life in those small towns that are often overlooked—like the group of kids riding their bikes down the side streets, or some grandparent working in the garden. In the country, they'd see farm animals and rows of crops. It was a view of how the "other side" lived. It was a life that Bill appreciated but had no concept of, at least not to the level of the people that lived in these small communities. Oil drilling rigs had dotted the land at one time, but there seemed to be fewer and fewer in the area every year. It made Bill think of his own trade. Once there had been tons of traveling shows and big top circus routes. And like the oil rigs, they seemed to have disappeared over time. Of course, you wouldn't notice it unless you really thought about or were in that particular line of work.

They had been on the road for a couple hours and were somewhere around the midpoint between their last gig and the area where Brownsville was supposed to be when Bill's beeper went off in that steady "bzzz bzzz bzzz" that he was so used to. He quickly pulled the little, black box from his pocket and looked at the LCD readout of the number of the person who called. He didn't recognize it, but assumed it was the pay phone that Jimmy was using to get in touch with him. He put the beeper back on his belt, then reached over and grabbed the CB to call Brad. "Tough Guy, Tough Guy. This is Daddy Donovan. Over."

"Go for Tough Guy," Brad's voice called through the CB speaker.

"I have to pull over and find a pay phone. I believe Smooth Talker just beeped me, so that should give us some information about the next spot," Bill said. "Smooth Talker" was Jimmy's CB handle. Sure, most normal people just picked their own handles, or call signs, but that wasn't the tradition of Donovan Delights Entertainment. It was established long ago and long before Bill was in charge, but it was tradition now. Their group didn't pick their own nicknames; someone else gave them to you. This would change over time, depending on the person and their position, however. Bill's call sign had been "Junior" for the longest time, while growing up. When he went away and came back, it changed to "Yo-Yo." Then, it slowly gave way to "Shadow," since he was basically his father's right-hand man, (you might even say he was his dad's shadow), making sure things were accomplished. When his father passed away, his handle became "Daddy Donovan," which he didn't like at first because that had been his dad's handle and he almost felt like it was a slight to his dad's memory. At the same time, however, it brought a sense of normalcy to the troupe, because that handle had been around forever. Brad's call sign was attributed to the fact that he had been the one to set many a wayward worker straight...and it wasn't surprising that he didn't always just use strong words to do it. He'd had the name so long now that he'd probably keep it until he was using a walker to get around, if he made it that far.

After Brad acknowledged, Bill looked for the next gas station. About five minutes later, he found one and pulled in.

"All right, kids, may as well use the bathroom while we're here because once we start again, we're not gonna stop 'til we get there," Bill said.

Everyone piled out of the vehicle, and Dani asked whether Bill wanted anything from inside. Bill shook his head "no," but then hesitated and asked for coffee. It couldn't hurt to have some caffeine because as soon as they arrived at the next spot, they would move right on into setting up shop. Where it took six to eight hours to break everything down, it would take two to three times as long to set everything back up. It was going to be hours before he would even think about stopping for the evening.

He walked over to the phone booth. This one was nicer than the one at the last location. It was clean, and the phone book was actually present and protected by a weatherproof, heavy-duty, plastic folder. Bill stuck his finger in the coin return and found nothing, then placed the handset up to his ear as he dialed Jimmy.

It rang a few times, and then he disconnected. He retrieved his quarter and decided to use the restroom himself while they were here. He would try Jimmy in five minutes. They had a system set up for the times when he expected to hear from Jimmy, and Jimmy didn't answer the phone when he returned the phone call at the next available phone. He would place three calls, five minutes apart. If Jimmy didn't answer, then Bill would get back on the road and drive for half an hour, then do it all over again.

After using the restroom, he walked out to see his family making selections on whatever they wanted, and checked his watch. It was about time for him to call again. On the way toward the door, he decided to stop when he saw the store clerk behind the counter. The clerk looked to be in his mid-50s, with a mustache and glasses that hearkened back to the 1970s. When he saw Bill walk up, the clerk asked, "May I help you?"

It was the kind of question that the man must have asked a thousand times, yet still had the ability to sound halfway interested in listening. "Yeah," said Bill, "My family and I are on the road and heading to a town a couple of hours from here called Brownsville. Ever heard of it?"

"Where did you say it was?" the clerk asked.

"I believe it's between Marion and Carbondale," Bill replied.

The clerk took off his glasses and, while holding them in his hand, he looked up while he pursed his lips. Wherever he was going in memory, he was going deep. Deep enough to provide an adequate and well-thought-out answer, anyway. The moment didn't last long, but to Bill, it seemed to drag. He waited patiently for the answer; it wasn't like he was going anywhere until his wife paid for the items she and the kids had picked up. Finally, the man ran one hand through his thinning hair and put his glasses back on. "You know, I don't think I ever have. I wanna say something was tickling my memory but can't remember why. I'm sorry."

"Oh, no worries, sir. Just thought I'd ask. I've never been there, so was curious," Bill said.

"Well, I'm sure someone will know about it. In fact, I could call my brother-in-law. He works at the local community college, as a history professor," the clerk said.

"That's okay...really," Bill said, thinking the guy was going way above and beyond to help a customer. Upon looking outside, Bill determined that the poor guy probably didn't get a whole lot of business and was bored half the time.

"Alrighty then; suit yourself," the clerk said, then transitioned to Dani as she walked up to the counter. "Will this be all for you, ma'am?"

While Dani took care of purchasing the package of red licorice sticks, soda, the cup of coffee and other snacks, Bill walked outside to try Jimmy again. He felt a sense of déjà vu since he had just done this a few minutes prior. He put the change in and dialed the number. It rang three times and he decided to try back in five minutes. When the receiver was halfway to the cradle, he heard a distant voice say "Hello?" Bill brought it back to his ear. "Jimmy?"

"Yeah, boss. It's me," Jimmy replied.

"Oh good. I called once already. Wasn't sure if I would have to wait," Bill said.

"Yeah, sorry about that, boss. I had to step away for a moment. Got hungry, you know?" Jimmy replied.

"That's fine. So tell me, how is everything at the next spot?" Bill asked.

"Um...well, you'll have to see for yourself. It's a bit weird to get to but once you get there, there's a town...though you wouldn't expect it to be there," Jimmy said.

"What do you mean?" Bill asked.

"The back roads to get to it aren't large, nor do they look heavily traveled. There must be other main thoroughfares to get to the town but if there are, I didn't see them. Anyway, it's a town, all right and bustling, too," Jimmy said.

"Did you meet the mayor, Mr. Bright?" Bill asked.

"Strangest thing, Bill... When I arrived at the truck stop, I didn't know who was waiting for me, but as soon as I arrived, the guy came straight up to me. It was like he knew who I was immediately," Jimmy said.

"What's strange about that?" Bill asked.

"Because it was midday, and the place was packed. There was nothing to identify me. I thought it was going to be a problem linking up with whoever it was, but it wasn't a problem at all. It was just strange...that's all," Jimmy replied.

"It might be your license plate; maybe I mentioned to the mayor we were from Kentucky. I can't remember. Or, could've been all the dust and dings on your truck," Bill said as he snickered. "Typical carnie truck."

"Yeah, maybe that was it. Anyway, how far out are you?" Jimmy asked.

"About two hours...maybe a little more than halfway," Bill said.

"Sounds good. I'll be here at the truck stop, waiting for you'uns to show up and guide you the rest of the way," Jimmy said.

Bill thought this was odd because usually, Jimmy would give general directions and set up signs or leave tied ribbon on trees to show where to turn.

"That tough to find, huh?" Bill asked.

"Yeah, I almost got lost finding my way back, but luckily, I took good notes," Jimmy said.

"Okay, sounds good. We will be there soon. Get some rest," Bill said.

"Oh yeah...I plan to take a nap in the truck," Jimmy said.

"Sweet dreams," Bill said, and they disconnected. When Bill hung up the phone, he heard the clink of change falling inside. The conversation didn't last long, and he had seen Dani and the kids head back out to the truck. He joined them and said, "All aboard!" The only one who seemed amused by this playful gesture was Laura. Jason seemed embarrassed and looked at the window. Even Dani seemed to be lost in thought. "Oh well," Bill thought to himself and put the truck in drive. They had no problems getting back on the road, as there was little to no traffic. As he was pulling out, he looked through the driver's side window, which had a perfect view of the store clerk watching them leave.

The store clerk watched the lone truck pulling an RV disappear down the road. "Ah, that must be the life," he thought to himself. "Better than being here at this crummy store." He looked around and sort of became disgusted at his lot in life. The store phone rang, which surprised him because that rarely happened. Usually, the only time it was in use was when he was calling his wife.

"Corner Mart, how may I help you?" the clerk said. After a moment, he continued. "Oh, hey. Sure, you and the boys can come over tonight. Your sister was thinking about making some barbeque and we'd love to have you.

You have to leave your students' papers behind, though,"
he said with a chuckle as he listened to the voice on the
other end. Truth be told, he was a little jealous of his
brother-in-law's success, but he always tried to be cordial.

As he listened to his brother-in-law on the phone,
he looked out the window again. "Oh, I'm glad you
called...too bad it wasn't a few minutes sooner. Your ears
must have been burning because I just told a family about
you."

The man listened to the quick reply and continued,
"Yeah, they were traveling through and making a pit
stop. Well, they weren't from around here—you could
tell—but while they were here, they were asking about a
town over near Carbondale, called Brownsville. You ever
heard of it? I can't say that I have. I reckon if anyone knew,
it'd be you."

The store clerk listened to the reply and as he did, his
eyes squinted in concern, then opened in surprised amazement at what his brother-in-law was telling him. "Really?! You don't say. Well, that's crazy. I never heard of that
town before. That's a shame that it was destroyed so long
ago...1800s, you said...yeah, that's a shame. I guess that
family won't be finding it. I wish I could let them know.

8

— > —

"**8**5 bottles of beer on the wall....85 bottles of beer..."
Bill heard Laura singing in the back seat, in such
a way to annoy her brother, but not succeeding. Bill
couldn't remember if there was ever a time when he ever
heard that particular song sung to completion and he was
pretty sure that it wouldn't be today. He was right, thank
goodness. As soon as she sang the chorus, she stopped.
"Dad, how much farther we got?"

"Oh, I'd say less than 100 miles," Bill replied.

They had been on the road 30 minutes since the gas station and in that time, he had relayed the information about
where to meet Jimmy to almost everyone else through the
CB. Those he couldn't reach himself, he could hear others
pass it along to.

He looked over at Dani and she was halfway through
a book, a thriller by the look of it. Then, he looked in
the rear-view mirror and could see Jason sitting with his
eyes closed, earphones in, listening to his CD player. No
wonder Laura's annoying song about beer bottles didn't

bother him. He was gone, listening to whatever was in the player.

Bill brought his eyes back to watch the road and take in the sights. They had caught back up to the convoy, which wasn't difficult, since they tended to inch along when they traveled. They were on back country roads, and they were in farm country. If Bill had a nickel for every barn he saw, well, he wouldn't be a millionaire but he would have had a pocket or two full of change. With the cows and horses that dotted the land, it made for a picturesque and pleasant drive.

The radio played softly. He could hear the weatherman come on, so Bill reached down to turn it up. "...High pressure system heading our way. The skies are clear and blue, and the rest of the week is going to be a hot one, with temperatures near 100. With virtually no chance of even scattered afternoon showers, there won't be anything to put a damper on any outdoor plans for the week. But stay hydrated, people! And that's all the weather from WK..." Bill shut the radio off. "Good," he thought to himself. That's about the best news a traveling carnival like theirs could get. Heat, they were used to, but if it was going to be a week of thunderstorms looming...well...it wouldn't be a good week at all. Bill really felt that his luck was looking up. They had found a spot, the weather was going to hold, and they had encountered no major problems on the road as of yet. Bill smiled—it was the first genuine smile that he had had in at least a couple of weeks. The rest of the time, he had been too stressed with trying to keep things humming along and staying afloat. "Yeah," Bill thought to himself, "it's going to be a good week."

Since he was a few minutes behind everyone else, he was the last one to pull into the truck stop parking lot. By the time he arrived, everyone was in the midst of gassing up their trucks one last time or filling up extra gas cans for the generators. Those who weren't actively pumping gas were milling around inside and out, getting drinks, or picking out snacks. Bill parked in the area where all the other drivers were. Thankfully, the truck stop had ample room for all the vehicles.

Bill saw Jimmy leave the front sidewalk of the store and head over to meet him, so he rolled down the window and waved. Before Jimmy arrived, Bill looked into the rear-view mirror and warned the kids that this was the last stop before arriving at their destination, so if they needed to use the restroom or stretch their legs, this was the time to do it. They declined, and Dani was still nose-deep in her book. When Bill looked back out the window, Jimmy had arrived.

"Hey, Jimmy," Bill said.

"Hey, boss," Jimmy replied.

"How was the wait?" Bill asked.

"Not too bad. This truck stop has a nice waiting room for truckers, complete with cable TV, and since there weren't many people in there, I watched a movie that was on," Jimmy replied. "It could have been worse."

"Yep, it could always be worse, Jimmy. So, how far is Brownsville?" Bill asked.

"Not far. But like I said, it's not an easy route, as in, it's not one you would typically follow to get to a town," Jimmy said.

Bill didn't understand what this meant, but figured he would have to wait until he saw it for himself. "How were the people?" Bill asked.

"Mr. Bright was...eager, I would say. He introduced me to some other folks but their names escape me. Overall, they seemed very enthusiastic in welcoming us," Jimmy said.

"Eager for the money we'll make on their townspeople that we're gonna split, I bet," Bill replied with a smile.

"Maybe. I'm not sure, but anyway, all that to say this—they can't wait for us to arrive and set up shop," Jimmy said.

"Good deal. I'm going to go inside real quick. Pass the word and tell everyone to be ready to go in 15 minutes," Bill said, as he opened his truck door to head inside.

The truck stop here was much more bustling than the last gas station. Plenty of people were coming and going. There were more gas attendants, too. As Bill approached, he passed a tall, young man with the truck stop logo on his shirt and trucker hat, who was heading toward the gas booth near the big rigs. With Brownsville on his mind, he had a nagging feeling that he couldn't shake, so Bill asked the young man if he had ever heard of the town.

"Sir, I've lived here most of my life except for when I was deployed to Iraq for Desert Storm with the Army. I've never heard of that town," the young man replied.

"Really?" Bill asked. "Not once? Apparently, it's not too far from here."

"I mean...there are small towns all over around here, and I know most of them, but that name I've never heard of...then again, mister, this area can be a strange place at times," the young man said.

"What do you mean?" Bill asked, intrigued now.

"Well, you live around here long enough, you see some weird things. This area has a long history, not all of it good from what I've been told by my uncle...and those sorta things kinda stick around, you know?" he replied. It seemed as if he didn't want to share more.

The conversation became suddenly uncomfortable, and Bill wanted to ask more questions but couldn't think of anything pertinent to ask. Then the young man spoke up, "Well, sir, I have some things I must do for work. Is there anything else I can help you with?" Bill shook his head and the young man walked away, heading toward the big rigs, leaving Bill alone with his thoughts. Bill stood there, motionless, for a few moments as his brain worked to make sense of a place that apparently no one knew about...at least no one he had talked to yet. He was beginning to have a sneaking suspicion that no matter who he talked to in this town or the surrounding areas, no one would have heard of this place called Brownsville. When he realized he had been standing there for a good minute, he shook himself out of it and headed inside to use the restroom. As he had gotten older, he'd come to understand the importance of taking a leak whenever the opportunity arose.

A few minutes later, Bill exited the store and stepped off the curb. From what he figured, they would head west from here, since the town was supposed to be between Marion and Carbondale. Bill looked westward and although it had been bright and sunny all day, he now saw a large, dark cloud in that direction, and it seemed to be growing at a rapid speed.

Remembering the weather report on the radio earlier made him think that there shouldn't have been any storms in the area. He guessed it just reinforced that the meteorologists the world over were rarely correct. It seemed that Kathy/Madame Zara would have better odds than the weatherman.

Jimmy's voice crackled through the CB. "We should probably get going. Be best to get there before that storm hits. I don't want anyone to get lost in the rain."

Bill reached over and picked up the mic. "I agree. Let's see what this spot looks like."

Command given, the convoy began to roll. With so many trucks, vans, and other vehicles, it took them a bit to all get onto westbound Route 13. It was late afternoon, with plenty of cars on the road and with the traffic light's rapid rotation through the red, yellow, and green, the convoy couldn't all get out at once. Jimmy was leading it, so he slowed down in the right lane until the last vehicle could get on the road and catch up. Brad was at the tail end.

Finally, when Brad said over the CB, "We're up!" the pace quickened in an accordion-like fashion, with the front stretching first, followed by the remaining vehicles. Eventually, they all fell in line together and were uniform. Halfway between Marion and Carbondale, Jimmy turned right onto Route 148, heading north, where they passed a couple of small towns—one called Energy, followed by another named Herrin. They passed a burger stand on the left that boasted "Serving You the Best Burgers Since 1931," which, apparently was true; the lot was packed out. Once past these towns, the rain started falling. It began with couple of large raindrops smacking the windshield, like an opening to a drum solo that quickly crescendoed as the bottom fell out, with the rain coming in nearly horizontal sheets. It was hard to tell when, but at some point, Jimmy took a couple of turns and they were on some county backroad. Another turn, and they were bumping along a gravel road. Bill thought this was strange, but Jimmy had warned him that this wouldn't be the typical way to get to a town—any town—but here they were. It seemed more like going down narrow trails to get to a remote cabin in the woods. They continued on, and eventually, even Bill (who usually had a pretty good sense of direction) became lost as to which way they were heading. With the storm going full force, it was easy to become turned around. Through the greyness of the rain, Bill was barely able to make out corn fields to the right and left. "Where in the world were they heading? What did he get himself into?" Bill thought.

"Where is this place?" Bill spoke into the mic.

"I told you, boss...this is a wild way to get there, but it was the only way they showed me. They said it wasn't on any maps," Jimmy replied.

George spoke up on the radio. "This is the wildest route I've ever taken."

Then Brad replied, "Gut Buster, everywhere you go is a wild route" and chuckled into the mic.

After that comment, all anyone could hear was a loud scratching sound over the radio, as presumably George took the mic and rubbed it on his shirt to make the annoying sound. This was done when someone wasn't too thrilled with a remark, not unlike giving someone the middle finger to make a point.

Bill looked at the compass glued to the dashboard. He had picked it up at a truck stop 10 years ago but it had never failed him. It was a cheap one—basically just a plastic ball filled with water; inside, the directional component was mounted on a small pedestal. Normally, whenever the truck hit a bump in the road, the compass would slowly glide back and forth until it settled in one direction. This time, though, it wasn't gliding back and forth smoothly; it was spinning. Bill flicked it and it momentarily stopped, but then began rotating slowly and picked up momentum until it was spinning just as fast as it had been. It was the darndest thing, he thought.

Driving in these conditions was disconcerting; the sheets of rain made Bill feel like he was underwater. No matter how fast the windshield wipers moved, they were unsuccessful at truly wiping away enough water for him to be able to see. Bill felt, rather than saw, the road go from gravel back to a hard top. It was an abrupt transition as the crunchy sound of tires rolling over rocks disappeared, replaced with smooth turnings.

As quickly as the rain came, it ceased, and the sun blazed through a haze overhead. Bill looked out through his side window. It wasn't quite grey, like being overcast or even foggy; it was more like a filter had been placed in the sky. Eventually, even the haze lifted, and it was a bright, sunny day again. He looked at the road and it didn't even appear as if it had rained here. He rolled down the driver's side window, stuck his head out slightly, and looked behind them for the storm clouds, but there weren't any. Bill twisted back and sat straight in the driver's seat. His eyes moved back to the compass, which was still steadily spinning, and it didn't look like it was in the mood to slow anytime soon.

A voice crackled over the CB radio. "That was the weirdest storm I think I've ever been through." Bill couldn't tell who it belonged to, with all the static.

There were no responses. It was such an odd event that everyone was lost in thought over the experience. Jimmy's voice came on, "Not much farther now, boss."

The road was much more conducive to safe travel at this point. At a huge, ancient-looking oak tree, the two-lane turned into a highway and at the corner was a small, neighborhood-type store. There was another, more primitive road next to the tree and Bill wondered where it went. Before long, they saw a town in the distance. Up until this point, they had seen no other vehicles since they turned off Route 148, but now, there was traffic passing them in the opposite direction. To Bill, everything looked normal, at least for now. He didn't want to admit it, but he felt relieved to be back in civilization. Something about being on that gravel road in the middle of that deluge was unnerving. Of course, for the obvious reasons, since he was responsible for so many people and vehicles, but there was something else he couldn't quite put his finger on. It was like a sense of impending doom or a distant, clawing fear, but he couldn't figure out why he felt that way. His heart rate and breath had quickened, but when he saw the other vehicles, the feeling subsided and he was able to take a deep breath.

"Wow! What do you think, kids? Wild storm, huh?" Bill said.

Instead of a response, Jason took off his headphones and said, "I think my CD player is broken."

"Why do you say that?" Dani asked absentmindedly, her nose still in the book she had been engulfed in since the beginning of the drive. Her response was more autopilot because as a mom, she knew she needed to attend to the needs of her child but was also invested in what would happen on the next page. Her mind was somewhere in between the journey of reality and whatever world of imagination the book created for her.

"I don't know. It just quit working after that storm quit," Jason said.

"Maybe the batteries are dead. When was the last time you checked them?" Dani asked.

"They were brand new. I changed them this morning," Jason replied.

"I don't know, honey. We can check it out once we get to where we're going and get set up," Dani said, then returned her full attention to her book.

Laura, on the other hand, was just like her mother but instead of her nose in a book, she was deep in an activity book of word searches, ad libs, and other games you can pick up for $2.99 at any gas station, to keep you busy all day long. Bill considered it a good investment.

Bill's eyes returned to the road during the exchange between Jason and Dani. He was taking it all in; it was picturesque and inviting in the approach to what looked like a really nice town. Houses on the outskirts were sporadic at first but grew in number and density to one another as they drove on. Side roads lead into neighborhoods and eventually into a charming downtown area. There was a large clock tower in the town square. They also passed a large, well-maintained shopping center. Brownsville looked like a quaint area to live in—a welcoming place where a townsperson would have a regular hangout where everyone knew their name, or a favorite pizza shop with a name like "Fatties" or something else cutesy like that. However, as they drove through the town, there was something about it that seemed familiar, though Bill couldn't quite place what it was. He knew he had never been to this town before. He would have remembered the name. Even in the long career that he had in the traveling show arena, he remembered all the locations they had ever been. Sure, the memories might be as fuzzy as old baseball card photos, but the name would spark the memories and essentially bring a magnifying glass in, so he would remember in stark clarity.

The convoy lumbered through the town and continued to a large parking lot that was darn near the center of town, not far from the clock tower. Weird location, Bill thought. Most towns didn't have such large accommodations in the center of downtown, but here one was. It was a vast, grassy area that had ample room for all of them to set up with space to spare. At the edge of the green field, town buildings were set up almost like a man-made fence, facing toward the center of the field. There was another large grass lot across the street, presumably for parking. Bill had seen other squares like this in other towns, but they usually had a courthouse or some large gazebo with benches placed like a centralized park. This particular lot was the perfect size, as if it had been created just for Donovan's Delights Entertainment. It had just enough room, not only for their rides, tents, and booths, but also for their own living spaces at one end.

The convoy slowly drove into the center and by now, everyone was experienced enough to know roughly where they would go to set up. Still, Jimmy was the de facto lot man and guided everyone to where they needed to go. Bill knew they would work long into the night and all day tomorrow in order to be ready for the show to open the day after. Bill pulled the family trailer to the back lot and set up the trailer first. When he completed that, he went to help others get set up. As he moved into the main area where the rest of the show would eventually come into being, he had a feeling of being watched. This wasn't surprising because every town they went to, there were always "lookie loos" that stood around and watched them set up, breakdown, or just watch in general. This time, it felt like he, personally, was being watched—not an overall observation of the activity and goings on. He didn't know why he felt this way, but he shifted his eyes around to see if he could spot whatever it was that gave him the unsettling feeling. He didn't see anything at first but then...wait a minute...was that a figure in the second window of the building in front? Bill couldn't quite tell, so he walked closer. The closer he got, the more unmistakable the feeling of being watched became. Sure enough, it was a person—or a shadow—in the window, looking down at the show...No, they were looking at him. Bill stared back and eventually, the shadow melted away from the window, leaving nothing but an empty window. "How strange," he thought. He turned around and walked back toward the center again. The feeling of being watched left him and he suddenly felt alone, a feeling that was quite at odds with what he had just experienced—so different that it caused him to pause for a moment to ponder what had happened. The tasks of setting up the show and the rides propelled him forward into not dwelling on it for long.

There was something else that Bill hadn't noticed right away. Where there were always bystanders watching in wonder as they set up, in pretty much every town they traveled to, he hadn't seen a single person milling around in this town yet, and that was peculiar. There was no one on the street, no cars driving down the side roads, no activity anywhere except for that strange shadow that Bill had noticed in the window. He quickly passed the thought because again, he had too many other things that required his mental capacity at the moment. That was odd, however, his next observation was even stranger. He saw a man, just standing there at a distance, dressed from head to toe in black.

9

—·—

The man was old, but how old, Bill couldn't tell or even begin to guess. The eyes set in that old face looked youthful in their clarity yet ancient with experience. There was also a twinkle in them that Bill couldn't ignore, as if they were privy to a secret that no one else could comprehend. The man wore an all-black, three-piece suit, complete with a black shirt and a matching black tie. It was the color of night, as if shadows became fabric and had been sewn together. The man was watching Bill. For a moment, Bill wasn't sure if it was the same person that he had felt watching him from the window, but obviously that wasn't the case, since the window was on the other side of the field.

Bill walked toward the man because he felt compelled to say "hello."

"Hello, Mr. Donovan," the man said before Bill opened his mouth to say a word.

Bill was stumped. He didn't know this man, but this guy must have sensed his consternation because he continued, "Yes, I know who you are. I am Mr. Bright."

The voice sounded similar—not quite the same—but close enough. "Oh, okay. Nice to meet you," Bill said and offered his hand to shake, which Mr. Bright took. He felt a sudden hint of a shock, which he assumed was static electricity. The grip was strong, however, it felt cool and clammy, reminiscent of touching a dead fish. Bill immediately felt the need to wash his hands or at least rub them against his jacket when Mr. Bright let go. He would wait to wipe off his hand, though, because he didn't want to seem rude.

"I'm glad you came on short notice. I know the town couldn't wait for you to join them," Mr. Bright said and smiled.

Mr. Bright's teeth were perfectly straight and white, and Bill thought they had to be dentures to be that flawless. His teeth didn't match his face and, come to think of it, neither did his voice. His voice was powerful, whereas it seemed like it should be frail. Then again, although Mr. Bright looked old, he didn't appear frail at all. Bill had to avert his eyes because he didn't want to stare, but something about Mr. Bright was like watching an optical illusion that you couldn't figure out. Your subconscious caught on, but unfortunately, that knowledge couldn't make the leap across the chasm to the conscious mind. But you knew something was amiss.

"Ah...right," Bill replied. "Nice town you have here. You were right; it was a bit tricky finding it. We should be set up by tomorrow evening and we'll be ready to go the next morning. Are there any concerns or last-minute issues that you would like to discuss? I'm sure you discussed them with my right-hand man, Jimmy, but since I'm here, we can talk about them now."

"No issues," Mr. Bright said. "It's been a long time since we've had anyone such as yourselves in town—a very long time—and we're glad that you're here. It will be memorable for everyone, I'm sure."

"Do you have a point of contact that you'd like me to go through if any problems or issues arise?" Bill asked.

"Please call me," Mr. Bright replied.

That was peculiar, thought Bill. Almost every other place they'd been, the mayor was rarely involved, much less the point of contact for such events. They were typically more of a figurehead and didn't really get into the trenches, so to speak. For a town seemingly sizeable, surely there were more important things the mayor could be doing besides dealing with a sideshow.

"Okay," Bill said hesitantly. "Is there anything about the town we should know? Any place you don't want us? Any special rules?"

Bill knew that carnivals had bad reputations and since that was usually the case in every town they landed in, it was best to get it out of the way by being direct about any special "rules." Each town had their own way of doing things and sure, America was a free country, but that didn't always remain true when it came to strangers. Everywhere the carnival went, the carnies were always the strangers, the outsiders...and often the scapegoats. Fear and uncertainty are powerful things.

"You and your people may go anywhere you like, Mr. Donovan. They will find their stay very welcoming. In fact, you may never want to leave." Mr. Bright smiled, but Bill noticed the smile didn't seem to match the twinkle in Mr. Bright's eyes.

Bill laughed lightly and nodded his head in agreement, not because he felt like laughing, but because it seemed like the polite and appropriate thing to do...also, maybe out of uncertainty. It was such an odd remark and rather than pointing it out, Bill had learned long ago to roll with such things. As long as they had a safe place, and the townsfolk didn't mess with his people, then he couldn't care less what was said.

"Well, Mr. Bright, I have to move along. Have to make sure everything is set up correctly. It was nice meeting you," Bill said, and began to move toward the tractor trailers that were unloading.

"Likewise, Mr. Donovan," Mr. Bright said.

After he had gotten no more than 30 feet away, Bill realized he had forgotten to ask about compensation for the town. There was always a contract drawn up and towns always took a slice of the proceeds. Bill turned back to speak with Mr. Bright, but...he was no longer there!

Bill quickly looked up and down the street they were standing by and saw no one except for the carnie workers moving like ants, setting up the show. There was no indication of where he had gone and in Bill's estimation, not enough time had lapsed for Mr. Bright to get very far, but he was just...gone.

A troubled sensation moved ever so slightly in the pit of his stomach, which he could have almost mistaken for queasiness, but he knew that the pink stuff wouldn't fix this kind of upset stomach. It wasn't bad yet, but his years of experience were being put to use. They gave him a hunch that, although everything was working out, something about all of this—the timing, the odd nature of getting the call, the feeling of the town, it was just...something that Bill couldn't put a finger on. He was not prone to paranoia. Lord knows that all these years on the road taught him to be adaptable and to sense danger. Was this place dangerous?

Maybe he was being paranoid. He was tired, as he had started the day early and he knew that could weather his thoughts. Maybe it was nothing. He eventually chalked it up to being exhausted, knowing that he shouldn't look a gift horse in the mouth.

First things first. He, along with Jimmy, went around to help the work crews get the rides set up. Each ride had its own protocol for assembly and they had developed a specific order to set them up. First up was the Ferris wheel. There was nothing like seeing a Ferris wheel to let people know they were in town. It was, by far, the tallest thing they had in the show and when that sucker was lit up, it would be visible for miles on a clear night with nothing to obstruct the view.

Kurt, the ride jockey for the Ferris wheel, took great pride in making sure all the lights were functional. Kurt was in his mid-thirties and didn't smile a lot. His teeth weren't the best set of chompers in the crew—a fact he was well aware of—but he was loyal, cordial to customers that came to the show, and didn't give off that creepy vibe. And though he may not have had the best dental hygiene, it didn't reflect when it came to his work. He was borderline OCD when it came to setting up the Ferris wheel and keeping it clean. Before he came to work for show, he had been in prison for armed robbery, except he wasn't the one holding the gun; he was little more than a kid, at 18, and to hear him tell it, he was just driving for a friend and got caught up in it by mistake. Whether he intended to be the driver or not, Kurt Longrid spent 10 years in the pen for it. Bill gave him a chance about five years ago. Since then, Kurt had been a stellar employee and since he didn't have family, he always ended up staying on at the winter's quarters, helping to make sure the show was ready for the next season.

Bill looked at all the other rides from the platform of the Ferris wheel. All the other ride jockeys and crew had similar stories. Some histories he knew, some he didn't, and he would never pry. A man's past was his own, as long as he did the work and was dependable and honest. In some ways, Bill thought of his troupe as his own personal foreign legion. Donovan's Delights Entertainment didn't care about your past; it only cared about your present and whether you would work hard without causing trouble.

"How are you doing, Kurt?" Bill asked.

"Doing great. I had to work on the lines. One of the bulbs was broken, so I had to replace that. Had to splice..." Kurt replied and kept going.

Along with his bad teeth, he also wasn't the greatest of conversationalists. He had a tendency to control the conversation—not really "control" as much as talk at a person instead of to or with them. Some people were natural conversationalists, and some, like Kurt, definitely were not.

"That's fine, Kurt," Bill cut in. "We're going to have a good week this week...just checking to see if you needed anything extra."

"No, I'm good. The ride here was kind of interesting with the rain and all. I thought we were going to..." Kurt began again and launched into another stream of conversational bits.

Bill interrupted again, "Right. We're here because it was a last-minute spot that desperately wanted us to come and it came at just the right time, didn't it?"

Without waiting for a reply, because Bill knew there would be one, he looked at Jimmy and nodded that it was time to move on. He said his "goodbye" quickly to Kurt, who surprisingly didn't say much in return. His reply was

quite conservative by Kurt's standards, but it was probably because Bill noticed that Kurt saw a dirty spot on one
of the Ferris wheel benches and headed toward it with a
rag.

Next, they stopped by the Scrambler, then the haunted
house. Everything was like clockwork. Everyone knew
what they needed to do. The amount of coordination
that went into it was spectacular and a sight to behold.
Deep down, it bothered Bill somewhat that most people
would never know enough about the process to fully
appreciate it. Things were moving along nicely but, with
that being said, it would still take long into tonight and
most of the day tomorrow to finish setting up everything
before it would officially open. Since Jimmy was around
to oversee what was already going well, Bill knew his main
"job" was over for the day, so he checked in on George to
see how the food booths setup was coming along.

George's people knew what they were doing, as well.
With the fact that most of the food booths were trailers,
it didn't require much more than parking, detaching the
trucks, then setting up all the inventory and supplies
to sell hot food and snacks as soon as the gates prover-
bially opened. Apparently, one of the food stands was
already complete because when he found George, he was
munching on a hotdog, moving from one stand to the
next to see about any last minute or ongoing needs his
people might have.

"Doing a taste test?" Bill asked.

"Every day," George replied. "How's your side of the house coming along?"

"Surprisingly well. You?" Bill asked.

"About the same. You talk to Brad yet?" George asked.

"No, I thought I'd see how you were faring first," Bill replied.

"Just fine though...ah...never mind," George began.

Bill was going to let it go, but he knew from experience that little remarks like that were indicators of sometime serious issues that sprang up later.

"What is it?" Bill asked.

George popped that last bite of hotdog into his mouth and said with his mouth full, "Ah, it's nothing."

"You sure?" Bill proffered again.

"Yeah, it's nothing...well, I don't know...maybe it's just me, but this town seems different to me," George said.

"How so?" Bill asked.

"Where are the people? We haven't seen one car or anyone walking by since we've been here. I wouldn't have noticed it normally, but we've been here a few hours already and the sun is starting to set. I haven't seen any townsfolk and, being that we are pretty close to the center of town, it's just.... I don't know. You know?" George said.

Bill had indeed noticed it, but like George, you didn't really notice until it was either brought up or you paid very close attention. Like a low key "eureka!" moment that you didn't know you were searching for. "Maybe everyone is working, and it is a bit hot...or maybe that storm we went through sent everyone inside. I don't know. I met the mayor, and he seemed agreeable," Bill replied.

"Ah, you did?" George replied. "I didn't know."

"Yeah, he was dressed all in black and you know, he was fully dressed in a suit, even with this heat," Bill said.

As if on cue, they both heard the engines of a couple of cars driving by on one of the streets along the perimeter of the field. More joined in until it was a steady flow, which more closely resembled what they had come to expect from small towns such as this one.

"Maybe we just didn't notice them," Bill said.

"Yeah, maybe," George replied and with that, he bid Bill a quick goodbye as he left to check on the last of his folks setting up. Bill watched him go and turned to look at the cars driving past. They were all immaculate, which was very noticeable—all clean and fully waxed, as if they were right off the showroom floor. From Bill's vantage point, however, he couldn't see anyone in the vehicles. Either the windows were tinted to the point where, in the waning daylight, he couldn't see in...or he couldn't see past the glare from the windows. This was another one of those things that he saw but wouldn't really notice until later that evening, right before he drifted off to sleep. He never saw any of the drivers or occupants.

Bill found Brad right where he expected he would find him—on his back, underneath one of the mechanical games. The only part of his body that was visible were two legs sticking out, with one of his guys handing him tools to fix last minute issues. It was a view that would be completely normal in a mechanic shop, but here on a field in some town, it always looked out of place. He was, by far, at that age where he could have let someone else take over the actual manual labor of repairing the games, but he was one of those people that if it needed to be fixed, he would take care of it himself, by golly. There were several reasons for this: 1) because he knew what to do, 2) it would take longer to direct someone else about how to fix it, 3) he wouldn't feel right telling someone else to fix it, even if they knew what they were doing. All in all, it was just easier to do it himself.

"Brad?" Bill asked.

A muffled reply came from underneath the machine.

Bill got down on one knee and looked underneath. Brad was tooling away on some bolt, tightening it, flashlight in one hand and the sounds of ratcheting "click click click" coming from the other hand. "Brad, you need anything? How's it looking for your folks?"

There was a momentary pause as Brad looked down at his feet toward Bill and focused his eyes. To Bill, Brad was deep in focus on what he was doing and almost felt bad about interrupting him.

"I'm sorry, Brad," Bill said. "I know you're busy. I just wanted to see if you needed anything."

"Oh...Hey Bill," Brad replied. "I think we're all good here. Everyone is all set, though I need to go check in on independent row."

Independent row was a term that, as far as Bill knew, was only used by Donovan's Delights. It referred to the row with all the sideshows that latched on to the carnival, like Kathy...or rather, Madame Zara when she was working. They were independent and gave the carnival a cut from whatever they made.

"I'll go check in on them," Bill said.

"You will?" Brad replied. "That'd be great."

"Yeah, I'll let you know if they need anything."

Bill stood up and smiled at Brad's helper, a man by the name of Phil Cummings, who ran the duck pond game. At this point, all Phil was doing was keeping Brad company while he worked on the machine. Phil nodded back and Bill walked away from the "clickety clack" tune of the ratchet going at it again.

It didn't take long to end up where he needed to be, and soon Bill saw all the tents. Surprisingly, Madame Zara's tent wasn't set up yet, but all the others were. There weren't really that many tents. One was a mini petting zoo, complete with rabbits, snakes, pygmy goats and whatever else the couple who ran it, The Thompsons, picked up along the way. The booth was "Wild Things Petting Zoo." They hadn't been with them very long—maybe a couple years. Seeing them didn't exactly brighten Bill's mood, not that he was in a foul one at the moment. Honestly, they didn't bring in much money. The overhead of keeping the little petting zoo running was more than it was worth. It barely fed the folks that ran it and the percentage of the cut that went to Donovan's Delights was peanuts. Bill had often thought about cutting them from the show, but every time he went to do it, he took pity on them and kept them on for another week. Another week turned into another season. For now, it worked out because they had room for them, but if Donovan's Delights ever grew to where it needed room, the Thompsons and the Wild Things Petting Zoo would be the first to go.

Not seeing Madame Zara's booth set up, Bill spoke to the Thompsons to see if they had seen her around. Mike Thompson was a tall, overweight man with a face that was framed in a wispy beard. In all honesty, his face probably would have looked better without the beard, but Bill didn't think that any amount of conversation would persuade Mike to shave it. His wife, Sara, was a waif of a woman who wore only homemade clothing. Her mousy brown hair always seemed to be a mess.

"Hey, Mike. Have you seen Kathy?" Bill asked, using Madam Zara's real name.

Mike, who was currently putting the finishing touches on the chicken wire barrier around their tent, stopped what he was doing and looked up at the sound of Bill's voice. He then turned his gaze to where Bill indicated, an empty spot down the way.

"No, haven't seen her. She was at the last town," Mike offered pleasantly.

"Well, if she shows up, would you tell her I'm looking for her?" Bill asked.

"Sure," Mike said and went back to working on the fence.

From there, Bill walked over to where the ticket booths were being set up and the unofficial gate into the carnival. There were no fences surrounding the field, but the ticket booths were intentionally set up to create a funneling effect so that customers would have to go through the ticket booth area before they went into the midway and the rest of the show. As such, just like Bill did during every set up, he personally placed the car at the entrance where every carnival-goer would see the '58 Buick Special. He went to the back, where all the trailers were staged after setting up the show, and found the one he was looking for. He grabbed the keys to the truck from one of the drivers and pulled it around to the front. He always did this personally because, well, it was his dad's car and he felt it was his ritual. To break it would bring about some curse...Bill was sure of it. Even if he was only sort of joking to himself about a curse, he had done it so long that he wouldn't feel right doing it any other way. He backed the trailer hauling the car in front of the ticketing booths, not in a way to crowd them, but in a way that took center stage. It was an attraction and even though it hadn't run in years, it looked beautiful. It was the kind of thing that old timers and young bucks alike would stop and wordlessly express their amazement at such a beauty. Of course, he never told anyone the car didn't run. He didn't want to ruin anyone's vision or dream they may have conjured up for themselves.

That was the way life went sometimes—people created dreams based upon what they saw and not necessarily on knowing all the facts about such things.

Once set, Bill unhitched the trailer and put chocks around the wheels so it wouldn't roll. To prevent anyone from taking off with the trailer during the night, he was always sure to put on a hitch lock. Next, he removed the car cover, as well the chains that secured the car during travel. Then lowered the sides of the trailer so that the car could be seen unobstructed. Bill then unfurled banners that would hide the ugliness of the trailer. Not that the trailer was really ugly, but compared to the car that sat on it, it wasn't pretty. He parked the truck back where he had gotten it and returned to make sure there wasn't a single speck of dust on the car. This was something that both he and his son Jason did at some point every day of the show, to make sure it was spotless. It was, after all, the symbol of their carnival. Bill knew he would have to eventually get it running again, but with the debts they had, he knew it wouldn't be this year. He hung on to the hope, as he imagined a future where he could use the car and the smooth rumble of its engine as an attraction on opening night.

With that task complete, he looked at his watch and noticed it was getting late. The sun had long since gone down. There were still cars sporadically driving by, but still no pedestrians. Come the day after tomorrow, the midway would be open for business and this place would be packed with families from this town. The mere thought of it was exciting to Bill. It was like having the best gift at the party, and anxiously waiting for birthday boy or girl to open it. The giver got just as much, if not more, than the receiver. Of course, in this case, it was a two-way street, and the carnival would be given cash gifts in exchange for giving the gift they had brought to town. It was a fair trade, Bill thought.

He walked toward the back, where everyone would go to sleep at some point. There would be one or two night owls that would stay up and watch over the lot to make sure nothing walked away. Sometimes they had to hire security, but this time, the spot opened up so quickly that Bill hadn't even had time to think about such matters. No biggie, though, as the town didn't seem very harmful, at least what he saw of it on the way in.

Bill noticed Jason walking in front of him and hurried to catch up. "Hey son, how are you doing?" Bill asked.

"I'm tired. I think I'm gonna sleep well tonight," Jason responded.

A thought occurred to Bill in passing, so he asked, "Did you ever get your CD player to work?"

"No, I don't know what happened. It just quit working. I put new batteries in. I guess it's dead," Jason replied.

"Oh, all right. Weird," Bill said, and then put his arm around his son. "I'll take a look at it and see if I can get it running."

"Sure," Jason replied.

"Anything else going on today?" Bill asked.

"No, everything went as usual. I helped Jimmy with setting up some rides and then got a cheeseburger from one of the booths that Uncle George had set up," Jason said.

The mention of food made Bill's stomach rumble. He had been so busy throughout the afternoon and evening, he had forgotten to eat. "I wonder what your sister and your mom are up to," Bill said.

"I saw them earlier, heading toward home," Jason said.

"Home" meant many things. There was "home" like winter's quarters, then there was "home" on the road, that being the RV for his family. For others, like the carnies that traveled with them that couldn't afford their own space, a bunk in the bunkhouse trailer was where they slept.

"We've never been to this town before, have we?" Jason asked.

"Nope, this is our first time here. Why?" Bill asked.

"No reason, I guess. There are just some things that remind me of other towns we've been to—almost identical, really," Jason replied. "Just thought it was weird."

Bill had noticed when they entered town that it felt familiar on some level and it wasn't until Jason mentioned it that he stopped to think about it...but his son was right. Bill could have sworn that he had seen some of the views before, in other towns. Which towns, he couldn't say. Over the years, he had racked up quite a number to choose from, but given some time, Bill was pretty sure that he could eventually identify which towns looked similar to this one. It was an absurd thought. There was no way a town could look exactly like another, was there? Probably used the same architect or city planner or something like that. If something worked, there would always be others trying to replicate it elsewhere. Be it a new act in a carnival show or an efficiency in a town, another town was sure to try and copy it, not that Bill knew this for certain. He had a mind for the traveling show—not towns—and he was basically firing blind with assumptions. It sort of made sense, though, and this quieted the alarm in the back of his mind that sometimes broke through the surface when his mind couldn't explain something. Once he had arrived at a reasonable explanation, that alarm would again submerge itself until the next time something didn't add up, then it would propel itself outward again.

"Good eye, son. Yeah, that is kind of weird," Bill said, then added his explanation of it possibly being a common city planner or similar city building code or...whatever. This seemed to work, because Jason nodded as if that was the truth, and it was all the explanation he needed.

Bill noticed this and imagined a potential future encounter in which Jason defended something because his dad had told him so. "Oh Jason," Bill thought to himself, "If you only knew how much I don't know. I'm making this stuff up as I go along."

He then thought about his own dad and smiled. The more things change, the more they stay the same. It was a generational curse of life—not a "curse," per se, but in the sense of repetitive behavior between generations and frankly, it was a miracle that anyone survived the ignorance.

"Well, I agree. I think we're both going to sleep well tonight."

They could hear some rides still being assembled, but it was subdued and didn't sound as bustling as it had earlier.

Dani and Laura were at the RV, getting ready for bed. The way the RV was set up, Bill and Dani slept in the area that could be closed off with a door. There were bunk beds at the other end where the kids slept.

Everyone else had already eaten, so Bill looked into the small refrigerator and made himself a sandwich out of lunch meat and added a slice of cheese. It wasn't gourmet, but it got the job done. He crawled into bed beside his wife, who must have had a rough day, because she was already out, snoring lightly.

As Bill drifted off to sleep, he couldn't get the thought of Brownsville out of his mind. He remembered where he had seen the clock tower before; it was exactly the same as the one in the nearby town of Marion. Before consternation could set in to break the surface of consciousness, the gravitational pull of sleep already had him speeding toward the black hole of slumber. He was out before his mind fully comprehended what was floating through it. His last conscious thought before sinking away was, "It couldn't be the same clock tower...could it?"

10

The next morning, Bill woke up surprisingly refreshed. The thoughts from the night before were long gone, as his mind had forgotten all about them. It was early. He could tell by the light coming in through the slatted blinds that the sun was waking up, just like he was. It was a dull blue at the moment, but give it less than a half hour and a blazing orange would replace it. He swiftly moved from the bed and went through his morning routine. His wife woke up, as well and moved to the kitchen to start the coffee. While she did this, Bill hopped into the cramped shower and took a quick one. With four people needing to take a shower, he didn't want to hog all the hot water that the small water tank held.

In 15 minutes, he was ready to go. Fully dressed, a cup of coffee in hand, and a moment of peace while Dani replaced him in the shower. The warmth and flavor of the coffee was a comfort, but he didn't have long to savor it. He knew today would also be a long one—one with a lot of tasks to be completed before the "grand opening" tomorrow.

They had to finish setting up the rides, booths, trailers and tents, then double check everything to satisfy safety requirements, both those placed by external safety-related organizations, as well as Donovan's Delights' own personal requirements, which went beyond the bare minimum. He learned this from his dad, who always said that if you took shortcuts, it would come back to bite you in the rear more so than if you had just made the effort to do it right in the first place.

He heard the shower shut off, and he yelled to Dani through the door, "I'm heading out! Love you!"

He heard her muffled reply and looked to the back of the RV, where he saw his kids still snoozing. He would let them sleep a little longer. He turned toward the door and walked out.

Mr. Bright was standing there, at the bottom of his steps, obviously waiting for him. Not expecting him, Bill jumped and let out a curse word.

"Good morning, Mr. Donovan," Mr. Bright said. "I trust that you slept well."

"Geeze, you startled me. I'm sorry," Bill replied.

"That's okay," Mr. Bright smiled.

"Yes, I slept well...but um...what brings you here so early...and how did you know which trailer was mine?" Bill asked.

His trailer looked like the other trailers in the parking area, with little to establish who belonged to which trailer.

By looking at it, no one outside the carnival would have known that Bill's trailer was his.

"I'm a good guesser, Mr. Donovan," Mr. Bright said, his smile still wide and lingering. It was an uncomfortable smile that didn't reach his eyes, at least that's the way it seemed to Bill. Or, maybe it could have been a shadow. The sun wasn't fully up yet and at that angle, it did cast an awful lot of shadows. At the same time, the smile seemed fake, almost to the point of being cartoonish. Before his mind went away with itself, he asked "What did you need?"

"Oh me? Nothing really. I wanted to confirm some things and see what your people thought of our town here. As I said yesterday, we are really excited that you're here," Mr. Bright responded.

Bill had never had a mayor or representative of any town do this before, so it stuck out like a sore thumb. "Oh...well..." Bill began, at a loss for words before he found them again. "Oh well, everything seems nice here. We should be finished setting up by this afternoon and be ready for showtime tomorrow."

"Good. That's excellent. I know the people of my town will be most looking forward to this," Mr. Bright said.

"Is there anything else?" Bill asked.

"No. Oh, and be sure to let me know if any of your people have any issues—any issues at all," Mr. Bright said.

"Did something happen to where my people would have issues? I believe you mentioned this yesterday," Bill reminded him.

"Yes, I did, but we are so excited to have you here, I didn't want there to be any problems that would cause distress for you or your troupe this early in your visit," Mr. Bright said. "We don't get many out-of-towners visiting here."

"Why is that?" Bill's curiosity piquing.

"That's a long and old story—one I will save for another time, perhaps later this week," Mr. Bright replied.

"Sure, that will be fine," Bill replied.

Bill walked down the steps and Mr. Bright stepped back to make room. "Is there anything else you would like to discuss?" Bill asked again, "because...well...no offense, but I really need to make my rounds if we are going to be ready to go for tomorrow."

"By all means," Mr. Bright gestured, that creepy smile still cemented on his face. "I will take my leave."

Mr. Bright walked away first, turned at the edge of the trailer, and disappeared from sight. Bill watched him go with a sense of peculiarity that rained down on him like his own personal black storm cloud. His thoughts were interrupted when he heard the door to the trailer open up and Dani stepped out.

"Oh, I'm surprised to see you. I thought you would be long gone by now," Dani said.

She was fully dressed in jeans and a t-shirt with her hair pulled into a ponytail under a ball cap. She came down the stairs and stopped in front of him.

"Are you okay?" Dani asked.

"Yeah, I'm fine," Bill replied. "It's the mayor. He was out here waiting for me this morning."

"Really?"

"Strange, huh?" Bill asked.

"I suppose. What did he want?"

"To ask if we had any issues?"

"That is strange. Usually any issues are on the part of whatever town we're in and they rarely care what we think," Dani responded.

"Maybe we should pack up and leave," Bill said absent-mindedly.

The look on Dani's face, complete with a dropped jaw and wide eyes, only led to the incredulity of that thought.

"What? Why?" Dani asked. "We're here, and we're almost set up. Why leave now?"

"I'm not sure. There's a little voice in me whispering that something isn't right," Bill replied.

"You tell that voice to shut up. We will only have to be here for a week. No matter how weird that mayor is, it's only for a little bit. We've dealt with overbearing townsfolk before."

What she said had been true. Bill knew it, but there was something different about all of this. His mind felt behind the power curve on something—not enough to be worried, but enough to give a person pause.

"I don't know. We need the money, but that mayor gives me the creeps...makes my skin crawl a little, too," Bill said.

Changing the subject to lighter things and to get his mind back on the chores for the day, Bill asked, "Are the kids up?"

"They were slowly moving. Should be coming out shortly," Dani replied. "I think Laura is going to help Brenda again with setting up the funnel cake trailer, then make some candy apples to be ready for tomorrow."

"Well, that's good. She wants to learn and help out," Bill replied.

"It's more than that, I think. She wants to get paid...be a grownup. She says she wants spending money of her own," Dani said.

Bill shrugged. "Might as well start paying her then..."

It wouldn't be any different than what they did with Jason. The only difference was that they started paying Jason last year, when he was 13, not 12 like his Laura was now. It's hard to give privileges to one of your kids without giving them to the other. Also, they couldn't have them on the books, with labor laws being what they were.

Bill remembered a time when it was expected that he would work with his dad, and he wanted to. Then somewhere along the way, politicians passed child labor laws and now you couldn't hire a kid without hassle, even if the kid wanted to work. But allowance and chores? Well, that was a normal family function, wasn't it? It might not hold up in court, but Bill felt it was probably safe. They were never in one place long enough to draw attention, and Dani was a pretty good bookkeeper to keep such things from prying eyes. They didn't cut corners usually, but this, they felt, wasn't the government's business.

"All right, well, I love you. Going to head over to see where Jimmy is and see what else needs to be done," Bill said.

They kissed quickly and went their separate ways, Bill heading toward the rides and Dani toward the HQ trailer to start the day. It didn't take long for Bill to find Jimmy, with his clipboard in hand. He was overseeing the crew and going over the safety checklist for the Gravitron.

The ride was already spinning, making whirring sounds as it picked up speed. Tomorrow and the rest of the week, that whirring sound would be accompanied by screams of terror and delight. Bill knew that the clipboard Jimmy was carrying had a checklist for every ride and it would take most of the morning—probably until mid to late afternoon—before they would be finished.

Jimmy, seeing Bill, greeted him, "Morning, boss."

"Morning," Bill replied. "Sleep all right?"

"All right enough," Jimmy replied.

"How's the list coming along?" Bill asked.

"Right as rain. A couple of joints and hoists had to be replaced. Thankfully, we had some spares, but overall, things are moving along nicely," Jimmy replied.

"Jimmy," Bill said and then stepped closer. "What do you think of the mayor, Mr. Bright?"

Jimmy shrugged his shoulders and thought about it for a moment. "Well, he's an odd one."

"Did you meet anyone else besides him when you first got here, like the deputy mayor, police chief, the fair board, or any of the usuals?"

"No, I didn't see anyone except for him," Jimmy said. "Funny you should ask that. I brought that up with the mayor, and his response was that they all answer to him, so don't worry about seeing them."

It wouldn't be the first town that was ruled with an iron fist, Bill knew, but he felt like he was at the edge of the known world about to step into the part of the map where, "here be dragons" would be marked. The sort of area where unknowns lie, and those unknowns were more often than not dangerous. Of course, Bill had nothing to base this thought or feeling off of, except for a few odd things.

"Not the norm or the usual, but not totally off-base either," Jimmy said, to fill in the silence left by the revelation.

"Jimmy, keep an eye out. It could be nothing, but something doesn't feel quite right," Bill said.

"Anything in particular, boss?" Jimmy asked.

"No, I can't think of anything. It's just this small, nagging feeling that comes and goes since it started a couple of weeks ago," Bill said.

"You think there's trouble?" Jimmy asked, his eyes shifting around to look at the buildings at the far end of the field from his vantage point.

"No, I didn't say that, but I do think we need to keep an eye out. If you see anything out of the ordinary, let me know?" Bill said.

Out of the ordinary was the ordinary thing for the traveling show, but if it were more abnormal than what was typical, Jimmy would know, and Bill wanted to know, too. With that business done, they both went back to the chores of getting the show up to snuff. If they kept at it at this rate, they would finish in the late afternoon, or very early evening, then have respite for the night until they had the "grand opening" tomorrow.

Midway through the day, once they had completed one of the rides and were on their way to the next, Bill broke off and went to check on both Brad and George to see how they were coming along. As he expected, they were in the HQ trailer, along with Dani, getting the tickets and arm bands ready for the opening tomorrow.

Coming into the trailer, Bill sat down at the table and grabbed a box to assist in divvying the arm bands and tickets. George ran his fingers through his white hair. "It sure is going to be a warm week," he said conversationally.

"Why do you say that?" Brad asked, "Did you hear it on the radio?"

"No, I just feel it...but funny you should bring up the radio. I couldn't tune in any station, not on FM or even AM for that matter," George said.

"Was it plugged in?" Brad asked, with a sly grin that plastered his jaw.

"Very, funny Brad...but no matter what radio I tried—nothing. I just know there are going to be some really bored concession workers this week. What do you think they do when they aren't serving at the windows and waiting for the next wave?" George said.

"Ah, could have been just a bad night," Brad replied. "That freak storm could have messed with the waves or something..."

George stopped counting and looked at Brad. "You have no idea what you're talking about, do you? Radios don't work like that." Sometimes these two were like an old married couple.

Brad shrugged it off. "Maybe I don't. Doesn't matter. I'm sure there is some reason."

Bill listened to this with little interest as he counted out, but when he finished with the current stack, he decided to join the conversation. "Out of curiosity, when did you last hear anything on the radio?"

"When we got into town," George replied, as he reached for another stack of tickets to divvy.

Dani spoke up suddenly, as well, "I think that's about the same time that Jason's CD player broke."

Everyone stopped counting and looked at Dani. George said, "Do you think it's a coincidence?"

"I don't know, but having you talk about no radio just reminded me of his CD player not working," Dani replied.

"Strange," Bill said. "Will you give me that hand radio right there?"

Dani turned around and grabbed the small radio off the counter and handed it over. It was a small emergency radio. Not only did it take batteries, but in the event that you were stuck somewhere, it had a hand crank that you could generate power with if you had nothing else. As it turned out, there was enough juice for it to blaze alive with static when Bill turned it on. The tell-tale sound of white noise littered the air in the small room. Bill turned down the volume so it wasn't so visceral. Now at the manageable level of a dull roar, Bill extended the collapsible antenna to full length and turned the dial on the side of the radio that moved the needle, searching for a signal. He turned the dial and there wasn't even a whisper of a voice or tune coming through, just the steady hissing of static.

"Hmm..." Bill mused, looking at the radio.

"See what I mean?" George said, as if looking for a confidant to prove that he was not lying. "Nothing."

"Yeah, you're correct—nothing. That's never happened before this close to obvious civilization like the town out there," Bill said, as he nodded toward to the door and the town beyond. "I mean...we've all been on the road seemingly in the middle of nowhere where you pick up no signal or worse, only country-western stations."

Bill turned the dial and slowly ran through all the frequencies on both AM and FM. The constant noise didn't change. Bill looked up and saw that everyone had stopped what they were doing and were watching him...no, not watching him, but watching the radio as if their mind couldn't make sense of getting no signal here.

Bill lightly slapped the back of the radio. "Maybe it's busted," he said.

"You keep hitting it and it will be," Dani said in a tone that, although sweet, let it be known that she thought his actions weren't the brightest move.

"If that's busted, then all the radios are...because they're all doing that," George said.

"Oh, that's right. You said that already," Bill said, looking back down at the radio.

This whole week, Bill felt like he was trying to solve a mathematical equation that didn't make sense—like the equivalent of two plus two equaling three. The little voice of caution that had danced at the periphery of his consciousness tapped a little louder and closer. Bill didn't remember a time when he had been in such a state of...well...not confusion. He wasn't confused, but was reaching a state of unknowns he had never experienced. On the road, there were always unknowns, but there was a sort of stability that went with that. Tires would always blow. Gas would always run out. Machines would always quit. But there was always a solution that went along with those variables. This time—or this particular summer—there seemed to be variables with no obvious solutions. It just felt weighty, without a name to give it substance.

Bill pursed his lips, and a small line of sweat beaded on his forehead. He turned the dial slowly one more time. He was giving it one more chance before he would turn it off. He didn't know why he cared so much, but something within him had to keep pressing...had to know for sure. An answer to a question he didn't know.

He kept turning. 90.1...90.4...90.6...90.8...91.2. Finally, "And here we are at WKHL, listening to the sounds of the oldies. Here and everywhere. Another round and 30 minutes of all music, no commercials..." a voice blazed through the speakers.

Bill breathed a sigh of relief for a breath he hadn't realized he had been holding. The whole room shifted in the same way, as if everyone had been unknowingly holding their breath. Brad smiled, "See George, it's just you."

George looked at the radio as if it were a viper coiling to strike. "There was nothing. You guys all heard it, too."

A song played, and the voice sang out, "Put your head on my shoulders..." It was a song from the 1950s by Paul Anka, and a welcome change to the consistent white noise they heard previously.

Bill twisted the dial, and the song gave way to sports. "And the Chicago Cubs are hanging in there..." Then a news channel came on. Then the top 100 Billboard countdown. Bill then switched from FM to AM and the same thing happened. Radio programs that weren't coming through a moment earlier were now streaming into the small room with high clarity. Talk shows and gospel squeaked through the speakers and finally, Bill turned off the radio. When he did, it was like a spell had been broken. He had no idea why he spent the last few minutes continuing to check for a radio signal, but part of him was glad that he did, even more so after he found live stations.

"Satisfied?" Brad asked.

"Suppose so," Bill replied, and put the radio back on the window ledge. With that little episode over, the conversation died down and they continued counting the admission tickets into stacks. With all four counting, it didn't take long to finish. Bill asked Brad about Kathy. He realized he hadn't heard from her and, since he hadn't seen her, was a little worried.

"Yeah, she set up late last night," Brad said, then shrugged as he thought it over. "Apparently, she was in the parking area all day and waited 'til the last minute."

"That's not usually like her," Bill said.

"Right...she's a stickler about being first to set up, so she can relax before opening day," Brad replied.

Bill made a mental note to head to Kathy's tent next to see how she was feeling. With the counting done, everyone moved on to other tasks and slowly, one by one, left the trailer. The dwindling occupants feeling each as they left, step by step, as the weight on the small steps shifted the whole trailer.

Eventually, the only one left was Dani. Since most of her chores were done for the day and she knew she would be up to her neck in work later in the week, with counting money, making sure inventory was stocked, payroll, and everything else, she took a break. She reached over to the radio that Bill had been messing with a few minutes ago with the plan to listen to music. That oldies station sounded relaxing, and it reminded her of what her dad listened to as she was growing up.

She turned the radio on and nothing came out, not even the static they had heard earlier. She checked the batteries and was surprised to find that there were none in it. She hand-cranked it a few times, which breathed a little life into it, but it didn't last long. Even when it did, no radio signal came through—only white noise.

11

—·—

As soon as he left the HQ trailer, Bill headed toward Kathy's spot, not far from the petting zoo, like usual. He nodded toward the Thompsons. They nodded back. Mike Thompson waved to get his attention and spoke. "I'm sorry Bill. I forgot to tell her to go see you."

Bill waved it away, showing that it wasn't a big deal. Mr. Thompson nodded back and continued to place the hay that had been in his hands around the small area for Gertrude, the goat, to lie in and eat.

Kathy's tent flap was closed. Across the top, a well-made (and well-worn), homemade sign was attached. At its center was a picture of a hand with colorful swirls indicating "Madame Zara's Fortune Telling." In smaller letters, you could make out "Palm Reading!" "Crystal Ball!" "Séances!" and "I will tell you your future. Inquire Within!"

Bill stopped short and called out her name, but no response came. He knocked on the pole that framed the entrance and called out again. He didn't want to walk in.

That was her private place, and he didn't want to be rude, but if she didn't answer soon, he was afraid he might have to poke his head in to see. She wasn't a spring chicken anymore. She wasn't elderly, but she wasn't young either...and things happen. When he raised his hand to knock again, the flap flew open and Kathy came out.

"I was asleep and didn't hear you," Kathy said.

"That's fine. I was coming to check on you. I didn't see you yesterday," Bill said.

"You almost didn't see me today, either," she said.

A puzzled look came over Bill's face. Kathy noticed it and looked around to see if anyone was within earshot. She moved with quick motions, as if agitated and unsure of anything. It was quite unlike her, Bill thought to himself. Kathy was usually solid, as in, nothing seemed to perturb her. To see her shifting glances back and forth...well...that wasn't her usual self.

"Everything okay? Did something happen?" Bill asked.

Kathy looked up and down the lane of booths and motioned for him to follow her inside the confines of her tent. He moved forward, just behind her. It was bright outside, so it took a moment to readjust to the dim lighting inside. After passing through a corridor of sorts, the main area of the tent was quite spacious. It had a sitting room with a table in the middle. There were dim lights strung across the top and the tent had been made of heavy material so that the sun didn't infiltrate the room. It kept it surprisingly cool inside, too. Of course, the portable air conditioner that Kathy had attached with long extension cords to the closest generator made it more than bearable. In fact, there were many a moment where a worker would come talk to Kathy just to get out of the heat for a few minutes. There was also a section in the back of the tent that was just for Kathy's personal use, where she slept and kept many of her belongings. Although she had a motorhome, its air conditioner hadn't worked well for years, which wasn't very conducive to restful sleep during the summer months.

Once inside, Kathy closed the flap shut and sat down at the table. Bill sat down at one of the chairs usually reserved for rubes and waited. Kathy looked more relaxed, not as on edge as she had been while they were outside.

"Bill, I stopped off at a library in the town of Marion and stole a book when we convoyed through," Kathy said.

Bill had a moment of relief. Kathy stole a library book? Weird, but that was nothing to be this worked up about.

"It's okay, I think you have like a week or so before you have to turn in back in," Bill said.

"No, I didn't check it out," Kathy said.

"Okay, then return it," Bill replied bluntly–kindly, but bluntly.

"I will, but me stealing it wasn't the issue. I almost didn't catch up with the convoy, but I did and when we finally got here, I parked and started reading," Kathy said.

"I'm not sure where you're going with this," Bill said.

"Well, what I read scared me, and I think we might be in trouble," Kathy replied.

"What book is it?" Bill asked.

Kathy stood up and disappeared to her personal area, then came back and placed the book on the table. It was bound in dark leather, slightly tattered, and looked very old. There were intricate designs on the leatherwork, but of nothing in particular that Bill could point out.

"Legends and Lore of Williamson," Kathy said.

"What?" Bill asked. The name meant nothing to him.

Kathy repeated herself and added, "It's the name of the county we are currently in."

"What about it?" Bill asked, looking at the book dubiously.

"There are some curious things that have happened here," Kathy said.

"How did you even find this book?" Bill asked, leaning forward to get a better look.

"You don't know this about me, but everywhere we go, I like to pick up a book about the local area. You never know if it may come in handy, especially in my area of expertise," Kathy said, gesturing to the tent they sat in. "Also, when we left Charleston, something about leaving there felt weird and when I get those feelings, I am inclined to listen."

"What did you find out in that book?" Bill asked, leaning forward in his chair and eyeing the heavy leather tome.

"This area..." Kathy began but stopped short, searching for words to give it the right amount of meaning, but not finding them, she continued. "Unexplained and bad things happen in this area."

"Like..." Bill nudged.

"I read this all day yesterday. I almost left but then decided last minute to stay. One, because we are already here and two, I was afraid to drive through town to get out of here on my own," she admitted.

Bill understood, beating around the bush to get to the point. When it came to being a showman, sometimes you had to dance around the subject in order to build up to the crescendo. It came second nature to storytellers and showmen and people like Kathy and himself. He understood this, but he was ready for her to get to the point.

Kathy must have sensed his growing frustration and started spilling what she had learned. "First and foremost, before native Americans settled the land, there was another people, centuries prior to the arrival of the Shawnee tribe, that lived there. Next to nothing is known about these people, but they disappeared abruptly and since then, bad things happen every so often in this place that eventually became Williamson county and the surrounding areas."

"Okay, so what's that got to do with us now?" Bill asked.

"I'm not finished yet," Kathy said and continued. "I read that in the centuries since the arrival of the Shawnee tribe, then the eventual arrival and flooding of white man into the area, there were massacres that happened with regularity."

Bill didn't say anything during the natural pause because he wanted her to finish her thought.

She continued, "In the middle to late 1800s, there was a horrible, bloody feud between several families. After that, in the 1920s, there was an awful massacre with the coal mine workers. I don't know...it seems to me that there is a spirit....or that this area is...tainted...and it drives people to do horrendous things. I'm not sure, but not only all that—out of everywhere in the area, most people disappear in this part of the state. This includes entire families, never to be seen or heard from again...and that's been ongoing since...forever."

"And you think we're in danger?" Bill asked.

Kathy sighed, "I don't know. Maybe I've worked myself up, but you know me. I'm not like this...and something about this town has gotten to me."

Bill didn't admit it out loud, but she was right about one thing. This town did seem a little odd and gave him cause for concern, though he didn't necessarily know why. Just an itch that he couldn't find to scratch, and Kathy, baring her soul about her own thoughts, only added to that phantom itch.

Bill put his hands on his knees and felt the rough material of his pants on his palms, as he rubbed them back and forth. He then stood up, not because he really cared to, but because he had pent-up energy swelling inside that he needed to let loose. He paced back and forth a couple of times, then looked at Kathy.

"Perhaps it's nothing. Maybe we're scaring ourselves for no reason," Bill offered.

"There's one more thing. The original town of Brownsville was abandoned after it burned to the ground, not far from where we are now," she added.

"Maybe they just moved and rebuilt it," Bill replied.

"It's not on any maps," Kathy said.

"And so, you think we're in some sort of trouble?" Bill reiterated.

Kathy nodded slowly as she looked back at him. Her eyes told him everything. Whatever it was, she believed it down to her soul. Everything about her was in unison about this. That scared him even more, though he had nothing concrete to go on other than a couple of weird happenings and a brief history about the place. Who knew if there was any truth to it? People write stuff to sell and what better way to sell a book than to scare the Hell out of people with stories of intrigue?

"So, you were too afraid to leave alone and that's why you stayed?" Bill asked.

"Partly...and I didn't want to leave my family behind to face something they weren't expecting, so I'm here. I've thrown in my lot, for better or worse...and I'm here with all of you," she replied. She spoke with confidence, but the paleness of her face spoke otherwise. She was terrified and looked like she might need a bucket to catch all the fear that might spew from her.

Bill stepped forward and put his hand on her shoulder. "It's okay. Whatever it is—if it ends up being anything—there's enough of us. We'll be all right."

Kathy relaxed under the touch, and she stood up and hugged Bill. With a voice that quivered with tears, "I'm not crazy, Bill."

"No one said you were, Kathy," he replied.

"I know, but it's been bottling up inside me ever since yesterday when I got here. Truth be told, ever since right before we left the last town. It's a relief to get it out."

"Well, you aren't just among friends. You're among family, and you aren't alone, okay? You feel worried about anything more than what we normally deal with, you come and get me. Until then, let's take it a day at a time until this week is over and we go on to the next town," Bill said.

Kathy didn't say anything. She was embarrassed over her emotion and wiped away her tears with her right wrist. She then nodded to let Bill know she was okay and that she understood.

A few moments later, Bill was again outside, under the blazing sun. He hadn't yet gone off the deep end with fear like Kathy seemed to have done, but being in her presence in the dark seemed to accentuate his anxiety. Being outside in the open, under the blazing sun melted the alarm like hot butter. Sure, it was still there, but not in the same way it had been just a few minutes prior. There had to be explanations for everything. Things like that don't happen in real life—only in books and stories—but that eerie feeling persisted. They just had to make it a week or so here, make enough money, then move on to the next town. Speaking of which, the town they were scheduled for next week had also canceled, which meant they needed to go ahead and contact other fair boards and/or town representatives to see if they could get squeezed in somewhere. The season was far from over and they still had some time to make money if they could square a place. In some ways, he wished it could all be as easy as it had been with Mr. Bright and this town, but he still had some misgivings, especially after the conversation he had just had with Kathy.

He shook his shoulders because a chill swept over him. He looked around and everything seemed normal outside. The Thompsons were messing with their animals. He could hear the whirls and dings of the different rides and electronic games, while being tested one last time before tomorrow.

The past week had been a constant tug of war with himself in questioning his own sanity. He kept the notions of the building sense of something inexplicable to himself because he didn't want to cause a panic or look foolish. Besides, it was just a cluster of minor events which happened to be a perfect storm of oddities happening at once.

"Maybe we're just road-crazy," Bill thought. It happened sometimes, from the stress of being on the road and constantly on the go. One thing was for sure, regardless of everything else, he needed to keep an eye on Kathy to make sure she didn't completely lose it; he'd have to keep a close eye on himself, too, for that matter.

As he headed toward the Ferris wheel, which was positioned at the back of the midway, he saw Peter slinking along the lane, near the gaming tents. Everything that he had been thinking about was momentarily forgotten, replaced by a seething contempt deep in his chest, which came out of nowhere. This kid basically got them kicked out of the last town. It surprised him at how angry he was. He knew that he shouldn't confront the kid at the moment because the tight rope he felt like he was on was unraveling and about to snap. He had to confront him, though, because who knew when the next opportunity to do so would come. He didn't want this punk to mess up anything with the current town, as weird as it was. Peter didn't see Bill as he walked up, but when he turned around, he jumped in surprise, eyes wide, and stuttered...but no words came out. Bill knew then that Peter had indeed been avoiding him. "Guess he isn't all that dumb," Bill thought to himself. He should have kicked him out the moment he had the chance. He knew it would have riled Brad a little because Peter was one of his guys, so it was his responsibility. Bill knew Brad would relent because, at the end of the day, Donovan's Delights was bigger than all of them. Brad was, overall, a reasonable guy and would understand that immediate decisions needed to be made. He would also make it up to Brad somehow.

The kid stopped trying to say anything and shut his mouth. Bill thought maybe Peter was surprised, then embarrassed about his reaction to seeing Bill. He could have just been mad at himself and the world, judging by the red face that replaced his stunned expression.

"Peter," Bill said.

Peter didn't say a word. He was waiting for the punishment, whatever it was. "Peter, you know they kicked us out of the last town because of you, right?"

"That wasn't my fault. That was that sucker...." Peter began.

"He wasn't so smart after all," Bill thought to himself before swiftly closing the distance and grabbing Peter by the front of his shirt and pointing his finger in his face. That caused him to put a lid on it. The kid was taller than he was, but anger, experience, and responsibility had a way of leveling the playing field.

"Stop," Bill said. "We are going to try this again."

Bill attempted to let go of Peter's shirt, which was hard to do with the intense anger threatening to take control. He still held on for dear life, like holding on to a bucking bronco. If he slipped, he knew he would pummel the poor kid and, even as irritating as Peter was, he didn't deserve a beating...well, maybe a small one, but not the one Bill would unleash if he let him go. Bill believed Peter sensed this, because the look in his eye was likely similar to that of a rabid dog, and Peter refrained from making any sudden moves. The thought caused Bill to laugh to himself. Maybe he was a rabid dog. Humor saves the day again. His rage was still there, but the hilarity of the situation blunted the dagger. In the back of Bill's mind, he was thankful for the innate gift to be able to see the humor of a situation at times.

Bill stepped back, giving Peter room. "Peter, we both know you were the reason. No more excuses. You can work this week and you're gone next week, unless, of course, you prove your worth in the next few days. Otherwise, you're out. Capiche?

Peter didn't say anything or show any response other than a glare, so Bill took a step forward, back into Peter's personal space, and looked at him with steel eyes. "Do. You. Understand?"

Peter nodded his understanding. Bill, relieved that at least this part was over, backed up a few paces and turned to the side to walk away, keeping an eye on Peter until he was at a safe distance. Bill didn't think that Peter would do anything, but some people were like wounded animals in that they could turn on you. It wouldn't be the first time someone thought there had been a resolution then discovered that that was, indeed, not the case once their back was turned. Bill knew he would have to keep an eye on Peter. He hoped he would clean up his act but, in all honesty, doubted it and suspected Peter would harbor some hate toward him.

Walking away, he felt a sense of relief. It had been nagging him ever since that altercation with the town kid and he knew he needed to resolve it. He was also glad for a diversion from the conversation he had just left with Kathy.

Before he left the lane that housed the gaming booths, he took one last look. Peter was still standing there. Anger was clearly conveyed on his face and his eyes bored into Bill. "Yeah," Bill thought to himself, "I'm going to have to keep my eye on that one."

12

The day passed rather quickly, and late evening had arrived. There were a few laborious chores that took up most of Bill's time, though he did have a moment that afternoon to pick up his little black book and call HQ at winter's quarters, the place they holed up in for winter. He still had an aunt that stuck around, taking phone messages for Donovan's Delights Entertainment. Whenever they finished setting up, he or Dani would call to let them know and to get any messages they might need. Since Bill had gotten a pager that sat on his belt, the need to call HQ in Kentucky wasn't as high on the list of priorities. Most of the time now, their phone business was handled on the road, with people reaching out for Bill to call them back. Old habits die hard, though, and he still kept Aunt Sue up to date about where they were, if only to let her feel like she was still on the road with them. Aunt Sue was his dad's sister. She had never married and helped out on the road for a very long time. As she got older, she couldn't get around as well as she used to and, thankfully, made the decision to stop traveling before someone else made the decision for her.

Bill crossed the street where he had seen a pay phone when they came into town. It looked brand new—a little kiosk-type booth, complete with shiny, unworn buttons. To Bill, it looked like it had just been placed. There was no grime or the appearance of having been weathered. He picked up the phone, checked the change slot as usual—nothing—and placed the receiver to his ear. No dial tone. He pursed his lips and used his finger to depress the lever a couple of times. Finally, he heard the clean dial tone and along with it, a voice cut in, "If you'd like to make a call, please hang up and..."

Bill punched in the quarters like he was shooting marbles and the dial tone returned. He dialed the number to Aunt Sue, and it rang. Normally, she would answer the phone quickly because she usually had it beside her recliner where she sat to watch TV. But today, the phone rang and rang, and oddly enough, the answering machine didn't pick up. Bill hung up the phone, grabbing his change from the coin release slot, and tried again. No dice. He tried a different number that he knew by heart—the local pizza delivery joint near winter's quarters. The phone connected and again, no one answered and there was no answering machine that picked up. He retrieved his change again and dialed zero for the operator. Seconds stretched into what seemed like minutes. The subtle sick feeling in his stomach was there again. He clicked the phone lever to get a dial tone, but the sound came in waves and eventually, there was silence. No dial tone at all. Then, after a few more seconds of fiddling with it, all that Bill heard was white noise, just like what had been on the radio. He jumped back from the phone as if he had been shot. The abrupt change from no tone to static was jarring, as it hadn't been expected. With the phone dangling by the silver cord, Bill heard the recording again, "If you'd like to make a call, please hang up..."

Bill gingerly took hold of the phone and looked at it as if it were a snake. He gently placed the phone back on the hook and stepped back. He looked around. No one was near, though he did see some cars parked on one of the nearby side streets. He then heard the phone ring and his eyes snapped back to it as it sang its tune to be answered. Bill hesitated before picking it up. He wasn't sure if he wanted to find out who was on the line, but his curiosity won out and he picked it up. "Hello?" Bill asked in a voice that sounded steady, but Bill felt for sure that it wasn't.

"Mr. Donovan," the voice said. Bill immediately recognized the voice as that of Mr. Bright.

"How did you know to call?" Bill asked.

"Are your people okay? Do you or do they need anything?" Mr. Bright asked.

"They're fine," Bill replied and then asked again, "How did you know I was going to be by this phone?"

"This is my town, Mr. Donovan. I know most everything that goes on here. Besides, it's the closest one to the lot you're setting up in. Lucky guess, I suppose. We are surely looking forward to your show this week. Who knows? Maybe we can get you to stay indefinitely," Mr. Bright said.

"I doubt that," Bill replied. "We do have other towns and other responsibilities to see beyond this one, though we appreciate the accommodations that we've had here so far."

"Oh, well...we will see. This town has a way of growing on you," Mr. Bright said. Bill didn't know for sure, but just from the sound of the voice, he could see Mr. Bright's creepy smile in his mind's eye...the one that didn't reach the rest of his face.

"Right..." Bill replied slowly, then remembered why he had been in front of the pay phone in the first place. "Do these phone lines reach out of town?"

"Oh, I'm glad you asked," Mr. Bright replied. "Unfortunately, that storm we had yesterday knocked down all serviceable telephone poles leading out, so no phone calls unless they are within town."

"I see," Bill replied. He didn't like the explanation and some part of him didn't believe it, but he wasn't 100 percent on anything at the moment. "Well, I guess I better get back to my people."

"Yes, if they ne.." Mr. Bright began.

"Right," Bill replied, quickly interrupting Mr. Bright. "If my people need anything, I'll let you know," he added, then he hung up the phone.

It would be a cold day in Hell before he asked Mr. Bright for anything. Something had changed, though what it was, Bill didn't know. It was the way that the air changed when a storm was on the horizon and you could smell the petrichor in the air. It wasn't exactly like that at the moment, but it was eerily similar to whatever it was that Bill was trying to piece together in his mind.

At that moment, he wanted to pack everything up and, come Hell or high water, just leave but...he knew everyone was tired, as they had just set everything up and were ready to start. The balance of strange occurrences didn't quite tip the scale enough to face financial ruin—just a bunch of incongruities and Bill's cautious nature.

Bill walked back across the street. The road noise from earlier in the day had died down and it was eerily quiet, except for the sounds that the carnival naturally gave off—the dings, whirs, whizzes, and occasional yells of workers to each other. That was normal, but this was like listening to all those noises in a vacuum, where there was nothing else. And that peculiarity wasn't so normal. Bill looked up the road that led to the center of town. No cars or people were seen in that glance. He stopped short and scratched his head. Now that he thought about it, he realized he hadn't seen any cars pass by since that morning, nor had he seen any pedestrians since they arrived.

Bill sighed and continued back onto the midway, stopping once to check on the '58 Buick as he passed by. Still pristine and beautiful. He thought about his father and wondered what he would do if he were in this situation. Would he have packed up at the first sign of trouble? Something told Bill that he didn't think so. He knew his dad had been a scrapper and had the ability and the stubbornness to meet everything head on. The good thing about it, though, is that his dad always seemed to come out ahead when everything looked bleak.

He touched the car lovingly one more time, then headed on. The carnies were almost done and were slowing down. It was about dinner time and tonight would be a time of celebration. They would be celebrating the fact they had a night of downtime before the show began the next day. This was always a relief, because they sometimes worked seven days a week, with little to no breaks. When everyone could actually experience some downtime, it had the feel of a New Year's Eve party. Everyone was light-hearted, but there had been more than one occasion in the past in which some had to be kept in check before getting a little too drunk or causing trouble with others. It was rare, but it did happen.

When Bill headed to the back end, he could see that his people were already starting. Someone fired up the grill and the smell of burgers wafted over to him, causing his stomach to grumble. Jimmy was already there, with a beer in one hand and a plate with a burger and potato chips in the other. He was talking with his mouth full to the guy behind the grill, which happened to be Mike McGee. Bill walked over and said "hello" and grabbed himself a burger. Then, he went over to an area where someone had placed folding chairs. It was a nice change of pace, and it was pleasant. With the sun deep in the sky, it was warm, but it wasn't unbearable with the breeze that was gently blowing.

He saw his wife and kids come to the group. They also grabbed some food and joined him.

"How was your day, Laura?" he asked his daughter.

"It was fine, but I'm tired. It's kind of boring in the little food trailers, especially after you set it up and there are no customers to talk to," she replied.

"Oh, just wait 'til you get put on ride duty," Jason snorted. "If you think that's boring, at least you're in the shade or might have a fan or air conditioning."

"Kids," Dani interjected, cutting them off at the pass before it became a bigger issue than it really was. They were just siblings being siblings, but everyone was tired. "There are pros and cons about everything. Now eat your food and don't antagonize one another...okay?"

It was a rhetorical question, and both kids looked down at their plates, not wanting to cause an issue with their mom. Bill couldn't help but be glad that they were still at that age that they didn't want to upset their parents. Bill had been like that, himself, until he was 16. After that...whoa... the fights he would have with his parents...well, they weren't pretty. He regretted that stage of his life every time he thought about it.

"Dani, how are you?" Bill asked.

She didn't say anything, but sat there looking off into space, deep in thought. "How are you?" Bill asked again.

Breaking the trance, she snapped back. "I'm fine. I was thinking about how to reply to that question. It's been a long day." Bill nodded his agreement.

"How was yours?" I haven't seen you since this morning," she said.

"Steady. I tried calling Aunt Sue but couldn't get a hold of her. Couldn't leave a message either," he replied.

"That's not usually like her," Dani replied. "Think she's okay?"

"I think it has more to do with phone issues," Bill replied. He briefly gave her the rundown on trying to call out and not making any connections, and then the follow-up phone call with Mr. Bright.

"Really? He just called you out of the blue like that?" Dani asked.

Bill nodded as he took a bite from his hamburger. Careful not to let the mustard he added a little too much of drip off the other side. When he had finished the bite, he looked back at Dani.

"Something about that Mayor Bright...I don't know. I don't like it," Bill said in a near whisper. He didn't want to create gossip when gossip was one of the only things around in outfits such as this one. It was a grown-up version of high school, where everyone talked about one another. It's what happens when you get a group of people that live together day in and day out. It was fine for the most part, just as long as it didn't turn mean and though it was rare, it did happen. There was no real privacy in the traveling show biz world, except for maybe the bathroom and taking showers...and Lord knew you couldn't stay in there very long. The warm water ran out quick when taking a shower in an RV.

Dani leaned forward. "I know what you mean. Since we've been here, I feel...a tinge of something in the air. Like you know how there's excitement in the air every time you open the park to new folks? You see the excitement on their faces and it sort of rubs off on you?"

Bill nodded.

"Sort of like that...but this isn't excitement. It feels stale, like a void or something. I know I sound crazy, but there it is," she finished.

"I don't think you're crazy, except for falling in love with me," Bill said, and a smile began to slowly form on his face.

"Who said I fell in love with you? I could have just been a desperate girl wanting to get out of my hometown," Dani replied, with a smile spreading across her own face.

Bill couldn't help himself; he was in love with her. Of course, a fault of his was to always try to lighten the mood when life got heavy. This particular conversation seemed like it was about to stray into that territory of heaviness.

"Well, whatever it was, it's been in my favor ever since," Bill replied, grinning ear to ear with his eyes mischievously twinkling.

Dani smiled, then took a sip from her red Solo cup of lemonade. The smile disappeared and she looked back at Bill. "We need to be careful here," she said.

Bill's smile lingered for a few seconds before it slowly dissipated. "Yeah, that feeling in my gut is real and although a couple of weird things have happened, I don't want to jump at my own shadow, you know?"

"I know. Heck, I'm the one who told you we needed to stay here for the money, and you're right, there hasn't been anything that breaks the bank but...we still need to keep an eye out," Dani said. Her eyes scanned the area and fell on the kids, who were off doing their own thing since they had finished their food quickly.

Bill followed her gaze, then scooted his chair over and put one arm around her, pulling her in. She felt good wrapped up in his arm. The warmth was comforting, but only for a moment. Even though the sun was taking a dive in the west, it was still warm.

"We'll be all right," Bill replied.

While most of the troupe was hanging out, talking, and joking with one another until later in the evening, Peter kept to himself. He sat outside one of the tents, sulking. He was pissed off. Ever since his run-in with Bill earlier that day, he had an anger that just wouldn't let go.

"Who does he think he is?" he thought to himself. "What does he know? If he paid more, I wouldn't need to steal." Although Donovan's Delights was known for being more than fair with what they paid their workers, at least in comparison to most outfits, that fact was lost on Peter at the moment. He was seeing red.

"I don't know why I put up with it," Peter said to himself, but deep down, he knew the answer. It was an answer he didn't want to admit. He had nowhere else to go, but that didn't stop him from feeling like he did.

"Peter, you okay?" another figure said from the dark.

Peter, surprised, stopped and peered into shadows. The figure stepped into the light of the nearby neon sign. It was Stan, another carnie about the same age as Peter—maybe a little older, maybe a little younger. Peter didn't know or really care. Stan sometimes worked at the shooting gallery with a girl named Louise, who was older by a year or two, and had stringy brown hair. Stan and Louise were always hanging together, but Peter didn't see her with him tonight. Peter thought Louise would be pretty if it wasn't for her serious acne problem. Of course, that didn't stop her from getting around. There wasn't much opportunity outside the carnie life, so he didn't look away when it happened to be his turn with her. Besides—in the dark, it didn't really matter. Peter turned and looked at Stan.

"Yeah, I'm fine. Why? You think I'm not?" Peter replied. Where Peter was tall and so thin that it seemed an errant breeze would knock him over, Stan was rotund and short. His greasy hair framed an equally greasy face, but he was friendly.

"No, I just saw you over here and thought I'd say 'hello'," Stan replied.

"Where's Louise?" Peter asked. Seeing Stan made him think of her and the way he was feeling. Maybe he could let off a little steam in the dark. That would make him feel better, especially if they had some organic herb they could enjoy before they took a roll in the hay, so to speak.

"Oh..." Stan said "She's with Clay tonight."

Clay was older than all of them—in his early 30s—and always had a joint ready to go and other, harder things at the ready. Peter never really thought about it before, but seeing Stan, he realized he had never seen or heard of Stan and Louise hooking up. It never seemed to bother Stan that he was the one person she didn't spend "quality" time with, other than all of her extra time.

"Damn," Peter replied. "Well, I don't have any money and nothing really to do tonight. I was sort of hoping for..."

Stan shrugged his shoulders. "Well, I have a 12 pack if you'd like to join me."

"Stan, you and Louise have never..."

"No," Stan replied. Peter couldn't tell if he was upset by this or not.

"Okay. Let's go get drunk, then. I think I may have a fifth of Jack that I, uh...acquired at that last town," Peter said, smiling at the memory. It was a mom-and-pop liquor store in the middle of the day, near where the carnival was set up in Charleston. He didn't get out and about often when the carnival was running, but he made it a point to explore the towns they visited when he could. He would make time—take an extra few minutes on a break, but those who covered for him, he didn't leave empty-handed. He never had time to case any joints. His crimes were always situations of opportunity, like the mom-and-pop liquor store with no cameras. He just placed a couple of bottles of whatever he got his hands on and placed them in his backpack. It didn't matter what he picked up as long as he picked it up. He wasn't picky about what would take him on a trip to "lose" his mind, be it booze or any of the harder stuff. Seeing the skinny, bald guy behind the counter who was more interested in the game on TV instead of what was going on in the store suited Peter just fine. Funny enough, it was the same day that he ran into that high school punk and stole his wallet. That punk that came to the carnival and got Peter in trouble with Bill. And all at once, the anger came back, and his smile morphed into a grimace.

"You better be glad that no one found out about that," Stan replied.

"Yeah...well...no one better," Peter said, his demeanor changing from friendly to threatening, staring knives at Stan.

"Of course not," Stan replied quickly with a sickly grin, a grin that spoke of uncertainty. Stan, Peter thought, was like an overgrown puppy that was quick to please and got along just to get along. You could kick him and he would still come back with that goofy-looking smile he always wore. It was really no wonder that Stan never had a romp with ol' Louise.

Stan wasn't really a friend, but then again, no one was really a friend when it came to Peter. He only hung out with people who could be used, stolen from, or manipulated for personal gain, but he knew it wasn't okay to be brazen about it. With all that being said, Peter also didn't like being alone, so friend or not, he'd pick hanging out with people he didn't really care for, like Stan.

"Well, good," Peter said. "Let's go get drunk and see if Louise is free later. I could use a good time."

"Yeah, I know what you mean," Stan said enthusiastically, now that he knew he was out of danger. Peter was pretty sure that Stan had no idea what he meant and most likely never would. Stan was a two-time loser that would never see the light of day or the shadow underneath some girl's skirt unless he was perving, which they all did from time to time. Some of those rides were not made for girls in skirts.

"Whatever. Let's go," Peter said.

Before they disappeared into the alley between tents to get wasted, Peter took one look toward the back of the midway, where he knew people were gathering. He thought about the encounter with Bill and his anger began to rise again. Stan was talking, but Peter didn't hear because he was preoccupied by the sudden fury and was lost in thought as he fantasized about how he was going to get Bill. He wasn't going to let him get away with it—making him feel the way he did earlier today or for that move he pulled on him last week. He was going to pay. And just like that, by making that decision, his tumultuous anger melted away.

13

—·—

The next day arrived, and it was showtime for the carnies, the ride jocks, the showmen, the show-women...it was on! Excitement was in the air. It was almost enough to cause Bill to momentarily forget his troubles and all the oddness of late. This day—the opening day—was why he kept coming back. It was the excitement. It was the adrenaline rush of putting on a show. It was all the laughs and screams. It was a synergy that created the strongest of highs for those who were into it.

Of course, there were some like Peter that would never understand the excitement of opening day. They were there to waste time and trade hours for a paycheck. The sort that was immune to the childlike wonder of the world and teetered on the edge of life and existence. It wasn't only the excitement of opening day that they were immune to; they were immune to life's abundance. Bill, however, had no such immunity and was caught up in the rush. He couldn't wait to see the crowd, though a sliver in the depths of his mind whispered for caution, but that cautionary warning had been drowned out by the thrill of opening day.

Bill bounded out the door and down the steps of the family's trailer. He was usually the first out every day, but this time, it was with gusto. His eyes twinkled and his smile was genuine, reminiscent of a kid at his first sleepover, where they had drunk too much soda and were bouncing on sugar highs.

He knew he had to tone it down. The show wouldn't go in full swing until this afternoon and later this evening. This morning, they would go over last-minute safety briefs, safety inspections, and all the other usual things that had become routine on the road, but the "sugar high" would see him fly through those.

Brad and George were up too, and already at the HQ trailer, having coffee and each holding a stack of cards. The cards were a system that they had come up with to show that inspections were complete for each ride, booth, or tent. When each was fully inspected, Brad or George would tag it with a card and upon completion of their rounds, go back around to collect the cards. This way, they would ensure that nothing was overlooked. The cards didn't come out again until the next opening day at the next gig.

"How'd y'all sleep?" Bill asked.

"I slept," George spat. "Not that it did much good. You'll find out once you get older that sleep doesn't provide the same kind of rest it once did."

"Speak for yourself. You're only as old as you feel," Brad interjected. "I slept great."

"Well, if that's the case, I feel like I'm 102," George replied.

They were both in their early 60s, but life on the road made them look much older. George looked a bit older than Brad because he was over the food vending and ate junk all the time. Brad also took a little better care of himself, whereas George didn't. They were the complete opposite of one another in that respect. George had quite the paunch and Brad didn't look to have an ounce of fat on him, but you wouldn't call him skinny, either. He was solidly built.

The banter went back and forth and they talked about nothing and had conversations that went nowhere, as they ticked off last-minute items to look at when they got started. After about 30 minutes, Dani came into the trailer, along with Jason and Laura.

"We just came by to see if y'all needed any help," Dani said.

"Yes, Daddy. Anything you need me to do?" Laura chimed in.

Jason just stood there waiting, didn't say a word, and yawned. Somehow, Bill thought it wasn't Jason's idea to be there, but the boy had chores and a job to do today, so here he was.

"Of course, honey," Bill said to his daughter. "You can stick with me...and Jason?"

"Yes, Dad?" Jason said, straightening up the moment he heard his own name.

"I want you to follow Jimmy around, okay, and see what he does," Bill said.

"I do that anyway," Jason replied.

"I know, but I want you to really pay attention this time. At some point, I'm going to have you replace him for the duties I currently have him doing."

Hearing that, Bill couldn't help but notice that Jason seemed to stand even a little straighter and taller, if that was possible. The chance to get more responsibility and maybe a little more money motivated him, all right, Bill thought. Dani already knew what she needed to do, so he didn't have to direct her, but looking at his watch, he knew it was time.

"All right, all right," Bill said. "We ready to start the countdown?"

The others looked at him and nodded their consent. "All right, it's Thursday and we will be ready to open at 1700, which gives us a little over under eleven hours," Bill said.

"1700?" Laura asked, a look of confusion on her face.

"Well, Miss Sunshine," Bill explained, "That's five o'clock this afternoon."

"Oh," Laura replied and flashed a big smile. With one more nod from everyone, Bill nodded, and the day began.

Bill hadn't seen or heard from Mr. Bright since yesterday afternoon, and all the strange or odd things in the back of his mind receded as the day wore on. In fact, even that morning, all the quirky things that had happened to cause his unease didn't cross his mind. The excitement of the "grand opening" drowned it all out and Bill, even if he had noticed this consciously, wouldn't have minded one bit.

They all left the HQ trailer and went their separate directions to do one last sweep. It really wouldn't take that long and they probably could have opened up earlier than five PM, but Bill learned long ago that it paid to start early with the last day and last-minute inspections. It gave them time to scramble and fix whatever problem presented itself, and there were always last-minute problems.

This had been his practice ever since an incident five years prior. They had opened the midway at some town in Ohio, and the Ferris wheel ended up not being ready because of something that was easy to spot and easy to fix but unfortunately, no one had caught it. Several customers ended up at the top of the wheel when it shut down. It took several hours to get it running again and by then, the families that were stuck were pissed off and threatened to sue. Bill was sure he was going to be fined by some authority and he was, but thankfully, not to the point of bankruptcy. That show ended up being a wash, with no profits being made that week. Heck, they may have actually been in the red. The story made all the local papers and Donovan's Delights became the laughingstock of the week in the traveling show biz world. They never returned to that town and its name escaped Bill at the moment. At any rate, ever since then, Bill was a stickler about starting the last day of inspections as early as possible and making sure all the i's were dotted and the t's crossed twice before showtime.

The first half of the day passed quickly, and all the rides, all the booths, and all the games were ready. The only thing left was for the last few hours to pass, then he would flip the switch to turn on the lights and open up the ticket booths.

There was one more pre-opening ritual that Bill had and he took Jason with him. It was something that he and his dad always did together before he passed, and although Bill didn't enjoy it then because he thought it was pointless, he would have given anything to do it one more time with his dad.

About an hour before showtime, Bill dragged Jason to the '58 Buick displayed in front of the ticket booths. Everything got an inspection and that included the car. It would be cleaned to perfection one more time.

30 minutes before it was time to open the midway, both Bill and Jason stood back to look at the work. They did one more last-minute wipe down, not that it needed it. It was a labor of love. They took their time, or rather Bill took his time, which is why it took 30 minutes. To Jason, this took an excruciating long time and was glad when it was over.

"Why do we do this every time?" Jason asked, taking in the view along with his dad. Where Bill's eyes twinkled in memory looking at the car, Jason's were dull with boredom.

"What?" Bill asked, not hearing since he was knee deep, reminiscing in memories.

"I said, why do we do this? Why do we clean the car before every opening? It was clean already."

"Because, son, it's my good luck routine. It's one that I picked up from your grandfather when I was your age and he made me do the same thing...understand?" Bill replied.

"I guess so, but I don't see how it helps."

"It probably doesn't, Jason, but you see, a person does something for so long that routine eventually becomes a ritual, and this is our ritual for what works. It gives me peace of mind. It also gives me a moment to think about that past. This isn't about just the car; it's about the moment in time," Bill said, looking at his son.

Seeing that his son clearly didn't get what he meant, he continued, "It's okay. You don't have to understand, but one day you will."

Jason shrugged his shoulders. "I guess."

Bill smiled and looked back at the shiny classic car that looked like it could go 120 miles per hour but couldn't move two feet, then he looked back at his son. "All right, it's almost time to flip the switch on all the lights! Ready?"

"Sure am."

The next 30 minutes went by quickly. A rising tension occurred within Bill at every setup. It happened every time and it would pop like a balloon to relieve pressure once they turned on the lights and opened. The relief and the excitement would replace the tension, then the almost adrenalin-like high would take over the first night and would carry him through the entire week of the show.

It was getting close and everyone was ready. Bill always liked to treat it like a rocket liftoff to the moon. "T minus one minute and counting," he squealed into the handheld radio. When it came time to launch, everyone holding their own similar radio would turn on the power of whatever they were operating, from the Ferris wheel all the way to the lights in the booths and tents.

"Ten, nine, eight..." Bill started that last count down. "...three, two, one! Showtime!"

There was an audible "click" that could be heard from several places all over the midway as people powered up their rides and lights. Everything was perfect...except that there were no people in sight. In fact, now that Bill thought about it, he hadn't seen one person since being in town, other than Mr. Bright. He had seen cars drive past, but he never got a clear look inside those cars. It was also peculiar that people didn't stop by to watch them set up. This was another first, but he would have sworn that there would have been at least one person ready to go at five PM opening night.

A minute went by as Bill stood at the entrance and looked across the road at the empty lot that was reserved for parking. Not a single car was there. He noticed that there were cars occasionally driving by earlier. Had Bill not been so busy, he would have noticed that the cars were indeed showing up and driving by on almost perfectly-timed

intervals. Since everyone had been preoccupied with setting up and other general things, no one noticed it.

A voice squelched on the radio, "How's it looking?"

It was Brad. He was in the back and wasn't able to see
clearly to the parking area.

Bill raised his radio to his lips. "Well, if we have excitement like this for the rest of the week, we may as well pool
for gas money now."

"That good, huh?" came the reply.

George piped in. "Well, maybe they didn't advertise as
much since this was a last-minute addition to our schedule."

"Maybe," Bill replied. "Well, if we don't get any visitors
tonight or tomorrow, we are packing up and leav..."

Bill didn't complete his thought on the radio because at
that moment, a line of cars came into view and drove into
the field across from the entrance. It was all very orderly.
It almost reminded Bill of a line of ants—evenly spaced,
going somewhere with a sense of organization and purpose. It wasn't just that; the cars were all from the...30s?
As Bill continued to watch, he thought maybe they were
40s models. He wasn't a car guru, but he knew they were
all classic and pristine, as if they had just rolled off the
showroom floor to end up here. They were all different
shapes and colors, but they were all old. There wasn't a
modern car among them. Bill wasn't aware of their show
coinciding with a car show, but maybe there was supposed
to be one that Bill didn't know about. It didn't matter to

him as long as they left enough room for paying customers to come enjoy the carnival.

They parked, perfectly lined up in rows. Then, one by one, the doors opened and families appeared. Without hesitation, they all started toward the entrance where Bill was located.

"I hear cars. Have some arrived?" Bill heard Brad's voice carry through the handheld speaker.

Bill lifted it to his mouth and replied. "Uh...yeah, they've arrived and uh...I think they've packed the parking area full...but you aren't going to believe this."

"Believe what?" came the reply.

"You'll just have to come to the front and see for yourself," Bill replied, then clipped the handheld onto his belt.

The townspeople had showed up, and it had turned into quite a crowd. Groups of people, ranging from couples to families with several kids in tow, crossed the street, heading toward the ticket booths. This had to be one of the most unique grand openings that Bill had ever experienced. The families closed the distance and lined up orderly. They all had smiles, but Bill noted they were strangely silent for such a crowd. He could see them talk to one another, but the usual jubilant whoops and screams of kids, teenagers, and other folks that couldn't wait to get on the rides or see the wonders of what Donovan's Delights had to offer, weren't there. In fact, it was a very subdued crowd, truth be told, but that wasn't the only odd thing. These people looked like they had stepped out of the past—like Bill and his troupe had ended up in a town full of reenactors that portrayed the 1930s to 1950s. Just like the cars that looked authentic, there were men in high-waisted slacks and button-up shirts, some with thick, black, Coke bottle glasses. Women were wearing conservative dresses and heels, and most had perfectly coiffed hair. Teenage girls were wearing poodle skirts and saddle shoes. Bill saw one greaser, complete with leather jacket and rolled up jeans around black leather boots. It was as if time had changed and the men and women of Donovan's Delights Entertainment were the interlopers.

As Bill's mind contemplated what he saw, he watched them pull out cash, and for all the craziness of what he saw in front of him, that was about the only ordinary thing he expected to see. It also helped keep him from getting too worked up about it. It was a quirky town. That was it. One thing was for sure, though, he would never put this spot on the schedule again. Everything about it had just been too weird up to this point. But in the back of his mind, he knew better than to shut out this town cold turkey so soon. He'd wait to see how they did financially while they were here. Who really knew? If they did really well, then Bill could stomach these weirdos and didn't care one bit what they wore or drove, for that matter. As long as his troupe remained safe and, so far, it looked like that they were because the crowd looked docile enough. Heck, they could have all been wearing ballerina tutus or dog collars and Bill would have been fine with that, as long as he saw that money change hands. That was the lifeblood of this outfit and Bill wouldn't get creeped out enough to run as long as the money flowed and everyone was safe.

The parking lot across the street was full and still more cars showed up—all classics— parked and lining the street now. Bill broke out in an uneasy smile. They were going to do well tonight. Nevertheless, this was definitely out of the ordinary.

Bill hopped into one of the ticket booths to see how the staff was doing. He opened up the back door to find Rita again, manning the counter.

Rita, with the frizzy red hair, looked up to see that it was Bill and turned back to the window to yell, "Next!"

While she waited, she looked back toward Bill, smacking her chewing gum, "Where's my quarter?"

Caught off guard, Bill immediately went digging into his pocket for one. He had meant to pay her back for using her quarter for that phone, which seemed forever ago, but somehow it had slipped his mind. Not finding one, he took his hands out and then palms facing out, he shrugged his shoulders in a gesture of "sorry, no dice."

"Uh huh, just what I figured. Rip me off," Rita said and if Bill hadn't known Rita for as long as he had, he would have believed she meant just what she said.

"Oh, come on. You know I'm good for it. I'll even pay you back with interest," Bill replied.

"Right, just so you can borrow 50 cents next time," she cackled back.

Bill stepped up to watch the crowd. "So, how's it going?" he asked, nodding toward the mass beyond the window.

"It's steady. I don't think I ever remember an opening night being so popular. Whatever they did for advertising worked," Rita said.

"That's good," Bill replied, lost in thought. He couldn't help but watch the crowd in wonder. Everyone looked like they stepped right out of the history books and now that he was closer, he noticed they all had the same look, more or less. Sure, their faces were different, but they all had the same type of smile that didn't seem to meet their eyes, so much so that it reminded Bill of Mayor Bright.

In some ways, all the townsfolk reminded him of wax figures, except these wax figures moved and didn't melt in the heat. Maybe wax was a bad example, Bill thought to himself. Plastic would be more appropriate. The smiles and mouths moved, but the eyes didn't. Even the small children looked more or less like they were delivering lines in a school play, but without emotion behind the words.

A couple came up to the window this time, paid their money, were almost overly pleasant, and received their wristbands. When they left, Rita yelled "Next!"

"Do you notice anything strange?" Bill asked Rita.

"I'm not paid to notice anything. I'm paid to take money and hand out wristbands and tickets," Rita replied, but continued, "But between you and me, I've never seen anything weirder than this crowd. I haven't seen dresses like that since I was a small girl and even then, it was out of place because it was old."

Bill didn't reply. He was busy contemplating what she said.

"Could be one of those towns that are just for cults, you know. Like the ones you hear of out west. You know those religiously fanatic ones?" Rita asked.

"Maybe so," Bill replied.

"The clothes don't bother me so much, but I will tell you what does. When I accidentally touch one of these people, they are as cold as stone and almost tingly-feeling. Is it cold out there or something?" Rita asked.

With the small air conditioning in the ticket booth on full blast, it was still a struggle to keep the room cool, due to the heat outside. Bill shrugged his shoulders but felt that he had to confirm her observations. He stepped up beside her and grabbed a wristband for the next person who happened to be a behemoth of a man in coveralls, who looked to be by himself. Even with the elevated booth that Bill and Rita were in, this figure was on eye level with them. He was bald and clean. No dirt anywhere that would be synonymous with what he wore. He looked to be a farmer, but again, a farmer from the 1940s—there was no going around it. The whole crowd did. Even though Bill made that connection before, it was still so peculiar that Bill's mind had to reconfirm it, like a tooth that had recently been pulled and the tongue had to keep re-investigating the vacancy.

"Hello, good sir," Bill said through the small hole in the glass, then told him the cost of the bands.

"Good day," the man said, smiling, but said nothing more. He just plopped bills on the counter and pushed them through the opening at the bottom of the window. Since the man didn't seem interested in engaging, Bill attempted again.

"It's a great day, isn't it? How did you hear about our show today?" Bill asked.

"It's a fine day," the man replied, but the reply lacked emotion. It was like he was going through the motions and only repeating or responding with generalities.

"All right, just give me your arm and I will snap this wristband on," Bill said.

The man slowly put his arm on the counter and pushed it through the opening. There was barely enough room to fit, but he made it. Bill took the wristband and wrapped it around the massive arm, where Bill invariably touched the skin where he fastened the band. Bill almost jumped back. That skin was cold to the touch—not cool, not lukewarm, not clammy—it was utterly cold. Bill didn't know for sure, but if someone had told him that that was what it felt like to touch a dead body, he would have believed them. Oddly enough, Bill had also felt a brief buzzing sensation in his hand when he put the wristband on the man.

Suddenly, Bill didn't want to engage the man any longer. Not that he had a problem with that, because the figure left as soon as he received his wristband. Once gone and after hearing Rita yell for the next person in line, he asked her, "They all feel like that?"

"Yup," came the reply, along with the sound of gum smacking.

14

— · —

Bill left the booth. He wasn't feeling well; he had the feeling of being in a room with the doors locked and the ceiling closing in. Maybe not that bad, but he did have a small line of sweat appear on his forehead that had nothing to do with the heat of the summer day. For some reason, in the back of his mind, the thought rang like alarm bells that he didn't want his kids or Dani to talk to any of these townsfolk. He wasn't sure why, but the constant "ding" drummed in his subconscious so loud that his consciousness was taking note.

As Bill walked through the midway, he felt he had to confirm his suspicions. With so many townsfolk at the carnival, it wasn't hard. He stopped and talked to a family of four. The dad was in pin-striped slacks, a button-up shirt, and thick, black glasses while the mom wore a floral dress and shoes that didn't seem to fit with walking through the grass or dirt. They were high heels and looked out of place. The children, both appearing eight or nine, didn't look at Bill, but they also didn't look at anything else with delight.

Every so often, they would whoop or yell, which conveyed excitement, but it didn't match their demeanor, which was totally void of emotion.

"Excuse me," Bill asked, getting the attention of the father.

"Yes?" the man asked. Bill introduced himself as the proprietor of the show and asked, "Are you enjoying yourself?"

"Oh, very much. We are so glad that you all came to our town to visit. We look forward to your stay here," the man replied.

"I'm curious, but how did you find out about tonight's opening? I'm...uh...doing research on best advertising practices. Whatever we did here seems to have worked. We've never seen the midway so full on opening night."

"We all knew the moment you arrived and we are all so very glad you came to visit us," the man said.

"How did you know?"

"It's a small town and we know everything that goes on here. It's so good here that you may find yourself wanting to stay."

"Ah...well...you know...my life is that of the road, but your town has been...um...pleasant so far. We're glad to be here," Bill replied.

With nothing more to say and the conversation at a standstill, Bill used his usual parting shot, "Enjoy your visit to Donovan's Delights Entertainment."

The family didn't reply. They all looked at him with expressionless faces for a moment, then turned in unison and walked away. The whole interaction made Bill's skin crawl. Something about this town was wrong. He knew it the moment he entered, but his mind had been clouded from the stresses of the world and bills to pay, so he failed to really realize it.

He watched the family disappear into the crowd and turned to find his own family when he thought he heard a whisper through the air. "Stay with us."

It was ever-so-slight, so he almost missed it. He stopped and looked around to see where it could have come from or to see if he even had heard it at all. It could have been his mind playing tricks on him. With all the "zings" and "whistles" from the nearby booths, it could have been nothing, but he could have sworn that's what he heard. The surrounding crowd moved as if he wasn't even there. No one looked at him. They all just moved forward, staring straight ahead. Maybe he really didn't hear it after all, he thought to himself. He started forward again, but the second time he heard it, there was no mistaking it. "Stay with us." It was a louder whisper and resonated from the nearby crowd of townspeople, but when Bill turned to look, he couldn't identify who said it. That particular group dispersed, leaving Bill by himself. His skin had stopped crawling, but there was a chill that ran up his spine. The old adage from his childhood echoed in his mind, "Someone walked over your grave."

He picked up the pace and went to the food booths, first looking for Laura. He didn't know what was going on, but whatever it was, he wanted to keep his kids in the trailer until he could figure that out and figure out what to do. As he walked, he could swear he was being watched. The feeling was unshakable but when he turned to look, no one was looking at him. He wouldn't have been surprised if, as soon as he turned around, they would start watching him again. A cold, sickly feeling started in the pit of his stomach. The sun was still visible and had quite a way to go before it went down, but he worried about what would happen once night set in. He also toyed with the idea that maybe he was losing his mind. He went to the food booth that made funnel cakes and caramel apples, where there was a line of people waiting their turn. Bill went to the back and looked into the open door. Brenda was standing at the cash register, along with another carnie worker that Bill didn't know all that well. Maybe Dan was his name. Laura wasn't there.

"Hey Brenda. Where's Laura?"

Brenda looked at Bill and replied, "I'm not sure. She was supposed to start with us here tonight, but I haven't seen her."

"Okay, thanks. I will go look for her."

"Send her our way when you find her," she replied.

Bill shut the door, walked away, and thought, "Not if I can help it." He would not be sending Laura to help anyone while they were in this town.

The midway was packed and on any other day in any other town, this would have been a very desirable sight to see, but to see it here and now in this particular town, Bill was wary. He made sure not to show his uneasiness. After all his years as the showman, no one—not even someone suffering from extreme paranoia—would be able to tell what he was thinking or feeling. Bill wrapped himself in the showman persona and it quieted his nerves. Sometimes, the mere act of pretending seemed to genuinely help balance things.

He caught a glimpse of Jimmy heading toward the fun house. He almost broke into a run but managed to hold back, though he did pick up his pace a bit. He wasn't at Olympic speed walking levels yet, but that wasn't far if he had to kick it up any more notches. He eventually caught up with Jimmy by the time he reached the fun house. It was a gaudy ride with all sorts of figures and clowns painted on the side. Bells jingled and whistles blew from inside, with moving parts that attracted the eye, such as the rotating barrel at the entrance.

"Jimmy," Bill called out.

Jimmy stopped and turned around. "Yeah boss? What do you need?"

"I need to talk to you over here," Bill replied, pointing to an area away from the crowd, between the fun house and the next attraction.

Once they were in the relative safety of the alleyway, Jimmy looked quizzically at Bill. "Everything okay, boss?

"Yeah, everything is fine. Where were you heading?"

"Well, you saw me. I was heading into the funhouse to check on José to see if he needed anything. We sure got a lot of people today. Isn't that great?"

Ignoring what Jimmy said, Bill cut in, "I need you to do something for me."

"Sure thing."

Bill stepped closer. The feeling of being watched felt stronger than ever. It hadn't lessened one bit. "I need you to go to the back, grab your keys and then I..."

Bill smiled a little, but with the showman bravado, didn't give way to his concern. "I know this is going to sound silly, but please just do what I say."

Jimmy's face was a blanket of questions. His eyes reflected concern, like he wasn't sure what was coming next. But he patiently waited for Bill to continue.

"Jimmy, I need you to go get in your truck. Act non-chalantly and drive around town. I remember coming in. There was a road that was little better than a country lane to get here. I didn't think about it much at the time, but I want you to see if there are any exits to other towns," Bill asked.

Jimmy's face twisted at the incomprehension of the request. "What? Of course, there are exits to other towns."

"I know and I'm sure there are, but just check for me, okay? And don't say a word about what you are doing to anyone," Bill said in hushed words.

"Bill, what's going on? Is there a debt collector on our heels? I know we're hurting for money, but it's not that bad, is it?"

Bill looked at him. The thought of debt and money was so far from his conscious thought, it took a moment for him to comprehend Jimmy's concern. "Oh no. It's not that, Jimmy. It's this town. I don't want to say, but it doesn't feel right."

"Well, sure, I've never seen anything quite like the crowd we're seeing tonight, but I don't think it's a bad thing. They're just different."

"I know, but just trust me on this. Something isn't square and for my peace of mind, I can only trust you to go check for me. I need to be here, otherwise I would do it," Bill said.

"Well..." Jimmy said with not quite a sigh but more of a resigned tone, "If you insist, boss, I'll go check."

"Thank you and come right back to me, okay? As soon as you get back. The sun is going to set in a couple of hours. Try to get back before then."

Jimmy nodded and headed toward the back of the midway where he parked his truck. Bill, on the other hand, put the showman's smile back on his face and left the alley. Bill's request to Jimmy was something that had been building on his mind for some time, though he didn't actively know it. He wanted to confirm that this was a town like anyplace else and, although it was more than likely just a strange town with strange inhabitants, Bill's upbringing and years of conditioning told him to double-check. You never just assumed a ride was safe. You checked and then checked again, and even then, every so often, you would check again.

Bill headed toward the back of the midway, keeping his eyes open for Laura, Jason, or Dani, but he didn't see them. He wasn't overly worried on that front yet. The sun was still up, and the show hadn't been open for long, but he knew he needed to find them. That nagging feeling of being watched wouldn't go away. He also noticed some customers fully engaged with the carnies at some of the booths. Most times, whenever the carnival came to town, the townspeople would show up and, although they relied on the ride jocks and game operators for the fun they had, they also had a tendency to ignore them. Almost as if they were part of the machinery not to engage with. Not tonight, however. He noticed his people were more engaged than usual and that wouldn't have been a bad thing in any other place, but this wasn't any other place, and Bill felt as if things were heating up. He wasn't in a panic, but he wasn't far from that now. He hadn't confirmed his suspicions on this town just yet, but he was on the highway there with all the moments that gave him pause over the past few days.

"Mr. Donovan," Bill heard his name called from closely behind him. He twirled to find Mr. Bright directly behind him. He hadn't been there a moment before. Bill had kept his head on a swivel, looking around for his family and he could have sworn...no, he knew that Mr. Bright hadn't been there a moment before, nor had he seen him in the distance walking up. Bill would have noticed him; he would have been hard to miss in his solid black suit, a moving shadow in the full sun as it began its descent.

Bill stepped back a couple of steps, in surprise. "Ah, Mayor. I'm sorry. I didn't see you come up."

"You just probably didn't notice me, Mr. Donovan."

"I would have," echoed in Bill's mind, reiterating his observation a moment ago.

"What can I do for you, Mr. Bright?" Bill asked.

"It's not what you can do for me, it's what I can do for you."

"I can't think of anything at the moment," Bill said.

"Are you sure? Aren't you tired of all that traveling? Maybe you would like to make this show a permanent fixture here?"

The smile, as usual, still didn't reach Mr. Bright's eyes and now, along with everything else that Bill experienced that day, it creeped him out even more.

"No, I don't think so. We stay here too long and people will get bored and we wouldn't make money. I'm sure you understand," Bill replied.

"Not in my town, you wouldn't. Everything has a way of working out for those that stay here."

When Bill didn't say anything, Mr. Bright filled the void of silence. "Ah...well, maybe you'll change your mind by the week's end."

"Doubt it, but I really must be continuing on to check on staff. With all your town's folks here, I need to check on inventories and make sure people have what they need," Bill lied.

Although that stuff needed to get done, Bill was using the excuse to walk away and go find his family.

"Please, continue, but before you go, do your people need anything from me or my town? Any concerns?"

There were plenty of concerns on Bill's mind now, but he didn't want to play his hand too soon or show his card. "No. No one has voiced any concerns or needs. We look forward to having a productive and lucrative week, then moving on."

"I see," Mr. Bright replied. "Then, I won't keep you. I'll be seeing you again, real soon."

Bill backed away, and the mayor stood, watching him go. Didn't bat an eye or blink. Bill turned and walked away quickly, and before he took a turn at one of the booths to head toward the rides to look for Jason and Laura, he looked back to see if Mr. Bright was still there. He was, and he hadn't moved one inch. The mayor still had that wide smile that looked as if it were made of concrete, never changing. Bill turned and thankfully, since he purposely enveloped himself in his showman persona, he didn't exhibit his alarm, though all the fibers of his being were feeling quite the opposite.

He stopped by the Gravitron, then the Scrambler. His son wasn't at either ride. Maybe they were helping their mom out with something, so he headed to see her next. At the HQ trailer, he bounded up the steps and found Dani inside.

"Hey, honey. Have you seen the kids?"

"No. What's up?" she said as she looked down at the table while going over records. After she read the last line of whatever she was reading, she looked up. "You're sweating. Everything okay?"

Bill wasn't drenched but his face looked like someone had taken a spray bottle and spritzed him with water. He could feel the sweat drip down his face. "I don't know what's up, but I think we need to find the kids and have them hang out here tonight."

"What's wrong?"

"Just a gut feeling, Dani. It's been going since we've been here, and I can't shake it. I want the kids and you to hang out here," Bill replied.

"I know we discussed our reservations, but what lit the fuse to make you think we should do this?" Dani asked. Her face didn't have a look of concern, but a look of extreme focus, to read whatever body language she could pick up from her husband.

"You will just have to trust me, honey. If I'm wrong, then I am totally okay with being the butt of the jokes that will surely follow, but I don't want to take any chances. I can't even explain it properly. All I know is until I'm sure one way or another, I want you and the kids to be safe. And if I'm wrong—which I probably am—then that's okay."

Dani looked at her husband. "Okay, I had the kids go help Kathy, the Thompsons, and everyone else on vendor row. When I heard we had a crowd, I thought they might need more help there, to help direct foot traffic or organize the lines through the petting zoo and the other attractions. I know they usually don't get many visitors, but with so many people here tonight, I thought that might be a problem."

"Good thinking. I will head over there now."

"I'll go with you."

"No. Please stay here."

"Why don't you call over the radio and have them come here?" Dani replied.

That suggestion was such an obvious solution that Bill felt dumb that he hadn't thought of it himself, as he looked down at his belt. Dani was so smart; that's why he loved her...well, there were more reasons than that, but all of it together made her and he loved her for all of it.

He took the two-way radio off his belt, lifted it to his mouth, and clicked the mic open. He asked if anyone had seen his kids, but no reply came back, only static. Normally, someone would have said something, but since there were no replies, Bill tried one more time. Again, no replies from anyone came. That had never happened before. Someone on ride or food truck duty would have had a little downtime to respond. Bill felt his body go incredibly warm. It felt like 100 degrees outside, as well as inside the HQ trailer. The struggling air conditioning unit barely kept it comfortable in there, but Bill's bodily response had nothing to do with the temperature of the day or the room. It had everything to do with how he felt and his gut instinct. He clicked the radio back on his belt and looked back at his wife, whose eyes turned to the radio on his belt with concern.

Dani stood up. "I wan..."

"Listen, Dani. I need you to stay here in case I miss them, and if they come back here first," he lied. Well, he wasn't really lying. If he didn't find them over there, he wanted her to be here in case they came back, but the reality of it was that he didn't want Dani to be out among the townspeople if they were tainted in some way or had something contagious. As far as Bill knew, they might.

Bill's excuse seemed to work because Dani sat back down and didn't say another word, though Bill knew she wanted to. "I'm sure it's all nothing. I love you and I'll be right back with the kids," he told her.

Out the door he went, heading toward the area where the petting zoo was located. He hopped down the steps and looked around. There was no one around, and it was quiet. Not even the "zings" and the "whoops" from the midway proper seemed to sound at the appropriate level. It was as if there was some sort of damper on the noise. It made the back lot seem all the more...not secluded...but frozen in time. A quietness that permeated everything and spoke of eternal things. Things that Bill couldn't hear, nor could he comprehend even if he could. Although he noticed it, he didn't have time to dwell. He needed to find his kids. He walked fast initially, then began trotting. Upon his entrance into the midway from the back lot, he saw Brad coming the opposite direction, whereupon seeing Bill moving with a quickness, Brad flagged him down.

"Where's the smoke?" Brad asked.

"No fire that I know of Brad, but I am looking for my kids. You seen them?"

"Yeah, they are over there near Kathy's mitt reading tent. You okay?"

"Everything is...Well, I'm not sure to be honest, Brad, but something about this town isn't sitting well with me," Bill confided quickly.

"It's sitting well with me." Brad let out a big laugh. "These people are spending money left and right and some of the nicest group I've ever seen. Reminds me of being a boy, it does, along with those cars out there. I've never seen so many vintage cars."

"That's what's worrying me. I've never seen anything like it, either."

"Bah...just a quirky town. That's all it is," Brad replied.

"Maybe so, but I'm going to go find my kids and have them work on next year's homework."

"What? That doesn't make any sense," Brad said.

"I know it doesn't. Nothing makes sense to me at the moment. I'm kidding about the homework, but I think they need to help Dani with some stuff at the HQ trailer."

Brad continued to look at him like a seriously endangered flower or bird that a botanist or ornithologist hadn't seen in a long time and was scrutinizing to be sure they were seeing what they were seeing. Then, as if coming to a conclusion, Brad said, "Um...Okay, Bill." It wasn't his concern; Bill could almost hear Brad thinking.

Bill put his hand on Brad's shoulder. "Be careful tonight, okay Brad? Something is in the air."

"You know me. I'll give them the what's what if need be, no matter who it is...but, who has you spooked? Anyone in particular?"

"No, like I said, just a gut feeling. I'll catch up with you later," Bill replied, exiting the conversation, then trotted on.

Had Bill turned and watched, he would have seen Brad watch him running away as he put a hand on his chin to think for a moment, then scratch his head in puzzlement. Bill didn't see that, nor did he see Brad look to the right, as if he heard something. Bill didn't see it, but he heard what Brad heard—a whisper through the air. "Stay with us."

15

— • —

The haunting whisper only caused Bill to pick up the pace; it didn't take him very long, even as he had to dodge families, to get to his destination on the midway—vendor row. This was the row that showcased trinkets and oddities. The sun sank in the west and shadows stretched, but there was still about an hour left before the ball of light would disappear from sight, and leave everything in darkness, except for flashing artificial lights. For now, the diminishing sunlight provided a sense of safety in its soft glow.

Bill didn't see Jason or Laura. He quickly walked up and down the lane, coming to a stop by the petting zoo. The low bleat of Gertrude the goat could be heard, and Bill yelled and waved his arms to Mike Thompson to get his attention above the noise from all the customers in the area. Even though the townspeople weren't loud, their collective murmurs were deafening in their own right.

Mr. Thompson came over at once when he saw Bill waving his arms. As he closed the distance, though, he had trouble wading through people in the petting zoo enclosure. "What's going on Bill? Isn't this great? I don't think we've done this well in...well...forever."

Bill didn't respond to this, but went directly to the question he was burning to ask. "Have you seen my kids?"

Mr. Thompson looked around thoughtfully. "No, I haven't. Were they supposed to be here?"

"Dani sent them over this way to help, since there were so many customers here."

"Hmm. Let me ask my wife."

Mr. Thompson disappeared and shortly reappeared with his wife, who still looked unkempt, with her frizzy hair jutting all over the place.

"Hey, Bill. Yeah, they were here earlier. I turned around, though, and then they were gone. I figured they got bored and left. Everything okay?" she asked.

"I'm not sure yet, but I'll let you know."

Bill left them there standing. The Thompsons watched him walk away, then turned back to give their full attention to the folks in the petting zoo.

Bill was on the verge of feeling frantic, but then he noticed that the "open" sign over Kathy's act wasn't there, nor was her table out front, which was peculiar. Anyone that looked at it would have guessed that her booth was closed. No lights on outside and nothing else to indicate that she was open for business. With nothing else to go on, Bill went there next. Kathy did voice her concern earlier and she might know more now.

He knocked on the tent entrance, where the heavy wooden tent pole kept the tent rigid. "Kathy?"

Bill didn't wait long. The folds of the tent opened, and hands appeared, pulling him just inside. The action was so swift that it caught him by surprise. Before he had time to react, he was already inside. He was about to lash out, because although there was a small light source inside the tent, he couldn't see anything while his eyes were adjusting to the dark from the dying light outside. Then he heard Kathy's voice. "Shh...don't talk so loud."

"Kathy, what are you doing?" Bill whispered.

"I'm keeping all of us safe," she replied in a voice that was dry, low, and reminded him of a flame moving across an open field of grass during a drought.

It took a moment for Bill's eyes to adjust, but as it did, he noticed two other figures in the dark confines of the tent. It was Jason and Laura playing a card game. He looked at them and then back at Kathy.

"They don't know anything...yet, but I told them you told me to keep them here," Kathy said.

The kids were at the back of the tent, sitting at a small table near the entrance to her living quarters. They couldn't hear the conversation because they were intent on playing whatever game they were playing.

"What do you think is going on and why did you decide to bring my kids inside?" Bill replied, keeping his voice low. He was glad she did, but since they had never discussed that, he wondered why she did it. This wasn't a practiced response, like one of those families that had fire drills and established a meetup point outside in case there was ever a real fire. They never did anything like that, so Bill had to know.

"I'm not sure, but I've been reading more of that book, and found out more disturbing things about this area. I was going to tell you about it but didn't have a chance to. Then when I saw the strange mannerisms of the townspeople here, something told me to be careful. I tried to use the walkie-talkie to call you, but it wouldn't work, which only added to my gut telling me to do something. When I saw the kids near the petting zoo, I figured I'd start there, and pulled them into my tent."

Relief flooded through Bill like an Arizona wash that hadn't seen rainwater in months. It flowed quickly and steadily and gave Bill a moment to breathe freely. He hadn't realized how much he had been holding it while looking for Jason and Laura. Quickly, he looked at his kids to see them smiling and lost in the moment of the game they were playing, without a care in a world. The relief was two-fold. One, because he found his kids, and two, there was someone else that seemed to have the same type of gut alarm that he seemed to experience.

It wasn't so surprising because they talked about it briefly before, but what they talked about before was an oddity. What they talked about now was danger on some unknown level.

"What did you find out?" Bill asked, as he turned his attention back and looked directly into Kathy's eyes.

"This area—the whole area in between the Mississippi and Ohio Rivers—is reminiscent of Egypt. There is no coincident that there are places here like the city named Cairo, or the nearby, large lake called the Lake of Egypt. It's like remnants of ancient Egypt ended up here, complete with other things that came with it. It didn't specifically say that in the book, but it was one of those, "if you read between the lines" type of things. The person who wrote it definitely had some thoughts on the matter. This isn't some country bumpkin place in the middle of nowhere farmland. There's something here. I don't know what, but it's here."

"I believe you. I wouldn't have believed it yesterday or maybe even this morning, but now I do. I agree that we're in danger." Bill said, then asked, "Are you hearing whispers?"

"What?"

"Whispers," Bill said again.

"No. Are you?"

"I think so. I can barely make them out and it's only when I'm near a large group of the townspeople."

Kathy's eyes grew in size. In surprise or fear, Bill couldn't say. "Well, that isn't good. I've turned off my light outside and covered my business sign. I've stayed inside since those people arrived, then brought the kids in here."

"Good thinking," Bill began, but then the kids noticed Bill standing in the shadows of the tent entrance.

"Daddy!" Laura squealed as she jumped up from the table and ran over to give her dad a hug. Jason stood up and trailed his sister, stopping short before speaking. "Why did you have Ms. Kathy keep us in here? It's busy out there and they need our help."

Bill returned Laura's hug, then turned to look at Jason. "I think it would be a good idea to hang out in here tonight or at the HQ trailer."

"That doesn't make sense. That crowd is the largest I've ever seen and I know I could make some money..." Jason began, but was cut off.

"I know, son. Don't worry about the money. I will make sure you get compensated like you worked...you too, Laura. I know you wanted to start working, too. But I need you both to hold off this week. I think something is wrong with the crowd out there."

"What do you mean? Like they're sick or something?" Jason asked.

"Yes, something like that. Whatever it is, I don't want you around it. You're just going to have to trust me on this."

"But what about everyone else? Are they in danger of getting sick?" Laura asked.

"I don't know, but we are going to wait it out tonight, then see what we can do about everything tomorrow," Bill said.

"But the sun isn't even down yet. We still have hours to go until we shut down at midnight," Jason said, his voice not hiding the fact that he was frustrated.

Bill grabbed his son and pulled him in for a hug. His son's body stiffened at the sudden movement. They all loved each other, but Jason was at that age where showing affection for his parents and his sister wasn't a top priority, but after a moment, his body visibly relaxed.

"I know it doesn't make sense," Bill said when he released Jason from his embrace.

"What was that about?" Jason asked curiously, his mind questioning the hug that came out of nowhere. "Are you okay? Are we okay here?"

"You are going to have to trust me, all right?"

Jason's demeanor showed no more signs of frustration. Instead, it was replaced by a look of concern and curiosity.

Bill said, "Okay, I'm going back to the HQ trailer. You can come with me or stay here, but we need to move before the sun dips out of the sky for the evening."

"I'm going with you," Laura stated with finality.

Jason nodded his agreement with his sister.

"Kathy, you want to come?" Bill asked.

"Me?"

"Yes, I think it would be a good idea if we stick together."

"Sure...oh...I hadn't expected to leave. Let me grab some things."

"That's fine, but hurry, we don't have much daylight left."

Kathy quickly grabbed a backpack and hurriedly went through the tent, stuffing items into the pack before disappearing into the back of the tent. She returned with a walking stick that looked like a staff.

"I'm ready," she said.

"Okay, let's go. Kathy, I want you to go first, followed by Jason, Laura, and then I will bring up the rear. I want you to head down the lane toward the back until we get to the Gravitron. Then take a left until we hit the main lane, and then move past the Ferris wheel to the back lot."

Kathy nodded her understanding.

"If, for whatever reason, we get separated or split up, stick together with whoever you're with and make your way to the HQ trailer," Bill continued.

"Dad, you're scaring me. Is something really wrong with these people?" Laura asked.

Jason quickly stepped in. "No, sis, he just wants to make sure we all know what we're doing and where we're going. Once you start setting up the rides like I do, you'll understand that you have to plan for everything."

"Oh, okay," Laura replied, relaxing.

Jason looked at his dad, and Bill gave a smile that spoke of appreciation. Bill could tell that Jason was worried, but he was using his own version of the showman persona to keep his sister from being scared.

"Okay, are we ready, then?" Bill asked, looking at the small group.

"I am," Laura squeaked.

"Sure," Jason replied.

"I guess I'm as ready as I'll ever be. I will have to padlock the tent entrance, so no one comes in and magics my stuff away," Kathy said.

Bill nodded, "All right, let's go."

Kathy started first and, like a line of ants, the rest followed, stopping momentarily for Kathy to close the tent flaps, wrap a small rope with loops at both ends through eyelets, then connect them with a padlock. Bill had never taken the time to see, or even really thought about what Kathy did for security, but he could see that the maneuver could be done from inside the tent, as well. Bill figured that's how she slept relatively safely at night. Moving forward, he would have to do a better job at thinking about the small stuff like this...that was, if they got out of here alive.

The sun was at the horizon now; they didn't have much time left. Bill wasn't really sure anything would happen that would be very different from what was happening now, but he couldn't help what he felt. It was a growing ball of nerves and he couldn't tell if it was that gut feeling on steroids or if he was really coming down with some sort of sickness.

Once done, Kathy nodded to indicate her task was complete, then led the group up the lane like they had discussed. They passed the petting zoo, and it was still packed, but that was every booth this evening. The whole midway was packed and the crowd only seemed to grow. Bill looked around and wondered if the whole town had shown up. The Thompsons were wheeling and dealing. Mrs. Thompson was collecting money at the makeshift gate and Mr. Thompson was regaling anyone within earshot with numerous facts and little-known stories about animals in their care.

Once past the petting zoo, they saw one of the food booths; it was little more than a hotdog stand. From the light glowing inside, Bill could see it was two new hires that had joined them this summer. He couldn't remember their names...Jodie or John and Betty or Beth, he thought. But whatever their names were, they were too busy to notice the small entourage pass by.

The crowd certainly wasn't rowdy. In fact, they were quite pleasant, but the strange dress and the whispers didn't jive right inside Bill's mind. He didn't suspect it ever would unless he found something that would logically explain it all. At this point, the only rational thing he could think of was that it was an elaborate joke, maybe like Candid Camera or one of those shows where jokesters take videos of people getting pranked. That would have been the only explanation that would have come close to making sense, but somehow, Bill knew that wasn't the case here.

They scurried on; the Gravitron was coming into view. The sun was setting. Shadows lengthened. Lights took over more of the darkness but created pockets of velvety night where it would be hard-pressed to look for anyone.

And, it would only get darker once the last rays of the sun disappeared from view.

Bill looked around and didn't see any other carnies beside the ride jock at the Gravitron, but he was too busy changing out passengers and taking tickets to pay them any mind. On any other night, Bill would have stopped to see if he needed anything, like food or a restroom break, but not tonight, at least not until he got his kids to what he perceived to be the safest place.

It only took about 10 to 15 minutes to walk to the back lot, but it felt like it took all day. When Bill looked at the Sun, however, it felt like it was dropping fast—faster than usual. They passed the Ferris wheel and were in the back lot. They didn't get separated, and all arrived in one piece. Walking up the steps into the trailer, Bill looked back to catch the last tidbit of bright, shining sun sink out of sight.

Inside, Dani looked relieved at the sight of her family coming through the door. She jumped up and came over to hug them. Kathy stepped to the side, and they nodded toward one another as Dani passed by her. Bill came in and closed the door behind them, then embraced the whole family in a group hug.

"How was it out there?" Dani asked, immediately after the hug.

"It was like any other night, except those people are dressed funny," Laura said excitedly.

Bill looked at his wife and shrugged. "I bumped into Jimmy and asked him to drive into town to check things out."

"That's good. He has his head on straight," she replied.

Now that Bill knew his family was safe, or rather, safer from whatever was out there on the midway, he was relieved. He still had no concrete proof of anything ominous or dangerous other than a strange town with strange people. And other than the whispers that he couldn't confirm others had heard, everything was going okay. No one had come to find him to tell him that someone was hurt, though if it was that guy named Peter, it wouldn't have bothered him so much other than worrying if the show's insurance would cover it. It was a fleeting thought and as quickly as it came, it went. It brought to Bill's attention that he needed to go back on the midway to keep an eye on things. Even if he didn't feel good about being here, he still had responsibilities. And if it turned out to be nothing more than a strange town in the rearview mirror, he'd be remiss if he didn't handle his daily chores of keeping a smooth ship running. That was the way of things—daily routines that kept things moving smoothly and safely. If a particular duty like checking on your people or equipment went by the wayside, things had a way of becoming unbalanced...and it would take more work to get back on balance than it would had everyone just done what they were supposed to.

"I have to go back out there," Bill said.

"But what if they're sick, Daddy?" Laura asked.

"I think I'll be all right, besides, what about everyone else? I need to make sure they're okay too, you know."

"Are you sure you have to go out there?" Dani asked, though she knew the answer. She had known his routine for the past...well...what felt like forever. He knew that she knew he wouldn't deviate that much from it.

It didn't require a verbal answer. Bill looked deeply into her eyes and nodded. Dani only nodded back with her understanding, though she wasn't happy about it. Bill felt like he was back in middle school...the times he went to an actual school and was faced with decisions he didn't know how to make. On one hand, he had his family that he felt needed to be kept safe. On the other hand, he had the rest of the people that worked for him, either directly or through Brad and George. And they were also family, of sorts. And all this over a heebie-jeebie feeling. He felt silly and absurd, but also "once bitten, twice shy." Not that he had ever faced this kind of situation before, so no, he had never been bitten in this way in the past. But being cautious...well...he'd had more than enough parallel experiences when his stomach screamed for caution that had kept him, as well as the show, out of serious trouble.

Kathy came forward and offered her long walking stick. "Here, take this."

"Why would I need that?" Bill asked.

"It's a blessed stick and who knows, it might come in handy," she replied.

"Blessed, huh?" Bill was on the verge of telling her to keep it, knowing full well that, in addition to fortune telling, palm reading, and tarot cards, she also sold "blessed" trinkets that were little more than dollar store junk that she doubled the price on by adding "blessed" to the description. But the way she held it out and the way her eyes were set, he questioned this and finally relented. What could it hurt? At the very least, he could use it to keep his mind preoccupied, like whipping a pen around while on the phone, or clicking the end of a pen in a meeting to get rid of nervous energy. Maybe having something in his hands would help him get rid of some of his anxiety. He nodded and reached to take hold of the long, thin rod of wood, which was about an inch and a half in diameter and about five feet long. The length of it came to the top of his chest. When his hand fell around the pole, he felt an immediate snap of something as if it were white noise in physical form. It was almost like a small, static shock but didn't cause pain or even a moment of surprise. It lasted but a split second and it was gone.

Bill looked at the staff in his hand. Looked normal to him but he felt a sense of gravity, a density of something beyond the norm of a regular walking stick. He looked back at Kathy and nodded. "Thanks, I'll take it with me."

Kathy nodded back and shortly after, Bill was out the door, down the stairs, and heading back onto the midway.

Kathy watched Bill leave. She had indeed picked up the staff at a roadside shop full of curios, many years ago. She didn't know why she brought it with her to the HQ trailer. Perhaps the weight of it in her hands felt comforting. She also didn't know why, at the last second, she was compelled to give it to Bill for protection. To her knowledge, there was nothing special about that staff, but Kathy knew the power of belief was sometimes all it took to make things happen. With all the eeriness of this town and the events leading up to this week, every little bit helps. Maybe a little nudge of magic would do them some good. It certainly couldn't hurt.

16

B ill walked quickly. His first stop was to check on George. He hadn't seen him since the beginning of the night and figured he would be near the concession area, keeping an eye on food and drink inventory. With the number of townspeople, the levels would run dry long before they shut down at midnight, and would have to be restocked.

He wasn't used to walking with a staff, but quickly moved in unison with it, tapping every other step as he walked along. Something about the rhythmic thumping along the ground kept his mind focused in a way that kept it calm. For the first time this evening, since the arrival of all those old cars and 40s and 50s-style clad people showing up, he felt calm...not okay or at peace, but calm in an indescribable way. Luckily, he was now far from letting his mind run away with itself and cause anxiety.

Thump...thump...thump...The rhythm continued and before long, he was where he thought George should have been. Bill knew George had a weakness for funnel cakes, a weakness that had left Bill many years ago, one night when he was 20. He had been drunk and had eaten his fill of funnel cake, because there was always an abundance of them on the midway. Well, that one night would last him for the rest of his life because the next day, he was utterly sick and thought he would never survive that event.

Sure enough, George was there in the booth, along with his daughter Brenda, and another worker. Brenda was busy powdering the cakes with confectioner's sugar and handing them out to customers, while the other girl handled the till. It was just as crowded there as it had been on vendor row. Heck, the whole midway was probably more crowded than it had ever been. Bill made his way to the back of the trailer, opened the door, and walked in.

"Hey you," Brenda said when she saw him. "Did you find Laura? We could really use her help."

"Yeah, I found her," Bill said, but followed up with a lie. "But Dani needed her for something, so I sent her there instead."

Brenda shrugged her shoulders, said okay, then went back to the routine of serving customers. George was hovering, helping a little in between bites of his cake.

"How's it going out there?" George motioned to the crowd and the midway beyond, then continued. "We're raking it in tonight."

"I don't think I've ever seen anything like it," Bill replied.

"You know, I don't think I have either, but I like it."

"What do you like?" Bill asked.

"Making money, of course, but seeing everything about this town...I don't know...just reminds me of being a little boy."

"Everything going okay here? How is your inventory?" Bill asked.

"We've already had to restock tonight, and I think we'll be okay, but if it keeps up like this every night, we'll run out way before the end of the week. Not a bad problem to have, I'd say," George replied as he rubbed the crumbs and sugar of the finished funnel cake on the shirt covering his pot belly.

"No...normally it wouldn't be," Bill murmured, but with the commotion of the sounds from the carnival and the conversations of the people nearby, the words drifted into nothingness.

"What was that?" George asked.

Bill looked at him as if he were just waking up from a dream and replied, "Oh, it's nothing. So, everything is good, then?"

"Yeah. Any reason it shouldn't be?"

"No," Bill sighed silently to himself. He wanted confirmation from more than just the small group he had hidden out in the HQ trailer that others felt something was amiss. Bill added one more thing as he looked at George with a focus that anyone else would have likened to that of a bird of prey. It was an expression of gravity that bordered on profound. "If you need anything, don't hesitate to tell me, all right?"

George, not looking at Bill, waved his hand in acknowledgement like it was a casual agreement that had been done many, many times over the years...well...because it had, and was indeed a routine. One of those dances that people developed and executed on autopilot. The only difference this time was that Bill had meant something completely different, and it was completely lost on George. Bill always asked if anyone needed anything. It was something everyone could expect and even admired, because Bill would do his damnedest to provide. This time, though, he wanted George to know that should he need him—no matter the depth of need—he'd be there.

Bill left George and Brenda behind as he continued on. The midway was in full swing now. The shouts and "zings" grew louder but underneath it all, there was something else. He had once listened to music that supposedly had something nearly imperceptible to human ears that would enhance the brain through altered waves. Whatever this was, it wasn't overt; it was very subtle, but if you paid attention, you could hear it. Bill felt no different after listening to that particular brain wave music but here, listening to the melodies of the midway, he could almost detect the same intertwining of...something...along with the normal carnival sounds. It was almost like a slow and repeated whisper, as if on a broken record that no one would hear unless they knew to listen for it. He could swear it sounded like chants of "join us" or "stay with us," but it was so faint, he couldn't quite make it out.

Bill felt the staff in his hand and continued to walk forward. Thump...thump...thump... The sound of the staff thudding on the ground brought his attention back to the present and disrupted the strange intertwining. Now, he only heard what was supposed to be heard on the midway—the nighttime carnival sounds. It was a night that normally would have been full of excitement, and tonight was indeed full of excitement, however, it was not the kind he had expected. This "excitement" bordered on sheer terror, though Bill still wasn't certain how much was truly an external threat or if it was merely his internal fear and anxiety. He knew, though, that he would soon find out. One way or the other, he would find out.

Bill continued with his own routine that he had built over the years, checking in with different carnies. For the most part, they were all fine, and Bill wanted to get back to his family. First and foremost, he needed to make sure they were safe but also, going back to the "excitement," he wanted that to be over. He also had to act the part of "business as usual" because if there was something externally nefarious going on, he didn't want to tip his hand too much that he knew. Like a gambler holding cards, he didn't want to give too much away, then have the consequences of whatever forces at play be too high of a price to pay.

Bill struck the staff harder against the ground to create even more of a buffer between the staccato of the thump, thump, thump and the now unheard intertwining of borderline imagined song.

Bill walked with purpose and ended up on the row that housed all the games. He passed by the milk bottle toss, and on the other side was the BB gun shooting gallery. Whoever was running the milk bottle booth this evening had apparently taken a break, because there was no one to be seen behind the counter. The BB gun shooting gallery, however, was currently being run by Stan, the chubby kid, and the scrawny, pimply-faced girl, Louise. Bill didn't know them that well, but he had heard stories about Louise; he treated no one differently, no matter what their reputation was. The only thing that mattered to Bill was their work ethic. He didn't care what they did when they weren't working. He didn't know much about Stan, other than the fact that he palled around with Louise, and come to think of it, he had seen both of them pal around with Peter. The sudden thought of Peter would have normally irritated Bill, but tonight, it didn't have the same effect because everything else preoccupied his thoughts. Since he was there, he said "hello" to the two behind the counter as they gave BB guns to three new townies who had replaced another three who wanted to shoot at the targets.

"Hey, Mr. Donovan," Stan said.

The girl looked over at him and gave him a smile to acknowledge him. He suddenly remembered why he opted to make sure he didn't deal with her often. Her smile was more than a greeting; it was crooked and coy. Along with her eyes giving him a look that Bill couldn't quite explain, it seemed to be an open invitation to come experience her nightly delights. Bill looked at Stan, who was obviously oblivious to the exchange, and ignored the girl.

"Everything all right here?"

"Yes, Mr. Donovan, everything's fine here. Having a good night. Better than I think we've ever had on an opening night," Stan replied.

Bill looked back across the crowded corridor at the milk bottle toss. It was still unmanned, and it was a growing itch at the back of Bill's neck. Even with everything going on and his mind preoccupied by the strange occurrences, he still couldn't believe that no one was there.

"Who's manning the milk toss?"

"Peter Thorston," Stan replied.

Louise sauntered over. "Yeah, he took a break, but he should be back soon. Do you want to go look for him in the alley?" she said as she smiled. He could have sworn she also winked.

Bill was taken aback by the apparent advance. It was done in such a way that if he called her out, she could play innocent, but there was no mistaking what she was really getting at. Let's go in the alley and screw our brains out. Bill wasn't sure if it was this town or if it was just Louise having an off night. She had never been this straight-forward with him before. There were boundaries that shouldn't be crossed, but tonight, for whatever reason, she didn't seem to think there were any boundaries left.

"Uh...no," Bill said.

"Suit yourself, but anytime you want to have a look...I mean...go take a look, I'm available."

"I'm sure you are," Bill thought to himself and shuddered. In all the years that he had been married, he had temptation maybe twice, but he had never cheated on his wife. And he certainly wouldn't have cheated on her with Louise. The exchange was so bizarre that Bill was still trying to wrap his mind around the whole situation when Stan spoke up. "Oh look, Peter's back."

Coming to from a mind full of fog, he turned to notice that Peter was back in the booth, calling out to people to toss the baseball and win a prize. "Three chances for a dollar!"

Bill nodded at Stan and Louise and walked away without another word, heading toward Peter. When he was halfway across the corridor, Peter noticed Bill was coming. He mouthed a curse word and rolled his eyes at his approach as if saying, "Puh-lease."

"Peter," Bill said when he arrived.

"Yeah."

"Everything okay? I didn't see you at the booth a few minutes ago."

It was customary, especially on a busy night like tonight, that you waited until someone could cover you while you took a break. In any other town, Bill would have been upset that Peter didn't follow protocol, but the feelings he had about their current location and its peculiarity caused Bill a fair amount of concern. He wanted to find out why Peter wasn't at his post, so to speak, hoping maybe it would shed light on something—anything.

Unfortunately, Peter became defensive and Bill's initial curiosity soured due to the haughty reply. "I had to take a break and besides with so many people, this booth has more than doubled what it would take in on a normal night."

Bill kept his frustration in check and asked one more question. "Peter, what do you think of this town?"

"Why? You gonna leave me here?" he asked.

"I hadn't planned on it. Did you want to be left here?"

The look on Peter's face changed from defiance to something that wasn't quite panic, but not far from it. "Could you make it the next town?"

"What?"

"If you kick me out of the show, can you make it the next town?" Peter said, looking beyond Bill at the crowd of 50s-style clad people milling about, going from booth to booth.

"Why?" Bill asked.

Peter looked back at Bill and then shook his head. "It's nothing."

Bill looked at Peter, then out to the crowd, which, no matter how many times he looked, gave him the hee-bie-jeebies because he felt like he had taken a step back in time. He then looked back at Peter. "Listen, I know we have issues between you and me, but I wasn't planning on kicking you out here."

Peter's demeanor changed from slight panic-stricken to relief, but also to a state of sullenness.

"What do you think about this town?" Bill asked.

Peter looked away while he pursed his lips, and his brow furrowed. Obviously, he had something to say but didn't want to talk about it.

"Peter."

Peter again looked at Bill. "I don't know, but I went for a walk earlier. I know—I'm supposed to be helping set up and do safety walk throughs but I wanted to check out town like I usually do..."

Peter paused to see if Bill was upset. Again, Peter wasn't doing what he was supposed to, but there was something different going on here. Peter continued, "So, anyway, I walked a few blocks over and decided to check out some shops..."

Peter then became quiet for a few moments until Bill nudged him forward. "And?"

"I...I don't know how to explain it, but I went into one of the stores and...there was absolutely nothing inside," Peter finally said.

"What?" Bill asked. "What do you mean?"

"Exactly what I said. I walked a couple blocks over, saw a store that looked open. From the outside, looking through the window, there were people and all kinds of stuff inside.

But when I opened the door and went in...there was nothing in there. It was an empty room."

Bill stayed silent as he tried to comprehend what he was just told. His silence seemed to nudge Peter on even more.

"And it scared me. Then, I went to the store next to it and the same thing happened. Busy from the outside, nothing on the inside. Then, I came out again and there were no cars or people... and then I realized I hadn't seen one since I left the midway. I don't know what's up with this town, but something about it's wrong."

Bill then saw Peter in a new light. Yes, he was a punk-ass kid but he was scared and to be honest, so was Bill. In situations like that, uncertainty had a way of bonding even the most unlikely pair or group of people. Although Bill wouldn't call him a bosom buddy, he could appreciate the fact that both of them were facing whatever this was together.

"I know. I feel the same way," Bill confided.

"You do?"

"Yeah, I don't think this place is like anywhere we've ever been before and we need to keep our heads about us. I'm not sure what's going on, but I don't think it's good."

Peter's shoulders slumped as if he had just dropped a heavy pack.

"I didn't think anyone would believe me," he said.

"I believe you. I just don't know what we're going to do about it," Bill said and then stepped closer, so his voice wouldn't carry, before continuing. "And we have to keep going on like everything is okay...at least for now. I still don't know if this is some elaborate prank, some twisted joke, or something else entirely, but I don't want whoever is behind this to know that we suspect anything, so we need to keep going like nothing is wrong. Got it?"

Peter nodded his head without replying.

Bill asked one more question. "Do you know of anyone else that feels this way?"

"No, I tried to explain to Stan and Louise over there," Peter said as he gestured across the lane to the shooting gallery, "But I thought they were going to think I was crazy."

"If you come across others that feel something, you let me know, okay? We may need to band together, but until then, it's business as usual unless they do something really crazy or threatening to us," Bill said.

"Okay," Peter said.

Bill looked at his watch, and time was flying. It felt like the sun had just gone down not long ago, but it was already 10 PM. Two more hours 'til midnight, then they would shut down for the evening.

"What time do you have?" Bill asked.

Peter looked at his own watch. "9:25," he said.

"What?" Bill said surprisedly, and that shock was only surpassed by Peter's, as Bill quickly moved forward to grab his wrist and look at Peter's watch.

"Get your hands off me, man," Peter replied, alarmed and angry as he yanked his arm away, then reared back and let his fist fly. Bill unexpectedly felt an explosion on his face and before he realized it, he was on the ground, looking up at Peter. A long stream of curse words was spewing from Peter's mouth—words he had held back for a while, and was now letting loose. "I thought we were cool, but you were gonna hit me again." Peter then gave Bill a final "F bomb" and told him where to stick it, before turning around and running off into the crowd.

Bill's stomach sank to the lowest point it could go. The churning of emotions in the pit of his stomach created an intense nausea. It felt like an old pirate ship, complete with full sails, caught in a dangerous storm on the high seas, fighting winds, rain, and high waves during a summer squall. All of it was so unexpected. All Bill wanted to do was confirm that the times were different, but now he was on the ground. His face felt numb, though he knew that at some point, it would start to throb. He checked his face and thankfully, it didn't appear that his nose was bleeding; the majority of the pain was from his left cheek, so at least his nose wasn't broken.

Bill rolled over and got to his knees, and then used the counter to steady himself and stand up. As he looked around, he became aware that everyone in the lane looked like statues. There was no movement, nor was there any sound coming from any of them. They all stood stock-still and watched him. But, he couldn't even say they were watching him because that word had a safe and familiar feel to it. They appeared to be staring, but that would imply that there was thought and a mind behind their eyes, but that wasn't quite right either. They all stood there focusing on him, then they all turned, as if on cue from some unheard whistle or bell. They then continued on with what they were doing, as if on a pre-programmed routine, like a needle on a record player that had been picked up, then returned to the exact same spot a few minutes later.

Bill watched as he massaged his face a little. He scanned the area for Peter, but he was long gone. He looked across the lane at the shooting gallery and found Stan and Louise staring dumbly at him. As they caught sight of him looking at them, they turned quickly like they hadn't seen anything, as if not sure what to do. Bill then looked up and down the lane, seeing no one else he knew. He couldn't believe he got decked. That kid was quicker than he thought and he had let his guard down, but he couldn't help but think that it wasn't all the kid's fault. If he was indeed scared and was in a constant fight-or-flight mode, any sudden movements like Bill reaching suddenly for his wrist would set him off. Instead of running, though, he fought and lashed out before running off.

Bill didn't like any of this experience one bit. He felt like he was losing control of his show. Ever since he had taken over for his father, the show had been his, for the most part, along with Brad and George. Bill made most of the decisions, but he was level-headed and never did anything too far out to rock the boat and cause the others to want to leave. He always felt like he had a pretty good handle on things and that's how it went for years. He fell into a routine, year after year, season after season, week after week and now, out of the blue, Bill felt like he was a passenger on a plane that had suddenly lost power. The plane was still in the air, but gliding. How it would end was anyone's guess, and Bill didn't like the feeling one bit.

He stood up straight, bent down to pick up the staff that went flying when he fell, and decided that he had had enough for one evening. He would check with people on the way to the back lot and then wait it out. Hopefully, he would see Jimmy. After Peter's tale of what he experienced in town, he wondered if Jimmy was okay and if he had unintentionally sent him into danger. He would have tried to reach him on the two-way radio, but Bill knew he wouldn't have picked up, even if he had tried. He would have hopped in his own truck and gone looking for him, but he couldn't leave his family behind to do so. He also didn't feel conformable sending anyone else. The responsibility weighed heavily and Bill's mind was filled with no good options, or at least any that didn't have unknown consequence attached to them.

He thumped the staff as he moved and true to his decision, he stopped off to check on different ride jockeys and other workers, none of whom needed anything, so he walked on. After talking to different souls, Bill decided that only a handful of people felt anything wrong about this town or maybe felt it wasn't wrong enough to voice it. He wondered what made the difference between those who felt something versus those who didn't.

The night began to cool now that the sun, with its warming light, was gone. Of course, "cool" was a relative term because in the middle of the summer, it was still rather hot, but compared to the blazing heat of the day, it was now comfortable. This time of day is when Bill would normally burst with excitement because this was when all the magic of the show would shine through—the crowd, the weather, the happy sounds—all culminated into the perfect moment. Had they been anywhere else, at literally any other spot, this moment as he headed toward the back lot would have been flawless...except that they weren't at any of those other locations. They were here...in Brownsville...a town that supposedly disappeared over 100 years ago and wasn't on the map anywhere. Yet here it was, and here he was. He was as far from that perfect moment as you could get.

He bumped into Brad near the entrance to the back lot. "Where are you going?" he asked.

"Heading back to see Dani and the kids."

"Oh, I just came from there as I had to grab a bottle of water. Kathy's in there with them. Surprising, though. I would have thought she'd be reading mitts or casting the bones...or whatever she does," Brad replied.

"Yeah, strange...but it's a strange time right now," Bill proffered. He wanted to see if Brad would give any inkling that he felt the same way he did.

"I don't know what's strange about it. This town is rather nice, don't you think?"

"Guess he doesn't," Bill thought to himself before replying, "I don't think I would say that, but it's certainly different from anywhere else we've been."

"Yeah, and I kind of like it," Brad said.

Bill had never heard Brad say anything like that about any other spot they had ever visited, and that caused a new spike of worry and caution. Bill had gotten so used to thumping the staff that to others, it looked like he was letting off nervous energy. Perhaps he was, but when Bill realized he was still doing it while standing still and talking to Brad, he wondered if the voices with the nearly inaudible messages of "stay with us" were having an effect on his people.

He momentarily stopped the tapping of the staff to see if the voices returned. A few moments went by as he listened.

"Hello?" Brad asked.

"Yeah, I'm still here. I thought I heard something and was listening for it."

"What did you hear?"

"Well, Brad, I've been hearing these voices," is what Bill wanted to say but couldn't because so far, he thought he was the only one hearing them. Even though he had known Brad ever since he was child and considered him family, he didn't want to go so far out on a limb that might end up with Brad thinking he was heading to the loony bin.

"I don't know," Bill finally said. "Have you heard anything that sounds weird this evening?"

"No...don't believe so," Brad replied and looked around, then concluded, "Nope, everything seems normal to me."

Every conversation has a natural starting and ending point and for the conversation that Bill was having with Brad, it was coming to an end.

"All right...well...I'll be seeing you later. I think I'm going to be hanging out back here tonight. I'm not feeling 100 percent," Bill said.

"You okay?" Brad asked, concerned.

"Yeah, I'm fine. I think it was something I ate," Bill said, and then he thought to himself, "or maybe it's just me going crazy."

Brad turned to go before Bill caught him by the arm. "What time do you have?"

Brad turned around and with the light now showing the part of Bill's face that had been in the shadows, Brad's eyes opened with alarm and a curse word rolled out of his mouth. "What happened to you? Looks like you're getting a black eye. You tell me who did it and I'll make sure they pay. Was it a townie?"

"No, no. It wasn't anything like that," Bill replied.

"Well, what happened?"

"I...uh..." Bill didn't know what to respond with. He looked down at the staff in his hands and lied, "Well, it's a funny story, but a little embarrassing. I was twirling this stupid thing. I have no idea why I was doing such a thing, but wouldn't you know it? It smacked me silly. I guess it looks worse than it feels."

And that was a lie because it was hurting.

Brad let out a huge guffaw of laughter. "Well, if that don't beat all.... Ha ha ha." Then, after he got that out of his system, "Yeah, you might want to go put ice on that. Looks pretty bad."

"Thanks. Yeah, I think I might do that," Bill said as he turned to go.

"Sounds good. I'll be seeing you," Brad said as he walked away and then called over his shoulder, as he lifted his left arm and pointed at his watch, "And by the way, I have 9 o'clock."

Bill quickly looked at his own watch, which still reflected 10 PM. When he looked up, Brad had disappeared from sight, moving down one of the lanes, heading toward the game booth area.

Bill headed to the back and saw Jimmy's truck in its usual spot. A wave of relief poured over Bill. He hadn't realized how much pent-up stress he was holding in, worrying about Jimmy and the errand he sent him on. He went over to Jimmy's trailer and knocked. The door opened and Jimmy stood there.

"Hey boss. I was just coming to find you. I got back about five minutes ago and needed to change batteries for my walkie-talkie. It doesn't seem to be working."

"It's okay. Is everything all right?" Bill asked.

"Yeah, sure," Jimmy replied, but then continued, "But I have bad news, boss."

"Yeah? What do you got?"

"The exit from this town? I couldn't find one."

17

"What?" Bill surprisedly asked.

"Just what I said, boss. I couldn't find a road out of here."

Bill stood stock-still, taking the information in, and though it looked like he was doing nothing, his mind was racing at what implications this had. Jimmy continued, "I couldn't even find the road we came in on. I thought I did as I backtracked and remembered some landmarks that I saw as we entered town—the clock tower, the corner store we took a right at—but heading out of town that way, the road curved and ended up circling back into town. Every road that I took that started in town and headed into the country would eventually turn and loop back into town. And of course when I looked at the map, this town's not listed, so I don't know. What do you make of it?"

Bill sighed heavily. He didn't know what to make of it, but he knew it wasn't what he wanted to hear. Down deep, however, if he were being honest with himself, this was the answer he expected. That was part of the reason he had sent Jimmy to go look in the first place.

Immediately, a thought raced through his mind of a rat trap that he had seen once. It consisted of a large mouth jug with a ramp leading to a trapdoor over its opening. As the rats were lured up the ramp with food dangling over the trapdoor, their weight would open it and they would fall through, with the door shutting behind them. They would then drop to the bottom of the jug and were trapped. Bill felt like one of those trapped rats. He'd been focusing too much on money and the show that he hadn't looked the gift horse in the mouth enough to explore what else could be going on. Just what strings were attached to this opportunity? Apparently none, so far...except being stuck in a strange town with no escape.

"Boss?" Jimmy asked, which brought Bill out of deep thought.

"Yeah, Jimmy, I don't know. I don't know what to think of it all. It worries me, though."

"That's not even the strangest thing. I stopped off at that gas station corner store, pulled up, and walked in. If I didn't know better, I would have sworn that it was the same little gas station that was on the corner of Oppenhiemer Avenue and Main Street back in Dovercity, where I grew up. I mean...everything was exactly the same, right down to the magazines. At first I didn't notice it but when I walked in, there was no one behind the counter, then the more I walked around the store, the more the memories clicked in place and I felt like I'd seen it before. Strange, huh?" Jimmy said coolly, but he was watching Bill's face for real answers.

"Jimmy, I don't think we've seen the strangest thing this town has to offer yet, but I'm afraid we're going to," Bill replied, then continued, "We're going to have to weather out tonight and see what tomorrow brings...but in the meantime, we need to make sure our folks are okay. I don't know what's at work here, but I've been holding my cards close because I didn't want whatever it was to have an idea I might know what they're planning. I mean...I don't know exactly what's going on, but I don't want anyone suspicious that I have any kind of inkling that's something's going down. Tomorrow morning, we're all going to meet up and maybe we'll pack up and leave."

"Yeah, but where will we go? Doesn't look like there are any roads out of here."

"I don't care. If we have to plow through cornfields, then that's what we'll do. We'll have to eventually hit something, won't we?" Bill asked.

Jimmy shrugged his shoulders. "I don't know, boss, but yeah, I think being on the move is always better than waiting for whatever's to come."

Another thought came to Bill. "Jimmy, what time do you have?"

Jimmy looked down at his wrist and with his right hand, reached over to press the button to light up the watch face. "I got 11:15. Why?"

Bill looked down at his own watch, which read 10:30. "I don't know. Everyone's watch seems to be off. Radios don't work, time is off, and I'm pretty sure that if we had a compass in front of us, that thing would spin like a top."

"Boss, I don't like this."

"I don't either, Jimmy, but I'm going to go close down the show. It no longer feels safe."

"Do you want me to come help?"

"No, I've already asked you to go out on a limb tonight."

"No, you didn't. You asked me to go for a drive," Jimmy replied.

"I know, but it's been quite the day. Why don't you go to the HQ trailer and wait with Dani and the kids? Have some water or coffee. You look beat. I'd feel better if someone else was with them."

"Okay, boss. If you say so," Jimmy replied, then saw the shiner bruising around his eye. "Are you sure you're okay? Someone sure gave you a good one."

Bill's hand instinctively reached up to his face to feel it. "Yeah, it's okay. A misunderstanding. That's all."

"I'd hate to see the other guy, then," Jimmy said and starting walking toward the HQ trailer. He called back, "But if you aren't back in 30 or so minutes, I'm coming to look for you."

"You do that," Bill said, but had a pretty good idea that any timepiece that Jimmy looked at wouldn't tell when 30 minutes had passed. It was a nice thought, though, but something he hoped he wouldn't have need for.

Bill, along with the staff in his left hand, stumped toward the entrance. The crowd seemed heavier, which didn't seem possible, but it was. They didn't get in his way, but they seemed to slow him down, nonetheless. No one overtly looked at him, but he could feel eyes on him. Bill felt that if he could just turn fast enough, he would see a whole swatch of figures standing there, staring at him blankly. Even if he had caught them, they would only turn around, as if nothing had happened.

In what felt like forever—certainly longer than it would have taken to get to the entrance and ticket booth on a normal night—he finally arrived.

He went to the ticket booth that Rita was usually in. He went through the back door and she was sitting there with her eyes open, but she wasn't moving, nor was she smacking her gum. She looked like a statue in one of those wax museums.

"Rita?" Bill asked.

No answer came. Bill looked closer and saw that Rita was breathing, so that was a good sign, at least he thought so. He moved a couple of steps until he was right beside her. He gently put his hand on her shoulder and said her name again, slightly louder. "Rita?"

She jumped and looked quickly up at him. "Oh! I didn't see you there. I'm sorry! I must have been lost in thought...but I can't remember what I was thinking about."

"Are you okay?"

"Yeah, I'm fine," she said and apparently, she was because her jaw began to work and the telltale sound of gum smacking came back. "What do you need?"

"Shut it down and turn off the lights. No more tickets. We are closing for the night," Bill said.

"Really?!" Rita asked. "We haven't been open that long. Why it's only..." she looked down at her watch and continued, "It's only 7."

Then she looked outside. "Awful dark for 7, though. Guess my watch is broken. People are still coming, though. Look."

Bill looked to where she gestured and sure enough, more people were walking up to be let in. The cars in the parking area hadn't changed, and Bill had no idea where all these new people had come from.

"I don't care. Shut it down," Bill said.

"All right. It's your show," Rita said. She reached for the shutter to close the window.

"After you're done here, tell the other ticket booths."

She nodded and Bill left to confront the new group that had arrived. As they approached, Bill thought he had seen them before—earlier tonight, near the petting zoo. They weren't the same people, were they? Bill couldn't guess. They were all wearing basically the same 1940's and 50s getups, which made them all look very similar.

"I'm sorry, folks, but we are shutting down for the evening."

The group came to a stop and didn't say anything. But then they moved forward again, closing in on Bill. Bill stepped back and said again, more assertively, "I'm sorry folks, but we really must be shutting down for the evening. Having mechanical problems. See..."

But the group still didn't stop. They continued on and walked right past Bill, past the ticket booth, and onto the midway. Technically, you didn't have to buy tickets to enter the show, but it was expected if you wanted to play any of the games or ride any of the rides. These "customers" who had just arrived didn't seem to be fazed in the slightest. It was as if they were on autopilot and on a loop of some kind as they mindlessly strolled past. He supposed that before they closed the ticket booth, the purchasing of tickets had been included in this loop. They walked up, got their ticket, and walked in. Now that the ticket booth was closed, they stopped short, then turned to walk right in, acting as if Bill hadn't said anything at all.

Bill looked over the whole midway and what he saw surprised him. Surely the whole town's population couldn't be here, could it? It sure looked that way. All the lanes were at full capacity, which was saying something since they were outside. Although it had never been a concern before, he also never thought they would ever reach an occupancy limit, however, this concern now bloomed in the back of Bill's mind.

"Rita," he said, looking back in through the window, "Stay here and turn off the lights, or go back to your trailer.

Whatever you do, tell the others here to do the same, and stay out of sight for the rest of the night until morning."

Rita looked like she was going to say something, but didn't. "Do you hear me, Rita? I need you to do what I said."

There only came a slight nod, then Bill turned and hurried along with the rest of the burgeoning crowd. This time, they slowed him from making headway more than they had before, but still maintained a bubble around him. The space around him was now smaller, and every once in a while, he would accidentally touch one of the figures in the jostle of hurrying. Each time, he would get a slight "finger in the light socket" sensation of a fuzzy electrical shock, but it was so small that it didn't cause harm, at least as far as Bill knew. It wasn't painful, but jolted a little bit, and that caused alarm.

Bill hurried as quickly as he could. His next stop would be the generators to turn off the electricity, then close the midway, and call it a night. He hoped by doing so, the town's inhabitants would lose interest and leave. He didn't see anyone else he that he knew along the way, and that worried him. He felt alone in a sea of people, but those people didn't seem real to him. They were like caricatures of the time frame from where they either came or that they represented.

He was getting close to the area where all the rides were. He planned to turn them off one by one, but he had to first instruct the ride jockeys to unload them and get everyone out of the fun houses, which he did. The first one he spoke to was Clay something or other. He knew he hung out with that Louise girl from time to time. Clay didn't understand why Bill wanted him to shut down, as his watch still reflected that it was early in the evening. But Bill was the boss, so what the boss wants, he gets. He told Bill that he would pass the word to the other ride operators. Bill left Clay with the instructions that once the rides were cleared, they were all to go back to the alley and signal him. With that business finished, Bill got off the lane and slipped into the alley behind the fun house. He could hear the whine and whirr of the generator that kept the fun house running. He turned the corner and Mr. Bright was there.

"What are you doing, Mr. Donovan? Shutting down early?"

He almost jumped out of fright due to not expecting anyone to be there, waiting for him, but luckily, his "showman" guise—his alter ego, if you will—took over and he was able to maintain his cool. He wrapped himself deeply into this persona to stay that way.

"Why, yes we are, Mr. Bright. You know safety measures. Honestly, I didn't think we'd have so many people from your town show up, but they have in force and, to be honest, we have an occupancy limit," Bill said, and it was the truth, sort of. He was sure there was some rule on occupancy limits but he had no idea what it was, or if there truly was one that applied to carnivals, but he was banking on the bureaucracy of it all. Surely, there had to be one, somewhere.

"Oh, really?" Mr. Bright said. The smile of his that never went away seemed sinister in the light, bouncing off the fun house on one side and one of the other rides on the other. "I wish you would keep it going. My people haven't experienced visitors like you in a very long time. That's why I wanted you to come...for my people."

"Well, rules are rules, Mr. Bright. As the mayor of this town, I'm sure you understand. I would hate to have my licenses pulled for not following safety regulations," Bill replied, so far into the lie now that he went with it as the God's honest truth. He continued, "And besides, there's always tomorrow night and the night after that."

"If we stay that long," Bill thought to himself.

"Yes...there are other nights. We just enjoy you and hope you enjoy us. There's no other place like this place."

That creeped Bill out even more than the smile that never seemed to falter. "That's a good one, Mr. Bright. I think every mayor says that and you know, it is true—no two towns are the same." Bill smiled his own smile, which, like Mr. Bright's, failed to reach his eyes.

"I see. Well, it's your choice to shut down," Mr. Bright said. "How are the rest of your people doing? Any problems or concerns? Do they like it here?"

And Bill could hear the second part of the question in his mind, though Mr. Bright didn't voice it. "Will they stay here with us?"

Bill stopped and looked at Mr. Bright more closely. The smile remained and Bill couldn't be sure, but his teeth looked like they may have grown larger. He surmised that it could have just been the low light in the alley. Continuing to play it cool, he said, "Everything is fine. Just need to shut down this evening...that's all."

For the briefest of moments, Bill thought this might turn into a standoff, a standoff in which Bill didn't know what he would do as Mr. Bright, the mayor, continued to stand in his way. Then, as if Mr. Bright came to a decision, he stepped to the side and said, "Yes, there are other nights indeed. Still plenty of time."

"Plenty of time for what?" Bill asked.

But Mr. Bright didn't reply. Instead he turned on his heels briskly and walked down the alley, leaving Bill by himself. "Plenty of time for what?" Bill asked, a little louder.

Before Mr. Bright disappeared from view, he turned and looked at Bill. There was no mistaking it this time—those teeth were a little bigger and appeared to be tapered into points. "Don't worry, you will find out."

The confusion from the reply caused Bill to blink and step back. When he looked again. Mr. Bright's teeth were normal, but before Bill could get a better look to confirm, the mayor turned a corner and disappeared. Bill wanted to chase him down and find out what he meant, but he was being very cautious. If this were any other town or, heck, any other situation in his life, he would have been bullheaded and either punched someone or packed up and left. He wanted to leave this town as a speck in the rearview mirror but something down deep kept nagging at him to stay calm, or as calm as anyone could be while facing this situation.

Growing up, Bill watched a show on TV, however, not often because his family was always on the road. Anyway, there was this one show that always had stories about strange, surreal events. Bill began to wonder if it had become reality and he was in one of those shows. He half-expected to see the host of the show standing off to the side in his black suit, talking about traveling through another dimension. But this wasn't some show. This was real, and it unnerved Bill.

He quickly refocused and hurried to the generator, where he waited for Clay or any other ride operator to come signal him. Bill waited a few moments, and no one came. He waited a few more and still nothing. Bill counted to himself. One. Two. Three. Four...When he reached 30, he walked out to see what was going on. He was sure that more than enough time had passed for the ride operators to clear the rides. From where he had been, he couldn't see anything except a long alleyway. He couldn't see the lane on either side, but as he turned the corner, he immediately noticed a difference. He still couldn't see all of the lane yet, but he could tell it wasn't nearly as crowded as it had been. When he emerged completely from the alley and into lane, the remaining people he had literally just seen, were no longer there. It had only been a few seconds, at most. Bill didn't think that it could have changed so quickly and a slight shock overtook him, though he knew he really shouldn't have been surprised, since nothing normal had occurred since they landed in this town. All that remained were the "beeps," "dings," and other sounds of the show, calling out to a crowd that wasn't listening—a crowd that, not more than a few minutes before had completely filled the midway, a crowd that was impossible to have disappeared so quickly.

18

He saw Clay just up ahead at his post, in front of the funhouse. Clay didn't pay him any mind when he walked up. "Clay."

"Yeah?"

"Where were you? You were supposed to come signal me that the ride was empty so I could shut down the generator."

Clay gave him a strange look, which was almost a mirror image of Bill's. "Why would we do that? Besides, it's been empty most of the evening. We had a ton of people one or two hours ago, but now it's pretty empty."

"What?" Bill asked, incredulously. "There was a ton of people here not five minutes ago."

Clay, not seeming to want to contradict the big boss of the midway, replied, "Ah...maybe...I didn't see it, but you know, now that you mention it, I vaguely remember talking to you earlier about...well, I can't remember."

Bill checked his watch and it was 11 PM. Where did the last hour go? The midway was empty and the ugly dragon of fear reared its scaly head and wrapped around Bill's guts, cinching down like a boa constrictor. Bill couldn't get a deep breath and felt like he was going to lose it and drift out of consciousness...and he probably would have had he not thought about his kids and his wife. He clawed at his sanity and held on tight. He breathed deeply. He focused only on that. Breathe deep, breathe long, in, out, slow, smooth. Out of nervous energy, he again thumped the staff against the ground. He thumped so hard he could hear small echoes being amplified as the percussion of the "thud" hit different objects around him. And suddenly, he was okay again. The panic and rust-flavored bile that had risen in the back of his throat was gone. He could think again.

"You, okay?" Clay asked. "That bruise looks pretty nasty."

Bill had completely forgotten about the bruise on his face and nodded quietly as he walked away, but he managed to say one thing before he was too far. "Shut it down. Shut everything down."

Whether Clay did or didn't, Bill didn't stay for confirmation. He needed to see his family. As he headed toward the rear of the midway, he looked down at his feet and at the ground. It was mostly grass, with patches of dirt here and there. He was alarmed, but he couldn't tell why he was alarmed. Just a sense of something unnatural that he couldn't put his finger on. It took a few moments before he realized what it was—it was the smoothness of the dirt. Footprints, or rather, a lack thereof. There were no footprints to be seen. Based on the sheer size of the crowd that came, that wasn't possible. Bill looked closer and saw the faint outlines of his own shoes, along with the circular outline of the staff he had been thumping along with. Those, he could see, but there were no other signs of traffic.

Sheer terror of the unknown cracked through him like the sound of a bat smacking a baseball out of the park. He ran. All pretenses of holding his cards close to his chest were gone. If Mr. Bright showed up again, Bill doubted it would be as peaceful as it had been. He'd be looking for answers—real answers. He was tired of this feeling of encroachment, but before he could do anything, he had to know how his family was doing. He picked up speed, going faster and faster.

He passed George on the way and even though George waved for him to stop, Bill ran past him. "I don't have time. I have to check on Dani and the kids. I'll get up with you," he half-yelled as he passed.

He finally made it to the HQ trailer and bounded up the steps, which caused the entire trailer to joggle slightly. He flung open the door and ran inside to the light. It had been dark out and the feeling of the dark was sickly, but coming into the light gave him more of a sense of wellness. With his family there, along with Jimmy and Kathy, he felt relieved.

When Dani saw the bruise, which, by now was a dark shade of violet, she jumped up and came over to him. "Are you okay?"

"Yes, I'm fine. It doesn't matter. How is everyone doing here?"

"We're okay, but what happened to your face? Did someone hit you?" Dani persisted.

"Yes...well, no...I mean yes and no. Yes, I was hit in the face, but no, I honestly don't think he meant to."

"Who?" she asked.

"Doesn't matter. We have bigger issues. What time does everyone have on their watches?" Bill said in a rush, as if he had a lot on his mind and, though he was patiently dealing with Dani's questions, he had another, more pertinent concern. The question went out into the room and five different answers came back. The only difference, though, was that with those who had been in the room together the longest, the time discrepancy was only a minute or two, whereas Jimmy's was off by 30 minutes and Bill's was off by 45 minutes.

"Well, that's weird," little Laura said.

The kids didn't seem bothered by the fact that time was off, but the adults in the room showed otherwise in their expressions. Of concern, of fear, of "what in the world is going on in this town," or a mixture of them all.

"Kathy, have you found out anything else in that book of yours?" Bill asked.

"I'm still going through it, but nothing new yet, except that...well, you know...bad things seem to happen here."

Bill looked at Laura and Jason, but they were busy reading a book and, in Jason's case, he looked like he was about to fall asleep.

Bill looked back at the adults and lowered his voice. "I think we need to think about leaving here."

"Pack up everything and go?" Jimmy asked.

"Yes, I think it's time to go."

Jimmy's face had a questioning look. Bill could tell that he was on the fence, even though he hadn't been able to find a way out. He wasn't totally on board that this town gave off creepy vibes and he wasn't 100 percent convinced whether the town was really dangerous or not.

"And if we can't pack up everything, we will leave and pick it up later," Bill replied.

"If you say so, though I'm not sure the rest of the carnies will be all that ready to move. We just got here," Jimmy replied.

Bill felt a pang of concern. He wasn't planning on leaving anyone behind, but what if they had to? What if there was no other choice? Bill would try his best and his best would just have to do, but if no one else left, Bill would make sure that Dani and the kids made it out. That was non-negotiable to whatever gods of chance that Bill made the plea to.

He wanted to tell them all about the lack of footprints and how it nearly instantaneously went from being busy to nothing at all, but he wasn't sure how to explain it. He wanted Jimmy on his side, of course, and he knew that Kathy and Dani were. He still didn't want to push them and cause them to panic or be close to the edge like he was; he was barely keeping it in. Only his years as the practiced showman helped him keep his cool. "Stay cool, Daddy O. I'm flying high all night and cool as a cucumber," he thought to himself.

"When do you want to go, boss?" Jimmy asked.

The word "immediately!" appeared in Bill's mind, but the words that left his lips were tempered down. "I think we should probably leave as soon as we can."

"Maybe we should at least wait until the morning so we can see better. You know as well as I do that it's not safe to dismantle in the dark. Even though it's doable with flashlights, it's not really a good idea," Jimmy continued.

And he was right, of course. It was only in extremes that they would do such a thing and Bill felt the situation was pretty close to being extreme, but that fine line between panic and calm swayed in the balance on a knife's edge, so erring on the side of caution, Bill said, "Yeah, that's fine. We will wait 'til the first light of the sun. Spread the word."

"You got it, boss," Jimmy said and left the light of the trailer and went into the darkness of the world outside.

"What are we going to do for the rest of the evening?" Dani asked.

"Just wait here," Bill responded.

"I better go to my tent," Kathy said.

A low warning bell rang in the back of Bill's mind. Suddenly, the thought of people being by themselves left such a bad feeling that Bill immediately regretted sending Jimmy out.

"I don't think that's such a good idea. Stay here this evening or come with us over to our RV. We have a couch," Bill said. "In fact, I'm going to go grab Jimmy. None of us should be alone. Whatever happens, I think the more we stick together, the better we'll be."

There was nothing specific telling him that, but it was a counter-feeling in his gut that balanced the warning bell he had experienced a moment before. He didn't know, but it felt right. Just like he didn't know why he suddenly felt bad about sending Jimmy out—it just felt wrong, much like how he was certain that the town was dangerous.

"Are you sure?" Dani asked. "I'm sure Jimmy will be all right."

"Yeah, I'm sure he will, but I still need to go. The quicker we can spread the word, the quicker we can all be ready to move in the morning. I'll be right back."

"Would you like to take some ice with you for that bruise?" she asked.

"Nah, it's okay. It barely hurts," he lied. It was hurting, but he had bigger things to think about. "I'm sure it looks worse than it really is, but I will let you kiss it and make it better when I get back," he finished as he winked.

She shook her head with a look of light consternation as if she was thinking, "I can't believe you could joke at a time like this...and if you were joking, I can't believe it's such a bad joke."

"Yeah, I know." Bill smiled back and kissed her quickly. He didn't want Jimmy to get too far ahead of him. He quickly went through the door and out into the night.

A fog had rolled in during the short time that Bill had been inside. He could see the lights still on from the carnival midway, but they were muted, like viewing something through frosted glass. The fog also muffled the sounds of the rides and games to a fraction of what they should have been. On any other occasion, Bill would have welcomed it. He kind of liked the fog. It had always reminded him of a sort of magic that obfuscated the world around him and left him with a small sense of manageable eeriness, the kind you get from reading horror stories. It provided enough intrigue but down deep, you knew there was a boundary of safety. Tonight, however, was completely different. The fog only added to the eeriness of recent events, and Bill could only assume that there was no boundary of safety tonight in this town.

He didn't see Jimmy, but he couldn't have been more than a few seconds ahead, so Bill quickened his pace to catch up. The fog cooled the area down considerably, almost to the point of it causing chills, but Bill couldn't chalk it up to the actual temperature or whether he was chilled out of fright. He continued forward. He looked at his watch. The dim green light told him it was 11:45 now, or rather it notified him of numbers on his watch. If it was really 11:45, Bill didn't know. He hurried forward and continued into the midway but immediately stopped, thrown off from what he saw. There was no one to be seen...anywhere. All the normal lights and sounds were there and some of the rides were going at full speed, but there was no one present. It was as if everyone had stepped away for a break, but they never took them at the same time.

Bill could feel his knees shake. He took hold of the staff he had with him because it gave him comfort. It was real and hitting it on the ground gave his nervous energy some place to go until his knees stopped shaking. He steeled himself because he knew in his heart that he had to continue, although he wanted to turn around and go back to the safety of the others. He was the leader of this troupe, so he had to be strong and carry on. He had to hold himself to a higher standard, so pushed himself forward, all the while cursing himself for this whole situation that he had gotten everyone into.

The fog grew heavier, making it harder to clearly see the end of the lane. It stunned him. Even as Bill watched, it closed in to the point that it became hard to see the next booth, making him feel isolated. It was a weird feeling of being closed in, yet having total freedom to move. It had not yet reached the level of claustrophobia, but it was getting there. The fog appeared to have tendrils that moved within it, making it dense in some areas and lighter in others, like strands of smoke within the fog. As the dense fog enveloped him, the tendrils moved over and around him, touching him, then backing away. Then he heard it again—the voices that almost pushed his mind to the 9th level of insanity. "Join us, Bill. You can be forever young."

Bill's chest heaved as if he had been running a sprint. He took the staff and pounded the ground in front of him. With each strike, it created a vacuum that grew, first around the end of the staff where Bill struck, then with each succession, the area grew as if it was a balloon with a slow leak being inflated. Strike...a little bigger...condense...strike...a little bigger...condense. It reminded Bill of his emergency radio with a hand crank. With each crank, the light on the radio would illuminate brightly, but then go immediately dim. Then you cranked it again, and the light would be slightly brighter and stay on a bit longer. It was the same type of effect with the vacuum that the staff created. With each hit, it would grow a little stronger and larger.

"Jimmy!" Bill yelled.

His voice went out, but into nothingness, it seemed. There were no replies and though Bill could still see the lights of the rides and booths, they were quickly diminishing and on the verge of snuffing out altogether, to disappear into the dark greyness that the mist created.

"Anyone!?" Bill yelled again and again. No reply came.

"What do you desire? You can have it if you decide to stay here, with us," a voice loudly whispered. It was the distant voice of Mr. Bright, and it was the only sound that had any sort of clarity. It surprised Bill because it was audible, even above the sound of the thumping staff, which had seemed to keep the other, softer voices that were pleading for him to stay, at bay.

"I will not!" Bill yelled into the fog, the tendrils of denser fog dancing in reply. "Whatever you have to offer, we want none of it. You will let us go!" But to whom or what, beyond a voice that sounded like it could be Mr. Bright, Bill didn't know. In some ways, he felt that even Mr. Bright wasn't who he said he was. And along that line of thinking, he wasn't really sure what Mr. Bright was, either.

"Bill?" a voice came from darkness. "Where are you? I hear you talking."

"I'm over here," Bill called out and eventually, the image of George materialized out of the fog, his stark white hair standing out, and his protruding gut preceding him as he arrived.

"I don't know what you were saying. To be honest, I could barely hear anything. This is crazy. I've never seen fog quite like this," George said when he arrived.

Bill was relieved to see someone he knew...and who was real. "I haven't either, George. Have you seen anyone else?"

"No, not since this fog rolled in, I haven't. I was on my way to the HQ trailer, but after this came in, I couldn't see a thing."

With the excitement of finding each other dwindling, George noticed the staff in Bill's hand and its constant motion of hitting the ground. George looked up and saw the small, clear space it created.

"And I've never seen anything like that, either," George whispered. "What are you doing?"

"I don't know," Bill replied. "I just know it helps."

"Helps what?"

Bill looked at George incredulously. "Helps all this?" he said, indicating the fog and everything that was obscured by its veil.

"Ah...okay. Well, I think I'm gonna keep going. I'm heading in the right direction, I think. You coming?"

"I gotta find Jimmy. I also gotta shut the midway down," Bill replied.

"All right, just let me know if you need any help. I would have shut things down myself, but my watch has been busted. It's scrolling through numbers like it has a second job."

Bill immediately looked at his own watch, and it was doing the same thing. The numbers were moving much too fast, sometimes moving forward, sometimes back. They sped up and slowed down, but never stopping for more than half a second. Bill had a feeling that they were somehow outside of time, in a pocket of uncertainty where time could go forward or back or...somewhere. Bill was ready to leave.

He looked back at George, but George had already shuffled forward into the fog, heading toward the HQ trailer. A moment later, Bill was alone again with his thoughts and he wondered if he should have gone back with George, for both of their sakes. He almost followed George back to the land of known safety, the HQ trailer. Almost. But Bill turned and walked deeper into the midway. It was dark, but Bill could see diffused cotton balls of light bleed through the misty veil.

"Jimmy!" Bill continued from time to time and at different intervals. As time passed (not that he could tell exactly how much, as his watch was still flipping through hours in short order), it seemed to him that the watch slowed down, then stopped altogether on what Bill could only assume was the correct time. It read one minute past midnight. The fog faded as well, but not in a normal way of rolling out and away—it just dissipated in place. It wasn't a quick process, but it was steady. And it wasn't the kind of environment where it would happen naturally, as if the sun burned it off. It was too cool for that. At first, Bill thought it was his mind playing tricks on him, but the cotton balls of diffused light became less and less fuzzy, with more light and clarity breaking through the confines of the mist.

Bill didn't feel so claustrophobic anymore, as if the door to the small room had opened and relief poured in. Although Bill could see better now, he still didn't see anyone around him in the midway. Shortly after he was better able to see, he turned off the generators one by one, just like he would have had it been a normal carnival night. "Good," he thought to himself, "a little normalcy in a day of utter strangeness.

He walked forward, and the lights, rides and sounds from different points along the lane winked out until all that was left was the night sky on a moonless evening. The fog was gone altogether now and in some ways, it was darker than it had been with the fog.

He saw a shadow appear, and realized it was Jimmy walking up to him. "Hey boss, time to call it a night. Everyone is shutting down."

"That's because I shut everything down. I couldn't find anyone, other than George. Everyone else appeared to be MIA. Did you see anyone?" asked Bill.

"Yeah, I saw some of the workers, but the fog was crazy. Made it harder to find people."

"Were they okay?"

"Yeah. Why wouldn't they be?" Jimmy replied.

Bill felt like he had to brain Jimmy over the head to make him understand anything. Why didn't he feel the same weirdness that Bill felt about the town? He wanted to confront him about the difference of opinion, or at least get him to admit that he felt something out of the ordinary was going on, but Bill held back. He was scared what Jimmy might say if he disagreed and felt something else about the town. When Jimmy came back that evening, he didn't seem to mind so much that there appeared to be no exit out of town. Was he surprised? Sure, but alarmed? Nope. Not even close. This kept nagging at Bill. And what if it wasn't just Jimmy who was oblivious to all the weird things going on? What if it was also everyone beyond the group that sheltered in the HQ trailer?

"Still carrying that staff, huh?"

"Yeah, it makes me feel safe," Bill said. "And it keeps the voices and the boogieman away," he thought to himself.

"So, boss...Tomorrow, we starting back up at normal time?"

This time, Bill stopped and looked at Jimmy. "Don't you remember we discussed packing everyone up and leaving?"

Jimmy stopped and looked back at Bill with a confused expression, then he reached up and scratched his head. "I didn't but now that you mention it, I do vaguely remember something about that. That's not usually like me. Strange. Well, I guess we'll see how that goes come morning."

The whole exchange bothered Bill. This town seemed to be a place not only beyond time, but also beyond rational thought, and the only way to stay safe was not yet known. In some ways, on this very question, Bill felt he was still stumbling in the fog, not knowing the answer.

Bill didn't reply. He kept pace with Jimmy, and they both returned to the HQ trailer. Dani, the kids, and Kathy were all waiting for him.

"Where's George?" Bill asked.

"He stopped by for a second, but then called it a night and went on," Dani replied.

"Boss, I think I'm going to do the same. A good ol' cold one is waiting for me in the frig."

"Okay, but don't get too sauced tonight. Let's meet up first thing in the morning and see where we stand as far as our people and the midway."

"You got it. I'll only drink half a six-pack, then," Jimmy replied as he left the trailer.

Bill turned back to the rest of the group. "I think we should stick here tonight. There's a couple of couches in the other room that we can all crash on."

The group had been cooped up in the room all night, and while Dani and Kathy were tired, the kids were wide awake and protested this proposal. They wanted to go back to their RV. At least there, they had items like books or games that would keep them occupied, but something about leaving the trailer to head that way felt wrong, like they just shouldn't do it. He could almost sense a voice over his left shoulder, telling him to stay, except he couldn't actually hear the voice. He half-expected its evil counterpart to hover above his right shoulder to nudge him to go, but thankfully, that never happened.

The excitement of the unusual events of the evening had waned. At least for the kids, it had. Something about being inside and out of sight from the midway and the town beyond seemed to help ease Bill's mind to some extent, but there was no real peace. It was similar, in a way, to what happens when a line of thunderstorms comes through. The water on a lake is all churned up and rolling around, then, in the aftermath, the waves are still choppy. That's how Bill felt—like he had been tossed back and forth and had survived the worst of the evening, as well as maintained his sanity. But it was still there—the concern, the worry, the uncertainty. Sure, it was a shadow of its former self, but it was there and it wasn't going away. Just like those who live on the coast, waiting for a hurricane to hit, Bill waited for this personal Hell of a hurricane to come at him full force. Except he didn't have a clue when it would come—only that it was on its way.

Things eventually quieted down enough for everyone to get to sleep or at least feign sleeping. Bill lay there in the dark, watching the ceiling. They kept the generator running, and he could hear the faint whine come through the wall, complete with a sputter here and there. Every once in a while, a strong wind would blow and rock the trailer. Bill waited and tried to go to sleep. He waited, then waited some more...

19

Bill woke with a start. He had been in a deep sleep—one where you wake up and don't know where you were, what time it is and, in the most extreme cases, who you are. This was, by far, one of the most extreme cases he had ever experienced. He looked around and everything looked unfamiliar to him, but then it slowly came back to him. He wasn't in the family RV; he was still in the HQ trailer. The sun was streaming through the blinds on the window. It took Bill a moment, but he realized that he had slept long past first light, judging by the sun's angle and brightness streaming through the window.

He looked quickly around the room and it was empty; he was alone. He had remembered falling asleep with Dani on the couch. The kids were curled up on the other couch, and Kathy slept under the table using a blanket that had been in one of the cupboards. The whole situation wasn't ideal, but they made it work. As surprised as Bill was at waking up so late, now that he had full working faculties again, he was more surprised that he had even fallen asleep. He stood up and walked around the trailer to find it was indeed empty. He looked at his watch and it was 11 AM. The watch wasn't scrolling through numbers as it had the night before, but the time worried him. He had wanted to wake up at the crack of dawn, take stock of everyone and everything, then pack up and leave this place, but that didn't happen. As it was, almost half the day was over.

Bill grabbed the staff and walked to the door, then stepped outside. The day looked normal. The sun blazed brightly, high overhead, and there were blue skies as far as Bill could see. It almost had a serene feel to it and at any other time and place, Bill would have taken the scene in fully, but considering where he was, the feeling of serenity slid off him like a rain drop slides off a windshield at 70 miles an hour. He had to find his family.

30 seconds later, he was at the family RV and went inside. At first, it seemed empty, since he heard nothing, but then his wife came out of the bathroom, with a towel on.

"Oh, hey you," she said cheerfully.

"Why didn't you wake me up before you left? And where are the kids?"

Dani's confused face said it all. She had no idea know what he was talking about. "The kids? They got ready earlier and went to help out on the midway. I think Laura went to go help Brenda at the funnel cake booth and Jason went to go help Tom Starling check on some rides. I felt disgusting, so took a minute to take a shower."

It took Bill a moment to process his thoughts as she whisked past him and into the bedroom area to get dressed. When Bill didn't reply, Dani asked, "is everything all right?"

"What do you remember from last night?"

"Nothing out of the ordinary. The townspeople were a little strange, but everyone seemed nice," she replied.

Bill's mind felt like it was being sucked through a straw. It was like last night hadn't even happened, or if it had, it happened differently for her than it did for him.

"Where did you go to sleep?"

"Here, of course."

"Where was I?"

"You were here, too, and you were still up when I went to sleep. You were gone by the time I woke up...which I don't appreciate you not waking me up, by the way," she said with a mischievous smile, then continued. "I guess you wanted to get a super early start. You may want to take a shower, though. Looks like you're wearing the same clothes you wore yesterday." She was fully dressed now and pushed him into the bathroom with a towel in hand. "You kind of stink."

Bill was dumbfounded—not by her comment about his smell, but the absurdity of the whole situation from last night to this morning. His brain felt like it was developing fuzz at the very end of his consciousness, and he was tired by it all. His energy sapped and now, just the mere act of thinking clearly seemed a bridge too far.

He numbly went through the motions of turning on the water. He caught a whiff of himself and she was right. He did stink, though he had been so focused and concerned, he hadn't been aware of it. He stood in the shower and let the warmth of the water cascade over his head and down his back. He was so confused. What was real anymore? Was he the only one that had any sense or memory of what really happened last night? They needed to get out of this town, and Bill knew it would only get worse if they didn't.

He finished the shower and when he opened the door, Dani was gone, and he was alone in the trailer. She had probably gone to the HQ trailer like she usually did. He stood briefly in the towel, still deep in thought about everything, then wiped off the remaining water and dressed in jeans and a T-shirt. Normally, he wore sneakers, but he went with a heavy pair of work boots that he usually reserved for the hard days of setup and breakdown. The steel toe came in handy and was important to have if something fell on his feet. When he finished dressing, he left the RV, but not before grabbing the staff again. For whatever reason, it had become a security blanket for him, or a night light that kept the darkness at bay. Although today was bright and sunny, there was darkness here.

He walked out and saw George, only he was different. His stark white hair wasn't as brilliant; it showed signs of dark color returning. He didn't look as old and something else surprised Bill—his signature paunch was nowhere near the size it had been the night before. He looked a good 10 years younger.

"Hey Bill! Isn't this town great? We made a ton of money yesterday and I don't know, I really like it here," George said.

Bill looked at him like he would have looked at a viper. It was a mixture of concern, curiosity, and fear, all rolled up into one.

"What's wrong, Bill?" George asked.

"Uh...you look different. Younger," Bill said.

"Oh yeah? I hadn't noticed. I feel great, though."

Bill didn't know how to respond. The shock of it all left him speechless. Even his perfectly honed persona of the showman wasn't there to help.

"I...uh...have you seen my kids?" Bill asked, changing the subject, because he couldn't think of anything to say and of course, was concerned about Jason and Laura. Like a tongue that kept exploring a newly broken tooth, his mind kept coming back to how differently George looked and the fact that he had to find out how his kids were.

"Yeah, Laura was with Brenda, but she's on break, and I saw Jason earlier."

"Okay, thanks," Bill said and didn't wait for a reply. He didn't know what George had done, but Bill's fear flickered into a flame down to his core. When Bill came into the midway, he could see the town inhabitants were back. Except this time, they didn't look like they were from the 40s and 50s. They were wearing bell-bottoms and most had long hair. The kind of style that Bill remembered from the time he was a kid. It was such a different look from what he saw yesterday that he couldn't help but stand there for a moment to take it all in. Most looked like they were straight out of a hippie commune, but not all of them. Some still looked like 1950s hold-overs with buzz cuts, beehives and horn-rimmed glasses.

He finally regained control of himself from the surprise and hurried forward. "Join us," he heard a voice say, and he got that weird feeling of being watched again. He thumped the staff again and again, just like he did the night before, and it seemed to ward off the voices. He made a beeline to the funnel cake booth and looked for his daughter. Brenda was there, but she too looked 10 years younger. The weight that she had previously carried was gone, and she looked much younger than Bill was now, but she was older than Bill by a few years. He almost didn't recognize her, but seeing George earlier had prepared him.

"Hey Bill. How are you doing?" she said.

"I'm okay, Brenda. How about yourself?" Bill asked curiously.

"I'm doing great. Feel wonderful. Haven't felt this good in years. I really like this town. It has done wonders for me."

Bill ignored the response and asked, "Where's Laura?"

"Oh, she's right over there," she replied, pointing across the lane at a young lady, perhaps 16 or 17, talking to some of the town's young men.

"Where? I don't see..." Bill began, but then stopped, stone-cold to the realization that the young lady was Laura, except she wasn't the 12-year-old anymore. She was on the cusp of young womanhood and looked almost completely different.

Laura saw him and broke away from the group.

"Hey, Daddy!" she said.

Her voice had matured, and it was beautiful, though it wasn't the same as it had been not more than eight hours ago. Bill had tears well up in his eyes. He couldn't think clearly.

"What's wrong, Daddy?" Laura asked. "I hope you aren't mad. I was just talking to those boys. Nothing else. Honest."

"No, I'm okay," Bill choked.

"Are you sure? You don't look it," she replied.

"You were just my little girl last night," Bill replied, almost whispering as he regained his composure.

"I'll always be your little girl, silly."

Bill had so many questions and didn't know how to bring anything up. She was a tween last night and this morning, she was anything but.

"What do you remember from last night?" Bill asked.

"It was the same as every other night. We all went to bed late after the close of the midway, but you weren't there last night when we all said 'goodnight.' Now that I think about it, where were you?"

"I was playing a game with the Devil," he thought to himself. Maybe not "the" Devil, but it was a devil, just the same. But he wasn't sure if it was the whole town or just Mr. Bright.

Laura continued to stare until Bill spoke. "I was at the HQ trailer."

"Oh, okay. Well, my break is about up, and I need to get back in the booth to help Brenda out. Love you, Dad. See you later."

Without waiting for an answer, she bounced across the lane and got back to work. Bill watched her go and with so many questions running through his brain about how all this was possible, he was left him motionless for several moments. How could she be older? Did she have new memories? Memories of things that never actually happened during the past few years? What year was she living in? In her mind, was it not 1995 but 2000 or something? But George and Brenda looked younger. No, they didn't just look younger—they were younger. Would they even realize it if they were questioned? Bill had a hunch that whatever was said, their minds wouldn't grasp, or rather, they would gloss over everything like it was normal. Whatever magic or evil could make some people older and some younger, surely the mind would easily be able to overlook it.

Bill staggered away, overwhelmed by it all. He didn't know where Jason was, but he wanted to see him next, so he went searching for him. He hurried, thumping his staff as he went. Bill didn't find his son in any of his usual places, so he headed to the gaming area. He heard the "ping" of BB guns hitting the tin targets. He looked over to see Stan and Louise, but they weren't the version of Stan and Louise that he knew. Stan was 50 pounds lighter and had a look about him that said he wasn't a pushover. And Louise looked...beautiful. Her pimply face was gone and in its place was skin that was smooth. Her eyes were bright and not as worn-looking. There wasn't a hint of stringy, greasy hair on either of them. They kind of looked like the townsfolk that were there yesterday, complete with slacks and a short-sleeved button up for Stan, and Louise was wearing a polka-dotted, navy blue dress with white shoes. Bill must have been staring hard because Louise noticed and waved with a beautiful, healthy smile that had no ulterior motives. It was open and fresh.

"Hey, Mr. Donovan. Come on over," Stan called out, motioning to him after he had seen Louise wave.

He made his way through the crowded lane and when he arrived, Stan said, "Hey, sir. I just wanted to say thank you for keeping us and everyone else around."

Bill had never heard Stan call anyone "sir" before, but this version? It seemed to fit. Louise came over and, in a bubbly, almost innocent, girlish way, "Yes, Mr. Donovan, we really enjoy working the carnival but Stan and I, we are really coming to fall in love with this town."

They looked at each other and there would be no confusion for anyone watching to take a guess that these two were an item.

Stan looked at her, down at her...he was taller, too! Bill hadn't noticed until he came over. "Yes, Darling," he said, "This town is swell. A place where dreams come true."

"Don't you agree, Mr. Donovan?" Stan said, looking back at him.

Bill wasn't sure if it was nerves or something else entirely, but the surprise of this impromptu meeting unnerved him and he stood there, staring blankly at Stan. It was almost as much shock he had experienced when he saw his daughter in the new world of today. The nervous energy traveled down his arm, into his fist around the staff and without thinking, he tapped the staff into the ground with more deliberate force. With each strike, he felt like he was grinding something forward. He did not know why he began, but immediately was met with some sort of peace that said yes, this was the correct thing to do. He then saw the reaction on the couple's faces. It hurt their ears as the sound waves, emanating from staff, moved with every strike and intermingled with the illusion of what was before him. Like a strong sound wave that rolled over the surface of water that caused it to ripple. Beyond each ripple, he could see Stan and Louise as they always had been. This picture-perfect couple in front of him was a façade, like one of those fake western towns that from the front, looked like real buildings but were only painted sheets of plywood. This couple was Stan and Louise's perfection, or rather, the perfection they yearned for in their lives, but the real Stan and Louise were still there, behind it.

They backed away from Bill and as they did, the waves stopped and their perfect versions were back. He caught a glimpse of them looking warily at him and sneering before they walked away. They had a taste of what they wanted from a life they could only imagine, and they were not going to let it go for anyone. Bill watched them walk away as he would have watched a bear or mountain lion walk away, coiled to spring into action should they turn on him.

Bill backed away, too, and the surrounding crowd parted around the bubble of safety that the staff created. He was on guard now, his wits about him again. Seeing his daughter years older than she was last night threw him off his game, but seeing Stan and Louise behind the guise brought him back. Sure, he might be losing his mind, but he was grateful for whatever powers that be that were guiding him and enabling him to see things for what they actually were. In a weird way, it gave him an edge. He realized that yes, there is definitely still a problem, but not to the point of being hopelessly lost in it.

He walked to the front of the midway and across the street, into the parking area, where there had been vintage cars from the 40s and 50s yesterday. The cars he saw today were vintage cars from the 60s and 70s, some of which Bill had wanted so badly when he was a kid. He also saw Rita through the ticket booth window, and she, too, looked different. She appeared 20 to 30 years younger, with a face that had a striking, unique beauty of its own. She waved at him through the window of the ticket booth and, surprisingly, she wasn't smacking on gum, nor was her hair dyed red. It was natural and healthy.

Bill turned quickly. He didn't want to deal with it. He knew it was fake, and it brought a sadness to him, though he couldn't put a finger on just why he felt that way. He then realized that some of these carnies weren't going to return with him. Whatever this town was, he knew they weren't leaving, but he was, and so was his family. By hook or crook, he would do whatever it took.

He then remembered that he needed to go check on Kathy. He hoped he would see Jason on the way. He trudged along. The crowds were just as bad as they were the night before, but they continued to part around him. The feeling of the crowd watching him couldn't be ignored. It was stronger now than it ever had been. He wondered if they were even real, and then he questioned everything he had ever known...or thought he had known. What was real? His fear was certainly real. So was his love for his family. And he would do anything for the latter.

He turned onto the lane that housed the petting zoo, so Kathy's tent wasn't far now. He looked over at the zoo and the Thompsons were there, but they had undergone a complete makeover, as well. Gone were the scraggly beard and twisted teeth he had always noticed on Mike. In their place was a gleaming smile that looked on par with a soap opera star. He was clean shaven, tanned, and by all accounts, quite good-looking. His wife, Sara, didn't look anything like her former self. Her hair was pulled into a tight ponytail and she wore makeup and stylish clothes. She was standing in a yard full of goats, so she looked a little out of place—almost as if she could have been a model in a photo shoot.

The goats were acting strange, though, especially Gertrude. They weren't allowing any of the townspeople near them. They ran and bleated in alarm and the strangest thing of all was how the Thompsons didn't even acknowledge this. They were busy mingling with the townspeople, who also didn't seem interested in the animals. Bill thought about interrupting, but something about the whole thing unnerved him. It told him they were gone and besides, if he approached them, he would only replicate what had happened when he saw Stan and Louise, with the ripple of illusion over reality.

He walked past them, and on to "Madame Zara's Fortune Telling." The tent was locked, just like he remembered it, but it was locked from the inside now. He knocked on the tent pole and had a moment of déjà vu from when he had done the same thing yesterday. He wished he could have gone back to that exact time. They would have left immediately.

He didn't wait long before he heard movement on the other side. The cable that wrapped through the eyelets slipped through and a slit opened in the dark fabric.

"Get in," Kathy's voice said, hurriedly and low.

He walked in and it took a moment for his eyes to adjust from the brightness outside. Again, it was surreal in how similar it was to what had happened the day before.

After a moment, his eyes adjusted and he noticed Kathy staring at him, but her face was blank.

"What brings you here, Bill?" she asked, her voice betraying nothing, but at least she looked the same. He wanted to respond, but he didn't know if she was the same person who he had spoken to the night before. She may be the same, but in this town, he couldn't be certain. Maybe she had some other desire that had nothing to do with outward appearances. He wasn't sure. He thumped the staff slowly, but nothing changed with Kathy. She didn't back away, and she didn't seem alarmed. She only continued to stare.

"I...I just wanted to see how you were, Kathy. Things aren't what they seem," he said. "Do you remember last night?"

She continued to stare. "I do, but you tell me—what do you remember about last night?"

"I remember we didn't end the night with you here in your tent," Bill said.

A wave of relief washed over Kathy's face. It was the first sign of any emotion she had exhibited. It was like a walled city that suddenly caved in so that an outside observer could get a glimpse of what the wall hid.

Not only did she look relieved, but her voice spoke in a tone that was more than relieved. It wasn't as on edge as it had been just a moment ago.

"I'm so glad you came, Bill. I'm not sure what's going on, but I know we're in trouble now," she said.

"What did happen last night?" Bill asked.

"I was about to ask you the same thing," she replied. "But we all ended up at the HQ trailer. You were there and so were your family. We went to sleep and the next thing I knew, I woke up here in my tent. I don't know how I got here. I peeked outside and noticed the crowd and that the Thompsons don't look themselves, so I locked the flap door and stayed here. I haven't moved since this morning, and it's been...very stressful."

Bill felt the same pressure valve type of release. Finally, something made sense that wasn't whispers in his own mind. Kathy was here, confirming that what he remembered was true and that he wasn't crazy or living in an altered state. Perhaps that last bit was true, and they were in an altered state, but there was someone else that could attest to what was reality. Bill quickly told her the experiences of his morning, to include meeting his daughter and how the others seemed to have changed, as well.

"Really? She 'grew up?'" Kathy asked, dismayed.

"Yeah, but I don't think she really has, just like I don't think the others are really any different. I don't know how to explain it, but when I strike the staff against the ground, the sound waves cause their images to kind of blink, and I get glimpses of what they used to look like."

Kathy looked at the staff in his hands but didn't say anything. She just had a look of mild surprise. "Did you find your son yet?"

"No, I haven't but we need to gather everyone so we can leave. I don't know how, but we need to go."

"I agree, Bill. I don't know what we're dealing with here, but I read more in that book that I picked up from the library. I don't have hard proof of anything, just what I told you before about this area of Illinois being an offshoot or maybe being truly connected to Egypt in some way. I can't believe I'm even saying it out loud, but maybe we're dealing with something from Egyptian mythology...or maybe we're dealing with something else entirely. Since the book also alluded to a people before the native Americans of the area, perhaps it's some curse they left behind. I just don't know. I've been racking my brain since all this craziness started, but one thing is for sure—this place isn't in reality. We could even be in a place that sits outside of time."

Bill took a moment to take it all in. It came out of her like a pot that suddenly boiled over, like it had been waiting inside of her all this time and now she was spilling out all her thoughts at once.

"I know it sounds crazy," she concluded.

"Did that book mention anything else? Anything at this point may help."

"No, not in that book. I couldn't glean anything else...but..." she replied, deep in thought.

"But what?" Bill asked.

"I remember something my grandma told me once when I was a little girl. She was a seer, and that's where I picked up my gift. She told me once that if I was ever in trouble, my faith would see me through. I didn't really understand what that meant, but it always stuck with me. It's something burned into my memory and I can remember it, clear as day."

"What do you think it means?" Bill said.

"I think it means that no matter what we face, our faith or what we believe to be true is what will see us through. I could be wrong, but why would that memory, of all memories, stay when others have faded into nothing? And it fits—just like your faith in that staff."

Bill didn't know what to say. At this point, anything sounded plausible, though less than a week ago, he would have looked at Kathy like she was nuts. Of course, a week ago, he would have also believed he was nuts.

"I need you to get Laura, then take her to the HQ trailer. I will continue to search for Jason. If you see Dani, get her to go with you. She's probably already there, but who knows? I think the town knows we know and will work against us."

"What will we do when we get there?" she asked.

"I don't know. We're making this up as we go, but I can't just sit back and let this happen. Be careful, though.

The crowd is strong and if you start to hear voices..." He looked down at the staff in his hands. "Here, maybe you should take this. If you hear voices, start striking it against the ground. It will help."

Kathy looked at the staff and then shook her head. "That won't work for me like it has for you."

20

Kathy could plainly see that Bill didn't understand, since it worked so well for him. But she knew the staff wouldn't work for her because when she handed it off to him, she fed him a lie that ended up being a bastion of belief for him. Unless, of course, there was something about that particular moment when she had picked up the staff in that secondhand store. Sometimes, coincidences are strange things that happen that, on the surface, seem for no reason at all. Maybe there was really was something about the staff. She picked it up for a reason, but she couldn't remember that reason now.

"Well, okay," Bill said. "But you might need something."

"I think I have just what I need," Kathy replied as she went over to grab her backpack, then went over to the bookshelf and picked up a deck of cards and a crystal ball.

"I have this," she said, showing the globe in her hands.

"You going to tell someone's future?" Bill asked. He meant it to be funny, but it fell flat since the circumstances were so dire. He felt dumb immediately as the words left his lips.

Thankfully, Kathy didn't seem to have heard what he said.

"My grandmother gave this one to me, and I've never used it. I use a prop when I'm with customers, because I can't bear to think of something happening to this one. My grandmother said that it will help guide my way someday. Perhaps that day is today."

"Let's hope so," Bill replied.

They both left the tent and out front, the lane seethed with people. Bill looked over at Kathy and down at the gleaming ball in her hand. The way the sun hit it caused a prism to strike the ground in front of Kathy. But that wasn't what surprised him. That was normal. What wasn't normal was what he could see in the ball. It displayed only their reflections in the refracted image, standing in an empty lane. No one else could be seen in the reflection, yet when he looked up, hundreds of townspeople were still there. Bill felt an icy finger of fear and adrenaline move up his spine, which caused his skin to break out into goose flesh, followed by hot flashes.

Kathy may have noticed it too, but it didn't seem to affect her. She closed her eyes to concentrate on the ball in her hands. To Bill, it looked like a bubble formed around her, similar to the sound waves from the staff that had surrounded him when he struck it. However, unlike his, which had flickered like the flame of a disposable lighter, only slightly illuminating the area around him momentarily before winking out, hers maintained. It was a steady, almost translucent glow of light blue.

Bill could see the crowd immediately move away from her. By this time, she had also noticed the crowd didn't appear in the crystal ball. She looked at Bill, her eyes wide. Bill shrugged his shoulders in return.

"All right, I will see you back at the HQ trailer. Be careful."

"You do the same," she responded before stepping off toward concession row to hopefully collect Laura on the way to the HQ trailer.

Bill turned and headed toward the rides again. The blue sky that had been overhead just a few minutes ago began to change, like a storm rolling in, but there were no sounds of distant thunder. Bill turned the corner and ran headlong into Tom Starling, almost knocking them both over.

"Hey Bill," he said as he stepped back, regaining his balance, then reached out to help steady Bill.

Bill felt Tom's grip on his arm and immediately, he had flashbacks to the man in the coveralls yesterday that he put the wristband on. The feeling was familiar but nowhere near as strong. It was there, like white noise in tactile form. His hand also felt cool against Bill's arm. Bill jerked back and looked at Tom.

"Sorry about that. Didn't see you," Bill said quickly.

"It's okay, boss. Many people here. It happens."

Bill noticed that Tom's lip was smooth. Any indication of a cleft lip was no longer visible. It was so strange to see it gone after so many years of it being there. It was like a man who always wore a mustache or beard suddenly showing up clean-shaven. They looked like themselves, yet they didn't. Tom was no different in that regard.

"What happened to your lip?" Bill blurted out, immediately regretting because it had always been a sore subject for Tom. He likened it to an extremely tall or short guy who gets tired of and a little touchy about all height jokes. This time, though, it didn't faze Tom in the slightest.

His hands went to his lips slowly and brushed his fingers across his mouth. "What do you mean?"

"Your lip. Your scar is gone."

Tom looked at Bill intensely with eyes searching for something, then a twinkle appeared, as if let in on a joke. "Oh, you had me going there for a second. Something on my lip..." he said as he smiled.

That's when Bill knew that this version of Tom had no recollection of ever having a cleft lip. Immediately, Bill struck his staff three times to power up the vacuum-barrier. When he did, he saw the illusion over Tom's lip shimmer. Bill could barely see that the scar was still there, and it wasn't as deep or noticeable as it was before—like something between the old version of Tom and the illusion that now replaced it were connecting and becoming one.

Of course, just like what happened with Stan and Louise, Tom stepped back and brought his hands to his ears. "Wow! That's loud, boss."

"I'm sorry," Bill said and let the bubble fade away.

"Where is Jason? Have you seen him?"

"He was near the spook ride just a couple of minutes ago. He was covering for Clay."

"Okay, thanks. I will catch up with you later, and Tom?"

"Yeah?"

"Be careful. Not everything is as it seems."

"Yeah, but it is what everyone wants."

Bill was mid-step in walking away but stopped short to look back at Tom, but he had already moved away and wasn't looking back. Bill wasn't sure he had heard correctly, but perhaps that was the truth. Did he consciously reply, or was it a subconscious thought that made it through? Like, instead of responding "take care" as a platitude to "see you later," the subconscious could step in and let something entirely different slip through. Tom might not even be aware of what he said. The thought gave Bill even more shivers, which was hard to do because this whole week had been one event after another that gave him the heebie-jeebies.

He wanted to follow up with Tom regarding the statement, but realized that he needed to find his son. The clouds in the sky were darkening by the second. There was no doubt that this spot was a spot for extremes.

He hurried along the corridor and made the turn, which brought him out near the entrance to the spook house. Tom was right. Jason was standing at the entrance with a long line of bell- bottom-clad people, all waiting their turn. Jason looked the same as he had the night before, except that his clothes looked...fresh? No, that wasn't it. New—they looked brand new and expensive. The shoes he wore, alone, were worth a couple hundred bucks. He remembered Jason had asked for that particular pair last Christmas and Bill hated to let him down, but there just wasn't enough money to get them. He also had on a brand-new baseball cap that didn't look cheap, either.

"Hey, Jason," Bill said as he came up to his side.

Jason quickly looked up and at his father, "Oh hey, Dad. You surprised me. I wasn't expecting to see you."

"Well, you know me. I like to be surprising," Bill replied.

"How are things here?" Bill asked. In the back of his mind, all he really wanted to do was grab Jason, pick him up like he was five years old, and carry him to safety, but Jason wasn't five years old anymore. He also weighed more too, and Bill didn't want to cause a scene, so he kept the conversation light.

"About the same as always," Jason replied.

"Nice shoes," Bill said.

"Yeah, they are really nice. I really appreciate you getting them for me," Jason replied.

"Right...Well, Jason. Do you know I love you?"

"Yes, Dad. Of course."

"Do you trust me?"

"Yes."

"I need you to come with me."

"Where?" Jason asked.

"We need to go meet up with the rest of the family."

"But Dad, I told Clay that I would hang out here 'til he got back. He's taking a lunch break."

"It's okay. We'll lock the gate here, and I'm sure he won't mind."

"But what about the people waiting to get in?" Jason asked.

"They'll either wait or they'll will hop the gate to go in."

"Dad, you've never acted this way when it came to our rides. What's going on?"

"I need you to trust me and just come with me."

Jason looked deep in thought, at the crowd before them, at the ground near his feet, then at his dad. "Okay, Dad. I'll follow you."

Bill didn't bother with locking the gate like he had told his son. It didn't matter and Jason didn't seem to notice, anyway. Bill thumped the staff as they walked, to which Jason initially put his hands over his ears, but only for the first few thumps.

"Are you okay?" Bill asked.

"Yes, my ears hurt there for a second. It was only for a sec, but they're fine now," Jason replied.

"Weird," Bill heard Jason say.

"What's weird?"

"My shoes. They aren't the same anymore," he replied.

And indeed, the nice shoes that had been there the moment before they started were gone, replaced by the well-worn shoes he had been wearing the night before. Jason shook his head as if awaking from a deep sleep, then he squinted, as it hit him. "You didn't buy me those shoes, did you?"

"No, son. I didn't. We couldn't afford them."

"But I remember...but it's slipping away, like a dream when I wake up. Dad? What's going on?" Jason asked.

"I'm not sure, son, but this town isn't what it seems, and I think we need to be careful."

Jason didn't say anything, which didn't really surprise Bill, since his son's mind had just been dumped into the vast sea of the unknown...with so many questions and concerns to chew on. And unfortunately, Bill couldn't do a darn thing to ease his mind or answer any of the questions. In times like these, it was best to stay busy.

"Come on, son, this was why I needed you to trust me. We need to get to your sister, your mom, and anyone else we can, and leave," Bill said.

Jason nodded his head and followed, keeping his mouth shut. They turned a corner and Bill saw something in his peripheral vision, down the alley. He stopped and did a double take. It was Peter, but he wasn't moving. He was on the ground and there were several of the townspeople standing around, transfixed. They had their arms down at their sides with their palms facing forward toward Peter.

Their mouths were agape and on their faces was a look of ecstasy. Whatever was going on, it didn't look good. He quickly grabbed his son and maneuvered them closer to get a look. As they got closer, Bill was astounded. Peter was on the ground, and he wasn't going to get up. From the looks of it, he was dead; he had a makeshift tourniquet around his upper arm, with a needle buried in it. It seemed that Peter had gotten exactly what he wanted...just like Tom Starling had said...but accidentally took too much. At any rate, he had been there a while—maybe a few hours. He appeared stiff, his skin was a greyish hue, and his eyes looked blank and cloudy. Bill immediately wanted to approach them and interrupt whatever the townspeople were doing, but he had Jason with him and didn't know what would happen.

"Dad, is that..."

"Let's go, son. We can't do anything for him right now."

"But, Dad," Jason protested.

"I know, but we can't stop. We have to go find your mom and sister."

Bill continued to thump the staff, and the surrounding crowds shied away from them as they moved, only to form again behind them. Bill wasn't sure, but he thought the crowds were worse now, almost as if they were at a general admission concert of a well-known and well-loved band. Perhaps Donovan's Delights was the band, and this was their final, goodbye tour.

They continued on, but Bill sensed something familiar and dark behind him. He glanced back and didn't see anything, but he knew there was something out there and it was coming. The clouds overhead were darkening and now there were rumbles of thunder, but Bill didn't see any of the usual lightning that came with thunder.

"We need to hurry. We don't want to get wet," Bill said, but really, he only said that for Jason's sake. He wanted to move more quickly because the darkness he felt seemed to be closing in on them.

They moved with a swiftness, and the crowds continued to part for them. When they made the last turn past the Ferris wheel and into the back lot where the HQ trailer was located, the darkness had caught up and he heard it speak.

"Where are you going, Mr. Donovan?"

Bill turned around and saw Mr. Bright, the mayor...or whatever he was...behind them. "Your people are doing good; they like it here. Why don't you stay and enjoy it with them?"

"Son, get inside now," Bill said quickly to Jason. "I need to speak to him."

"Okay, Dad," and Jason quickly went up the stairs and into the HQ trailer, out of sight. Bill then squared up and stood in front of Mr. Bright. The only thing that separated them was about 20 feet. The confrontation felt like an old western showdown. All they needed now was a clock tower to ring the bell at noon, then the show would begin.

That's when Bill heard a bell ring, off in the distance near the center of town. Probably the one he saw on the way in.

"Nicely done," Bill said, referring to the timeliness of the bell.

Mr. Bright's smile grew wider. "Yes, it was a nice touch, wasn't it? You can have anything you want here, Mr. Donovan. As you can see, whatever you desire can be yours."

Tempting, but there was always a catch. Bill had been in show business a long time, and nothing was ever free. Like a thistle or a rose bush with pretty flowers—Looks nice, but when you wrap your hand around it, it will hurt you. This place was no different.

"It would be a lot easier if you cooperate, Mr. Donovan. You can't leave."

Bill gripped the staff harder. His knuckles became bone-white from the strain. He was scared. It was like that song from the 70s about checking into a hotel but not being able to leave. As the fear soaked through him, he held on for dear life. He could feel his knees and hands quiver, his stomach clench, and in the back of his throat, a metallic taste crept up into his mouth. He felt like he was going to vomit, but he kept holding on.

"It will also be a lot easier for your people," Mr. Bright said.

Bill was just about to teeter over the edge and lose it, but then those words...those simple words from Mr. Bright changed everything for Bill. It was one thing to make veiled threats against him, but threatening his people? His family? The nauseous feeling that, just a moment ago, had encompassed his entire stomach, became something else altogether. It shrunk down to the size of a grape, but was hard and on fire. He could feel the heat and it warmed him. Whatever cold fear he had been experiencing was replaced with a burning anger. He could feel the resurgence of strength to his legs and his hands. "Yeah," Bill thought to himself, "I may not be able to leave, but I'll be sure to make it hurt for you on my way down."

Mr. Bright's smile lingered a moment and then, for the first time since Bill had met him, his sugary-sweet smile became something of a grimace. There was no humor, nor any façade of congeniality left in that smile, but the sentiment behind it finally reached his eyes.

"Fine, have it your way, then," Mr. Bright contemptuously replied.

And that's when the real terror began.

21

The anger that built into Bill's soul needed escape, so Bill focused on allowing that anger to flow into the staff. He raised the staff high and drove it into the ground one more time. The sound of the thump exploded around him and created a shockwave that flowed out from him, passing by Mr. Bright. As the shockwave reached him, any pretense of kindness or gentleness was gone, but there was more beyond that mask that Bill couldn't see. It was an ancient evil. A trickster. Something that devoured souls. An ability to see its face fully would invite madness. Bill was thankful for the veil that remained to obscure its true form. It had faded just enough to peek through, but it remained somewhat transparent, like watching something through a steamed up glass shower door.

The storm had arrived, and lightning began to strike all around the midway, first hitting the Ferris wheel, then other rides and booths. Sometimes it struck its target directly and other times, it would strike and bounce from structure to structure in a daisy chain of electrical activity.

Sometimes, multiple strikes would occur at once and connect, much like neurons communicating via synapses. The sounds of the midway ceased and were replaced by screams in the distance. Bill didn't know whose screams they were, but had a nagging, gut feeling that those who were "living their dreams" had experienced a rude awakening to what was and wasn't real.

Mr. Bright didn't step closer. He stood there with his eyes transfixed. This was the only time that Bill could see any kind of emotion reach his eyes. That emotion was hatred. "All you had to do was say 'yes' and we would have given you what you wanted...for a time."

"But it ends in death, doesn't it?" Bill spat back.

"Everything dies eventually, but here, you can become part of me and live forever."

In the back of Bill's mind, a quick flash of understanding struck. All those customers, all the townspeople, were real people that had come here before, but they were no longer themselves. They were now extensions of whatever Mr. Bright was, but they were no longer living, breathing humans.

"That ain't living and I'm no one's source for energy," Bill replied. He didn't know why he said that, but it felt right after he heard the words flow from his mind.

This evil had been tricking people to do its bidding for years, surviving off the energy, both good and bad, of what it did to people. Extreme happiness and extreme sorrow...it didn't matter. They were all forms of sustenance for whatever Mr. Bright was.

Mr. Bright raised his right hand to the side and snapped his fingers, which made an abnormally loud sound. A moment later, the crowd flowed into the back lot, surrounding them. Bill was heartbroken because he could see Jimmy, along with Stan, Louise, the Thompsons, and others among the crowd. Their forms were there, but they were no longer themselves. Whatever they had been was now replaced with a shell. Most surprisingly, he noticed Peter in the crowd, but Bill knew he had died. He had seen his body.

As if he could read Bill's mind, Mr. Bright said, "Yes, he did, but now he is alive and a part of us. You can still be a part of us, too."

"I will never be a part of this, and I will never be a part of you," Bill said again, striking the staff again. This time, instead of the soft blue bubble, what emanated from the staff was a solid line of blue that exploded from the ground and flew forward, toward Mr. Bright. Before it hit him, Mr. Bright snapped his fingers, and he disappeared in a puff of smoke. The line of blue shot through the smoke and into the crowd, knocking back several figures onto the ground, but they got back up and they all began to slowly close in. Bill turned and ran up the stairs into the HQ trailer.

He burst into the room and shut the door behind him. Everyone was there—Kathy, Jason, Dani, and thankfully

Laura was there too. She looked like the Laura he knew; she no longer appeared to be an older teenager. He would have to find out later how that had happened, but right now, he had to figure out how to keep them all alive.

The rumbles of thunder and the wind intensified even more. There was the kind of lightning that temporarily blinded you. By this time, the generator that kept the lights and air conditioning running had stopped. The gusts buffeted the trailer and caused it to rock.

"What's going on, Daddy?" Laura cried out.

Dani went over to the table and put her arms around her daughter, holding her tight. Jason was standing near the table and Kathy, who looked relieved at seeing Bill, sat on the other side of the table.

"It's going to be okay," Bill said, hoping that he wasn't lying. Even in the midst of all the strange, terrifying events, seeing his little girl whole again gave him such elation. A sense of normalcy that, even in the dark void of the unknown, was a bright light that brought relief and comfort. He was grateful that at least on one front, things were back where they should be.

"Bill, is everyone okay? I saw Brad, but he didn't look himself. He looked...different," Dani said. "And about this morning—I can barely remember what happened last night. I know that what happened this morning and what should have happened are two different things."

"There's a lot of that going around," Bill muttered to himself, but then louder in response to his wife's question,

"I don't know, honey. I honestly don't know how everyone is. Everyone is caught up in their own thing. Their wellbeing depends on whether they accepted what Mr. Bright offered or not. And even that I can't explain very well. The only thing I know for sure is that we are okay." With the words "for now," silently sweeping through his mind.

Bill went to one of the windows and looked out. The crowd outside showed no signs of slowing down, but they weren't hurrying either. They had all the time in the world as they thronged forward.

Bill's mind raced. "Dad, if you are out there listening, I could sure use some help," he thought to himself.

"What was that?" Jason asked.

Bill turned and looked at his son, surprised. He just then realized that he had spoken that last bit out loud, but no more than a whisper, if anything more than just mouthing the words.

"Oh, it's nothing Jason. I was just talking to myself."

"Kathy, did you have any trouble getting to the trailer?"

"No, I didn't. I think that crystal ball of mine kind of made them disappear. And I've had a moment to think about it, too. It was like there were two worlds that were connected; if I concentrated on that, I moved freely. It really was as if what I saw in the ball was reality. I don't think they were actually there in physical form," Kathy said.

"Well, we may need that trick again. The crowds outside are closing in and we need to get to a truck or something and try to get out of here," Bill replied.

Kathy nodded her head in understanding.

Bill then turned to everyone else. "Okay, everyone, grab what you need. I don't think we will be coming back anytime soon. We are going to try to make it to our truck and drive out."

Those that sat at the table scooted their chairs back, making slight sliding noises as the chairs glided across the floor. After they stood up, they rounded the table to prepare to leave.

Since they were all in close proximity, Bill wanted to take advantage of the moment. He put his arms around his family and held them close and for a moment. "Once we go through those doors, I want us all to stay close to one another. I don't know what dangers are there, but I know it won't be safe. I just want you all to know one thing...I love you. You all make my life complete, like nothing else does. I just want you to know that before we head out."

He popped his head up and looked at all of them. There was a warmth of love and belonging. It felt real and it felt good. He noticed Kathy wasn't in the hug. She hung back, watching them.

"Kathy—you too. Get over here," Bill said, holding back tears. He was scared, but this was the most important thing he felt he could have done during this moment. No matter what happened here in a few minutes, he didn't want this group to not know how he felt about them. Kathy came into the circle, and they all shared another bear hug before separating and gathering their belongings.

They were about to leave, so Bill decided to look out the window once more. The crowd was now surrounding the trailer. They all could hear whispers coming in, along with the rumble of thunder and claps of lightning. It was a cacophony of "join us," "stay with us," "stay here," coming through the walls. The wind no longer rocked the trailer, but it rocked just the same. Now, the rocking was a result of the figures outside. What saddened Bill even more is that he caught a glimpse of both Brad and George, and they were no longer themselves. George was now a young man with no hint of a paunch, and Brad now displayed muscles like a bulldog. It was reminiscent of Bill's memories of Brad when he was a kid, except Brad's face didn't appear younger. He looked like a 60-year-old with the muscles and fitness level of a 20-year-old athlete. They weren't the only ones that Bill saw; everyone was there outside. Bill didn't know what they all had traded their souls to the town for, but they certainly were no longer themselves. Their eyes had a glazed, almost rabid quality to them. There was no thought behind them.

Bill wasn't sure what to do. The door was locked, but he knew it wouldn't hold them for long. The plan was for his group to leave anyway, but now he had hesitations. They couldn't wait, but they couldn't very well leave, either. That was, until lightning struck the RV and made the final choice for them, to get a move on. The sound of the lightning strike was deafening and everything immediately became dark. Although it was no more than a few moments, time seemed to have stretched, then came smacking back to real time. Bill saw smoke billowing from around the closed door that led to the back room of the RV, where the lightning must have struck. The smoke moved quickly and filled the room, creeping along the ceiling. A moment later, flames were trying to escape from under the door. It wouldn't be long before everything became engulfed in an inferno.

"I guess we can't stay here," Bill yelled. He had to with the thunder, the whispers, and now the crackling of flames.

"Daddy, I'm scared," Laura yelled, and looked on the verge of tears.

"I am too," he replied, "But we will get through it."

Bill then remembered Kathy's crystal ball and hoped that whatever she did the first time she pulled it out would work again. "Kathy, I need you to go first...but slowly, so we can stay within your sphere of protection."

"Okay, but where are we going?" she replied.

"We'll head to our truck and go from there," he yelled back.

Dani grabbed both of the kids and put her arms around them, then moved closely behind Kathy. Bill brought up the rear. Kathy looked back at Bill one more time for approval, or assurance, or maybe both. When Bill nodded back, she nodded and didn't hesitate to open the exterior door.

Bill had never seen so many people in one place; it seemed like the population of the entire state of Illinois was standing outside. There was no telling how many souls had been tricked by this entity throughout its many years of existence. In the back of his mind, Bill was a little worried that maybe Kathy's crystal ball might not work, but it wasn't up to him whether it would or wouldn't—it was up to her and her faith in it. Luckily, it came through again. The crowds moved back from her as if they weren't there. But as soon as she passed, the crowd began closing in again, behind her. The sphere it created around her was small and barely encapsulated Kathy, Dani, and the kids. There wasn't enough room for Bill, so he began thumping his staff, which created a smaller, shorter-lasting protective sphere around him with each strike on the ground. It was slow going, however. When they were about 20 feet away, Bill looked back at the trailer. It had become fully engulfed in a matter of seconds. In the shuffle, he couldn't get a good look, but as he glanced back over the midway, he could see plumes of smoke in the distance, presumably from random booths and tents that had been struck by lightning. The only structure that Bill could clearly see burning was the Ferris wheel. It looked strange and out of place as the flames licked along the spokes of the wheel and enveloped each cabin like multiple small bonfires. The wind was heavy but didn't seem to have any effect on the smoke. The large black pillar lifted into the heavens until it seemed to become one with the dark and stormy roiling sea of clouds overhead. Bill almost felt as if he was in an enormous cave with columns of rock that connected with stalactites above, except it was all moving in turbulent waves of air.

They moved about 10 more feet when Jason strayed too far to the side of Kathy's protective sphere and his arm became momentarily unprotected. One of the towns-people lunged and seized his arm to pull him out. Jason screamed and Dani grabbed on to him. The commotion caused Kathy to briefly lose focus as she took her eyes off the crystal ball in her hands. Bill could see the sphere waiver around the small group. It was on the verge of collapsing and winking out, leaving them all vulnerable. Bill's heart leapt into his throat. His sphere remained, but it was barely large enough for him and he needed the freedom of move-ment to repeatedly strike the staff in order to maintain his area of protection. He could see all the townspeople around them. They all looked hungry, their eyes blazing in anger and focus. They only had one goal, and that goal was to stop them, no matter how. The figure that grabbed Ja-son yanked and pulled him completely out of Dani's grasp and out of the protection of the sphere. She screamed and poor little Laura was so scared, she was sobbing in fright. Jason was thrown to the ground and the crowd collapsed on him, similar to what you see in a zombie movie, where they all move in to feed.

Bill's anger surged in him again. There was no doubt he was afraid, but if there was a guage to measure his emotional state, he would have been redlining it. He lifted his staff like he had with Mr. Bright and brought it down before him, slashing it diagonally through the air and striking the ground with force. What was produced was like a blade of blue light that traveled in the direction he struck. Every one of the townspeople that the light reached flew backward through the air. It cleared the area to some extent, but Jason still had people surrounding him. Bill struck again, sending out another flashing blade, which resulted in more figures being thrown into the air. He rushed forward and now that Jason was clear of the figures around him, Bill quickly bent down, grabbing him and bringing him to his feet.

"Are you okay?" Bill yelled into his ear. It was still so loud that any communication could only be made by shouting.

Jason nodded, though he held his arm where he had been grabbed. Bill noticed it was bright red, as if he had been burned. Bill's anger exploded, and he brought his staff down several more times, taking it out on the figures around him. Even the figure that had been George was thrown back violently.

Bill pushed Jason back into the sphere with Kathy, Dani, and Laura. Kathy had quickly regained her focus, and the sphere had reappeared in full force.

"Quickly, while we have the time, let's go!" Bill yelled.

So, that's what they did. They took off running. The crowd was still heavy, but Bill's blades of blue lightning cleared out the area for the moment, though the figures would fill the space again shortly.

They ran to the side of the truck and, damn it, it was locked. Bill dug into the pockets of his blue jeans and brought out his keys. The crowd was closer now...and closing in. His hands trembling, he fumbled to find the correct key, then with trying to get it into the lock. He wasn't sure how, but he finally rammed the key home and turned, unlocking the door. He flung the door open and unlocked the back door. They all piled into the back seat, Dani moving to the front passenger side between the front two seats. Once in, Bill slammed the back door, making sure it was clear, then jumped into the driver's seat, just in time. As he reached to close his door, one of the town figures grabbed it. Bill almost lost the fight to pull the door closed, but using all the strength he could muster, he forcefully reversed the direction to push the door outward, flinging the man off his feet and causing him to lose his grip. Bill quickly closed the door, locking it. The crowd had reached them and surrounded the truck. They were beating on the doors and windows. Some had even climbed into the bed of the truck and were beating on the back window. All the while, they never slowed or stopped with their constant requests to "stay with us." It was all so surreal and even after everything they had been through, Bill still couldn't believe any of it was really happening.

But it was. It was as real as flesh and blood. As crazy it was, he knew not to underestimate it or slow down for even a second, imagining that it wasn't real.

Bill fumbled with the key again and stuck it into the ignition. The back and side windows were staring to crack under the incessant strikes. The rain poured and along with the smacks of palms and fists against the windows, the sound of the splatter from each large drop intermingled with the pounding. He turned the key and the vehicle chugged but didn't turn over. He tried again and it revved, but it didn't kick, much like a joke that had a sub-par punch line. It was very underwhelming to the point of being overwhelming, adding in their current situation to the equation.

Figures jumped on the hood and pounded on the windshield. Bill was at his wit's end. If this vehicle didn't start, then that would be it for the Donovan family. The windshield cracked. It wouldn't be long before they would all be within arm's length to be dragged out of the truck. Bill's mind raced. He figured he could get out and throw blades of lightning about, but how long could he realistically do that? One hour? Two hours at the most? If it came down to it, he would go the distance until he couldn't lift that damn staff any longer, but he hoped it wouldn't come to that.

"Please, please, please start," Bill prayed aloud and tried one more time.

Rrrr...rrr...roar! The engine kicked over like a lion's roar, and it was music to Bill's ears. He would have kissed the dashboard with relief had he had time for it, but he stepped on the gas and the truck lurched forward. The bodies, real or not while looking through the crystal ball, were real enough to make it difficult for the truck to break through. Although the truck was moving, there were so many bodies in the way that it was barely crawling. The wheels were spinning and since it was pouring so hard, the ground had already turned to slippery mud, which only added to the slow gain of the truck's momentum. Eventually, the rubber caught traction on hard ground and bolted forward through the crowd.

Half of Bill felt sick with the craze of thinking "what if these are real people?" but the other half was relieved to finally be moving and he just didn't care. They had to get out of there. He hadn't asked for them to get in his way. They chose to be there. He hadn't. He could feel the "bump" when the wheels rolled over people. He could feel the "snap" and tearing of bones as the truck moved forward, creating a chaotic swatch of mangled body parts in the truck's wake. The truck picked up speed, and the crowd thinned. Once he broke through and could more clearly see what was in front of him, he saw that there were even more of the townspeople on the road where the exit had been, so he turned and drove onto the midway, figures chasing him. He looked in the rearview mirror and saw that there were people still in the truck's bed, so

Bill swerved hard to the right, then to the left, knocking them off balance. Over the side they toppled. Before long, they were free from the encumbrance of the townspeople. Flooring the gas pedal, the truck jumped forward like a hiccup, then flew forward like a fireball as it picked up more speed.

As he approached the end of the midway, he realized that another large cluster of townspeople was ahead. He knew that if he drove straight into the crowd, he would only be able to go about 20 or 30 feet before losing momentum and stopping. He checked the rearview again and saw that the crowd they had just left were now approaching from behind.

The insane whispers were still audible and wouldn't stop. "Join us, join us, join us," as if it was a slow, broken record that just wouldn't quit. He didn't have much of a choice, so he decided, "to Hell with it. I'll drive straight ahead and take out as many as possible." However, when he straightened his wheels for the final straightaway dash and began to accelerate, he heard a loud "pop" and the steering wheel wobbled. Evidently, his front right tire had blown and Bill struggled to regain control of the truck. It swerved to the right and then to the left as he tried to correct it. Unfortunately, Bill overcorrected the first couple of times and just when he felt he had regained control, they crashed into the ticket booth at the entrance of the midway. They jolted to a stop. The truck's right side was buried in what remained of the destroyed ticket booth.

"Everyone okay?" Bill yelled.

"Yeah!" he heard from the back.

"Okay, we need to get out of here and head to the left."

And without waiting for a response, Bill opened the door and promptly fell to the ground. The adrenaline that pumped through his veins caused his coordination to go out the window; his legs were already wobbly to begin with. The others piled out after him, and Dani bent down to pick him up.

Bill kissed her quickly and looked her straight in the eye. "I love you. Don't you forget it...ever."

He then turned and held the staff in front of him. "Stay behind me!" he yelled.

The small group huddled behind him, and Kathy brought her crystal ball to the front to add to the defense. The crowd that had previously been running toward them slowed down to a walk. It was apparent that their prey wasn't going anywhere. Bill was miserable. The rain hadn't let up. They were all thoroughly soaked through, which only added to the gloom and despair of the situation at hand.

Bill hurriedly smacked the staff on the ground in front of him in a way that produced the blade of lightning to flow away from him and into the slowly approaching crowd. Had he been anywhere else, he would have remarked on how amazing the whole thing was that he could even do such a thing, but this wasn't the time. He held on to that ability like a drowning man holding on to a piece of driftwood that wasn't strong enough to hold him, but grabbed it anyway, because anything was better than nothing.

The blade of blue tore into the crowd and wherever it struck, the crowd backed away, but then slowly began advancing again. Bill noticed that all the townspeople were now smiling. It was eerie in its similarity to that of Mr. Bright.

Even with the thunder and the crowd's whisper-shouts, Bill heard an undeniable crack and a metal on metal screech that dwarfed everything else. He looked up to see the huge Ferris wheel, which was like a mountain towering over the midway, wobble, slowly shift, then collapse to the ground, sending debris and more smoke and fire into the air. The crash caused the ground to rumble, as if a group of stampeding horses was rushing by. His gaze returned to his immediate surroundings, where the townspeople edged closer. He sent another blue light blade and they again retreated, but only slightly. His protection seemed to be more of an annoyance to them, as it wasn't really stopping them, only delaying them.

Bill was convinced that the crowd was toying with them now. They had no way out and with every blade he sent, the townspeople would fleetingly back up before again filling the void to advance toward his group. He heard Laura crying behind him, as well as Dani's muffled whispers in an attempt to console her. It broke his heart.

"Please..." Bill whispered. Who this was intended for, he wasn't sure, but he inwardly pleaded to the cosmos? God? Jesus? His father? Anybody or anything that was listening.

Mr. Bright appeared in the crowd and walked to the front. With his broadening, sharp-toothed smile, he spoke. "There is no one to help you, Mr. Donovan. You are on your own here."

Bill wanted to say something poignant, or defiant, or at least manage to give a snarky comeback, but the only thing he could muster was a curse word and a snarl. Bill lunged forward and sent another blue blade of light toward Mr. Bright, but before it could strike him, he nonchalantly raised his hand and snapped his fingers, as if waving a fly away or summoning a waiter. It was a gesture that wasn't hurried and displayed complete control, almost lackadaisical. The blade disintegrated and disappeared.

"We've had enough of your games, Mr. Donovan. It is time for you to join us, whether you want to or not. We must feed and you will become one with me and with the town," Mr. Bright said as he gestured to everything around him.

Bill's mind was on the verge of breaking down. He was unable to form words. The only thing left was emotion—fear, along with swift breath and the feeling of his heart pounding a mile a minute. If he was lucky, he would have a heart attack before anything took place but then again, he couldn't bear that thought. Even if he died, his wife and kids, not to mention Kathy, would still have to deal with this.

He felt the pressure to his core, so did the only thing he knew he could do—throw another blade of energy. And again, it faded before it even reached the crowd as they crept closer. He knew that it wouldn't be long before they were within arm's length and Bill could only imagine what would happen then. He looked for possible exits, finding none. He scanned for anything and as he swept from left to right, his eyes came to rest on the 1958 Buick Special.

22

— . —

The Buick gleamed, even in the darkness. Bill didn't understand why he hadn't seen it before. Even with all the rain, wind, fire and smoke, the car was still spotless. He then made a decision.

Yes! That was it! The old car would be their last bastion of defense. If this was going to be the Alamo, then it might as well be in something that had brought him good memories and good luck throughout the years. The crowd had not yet blocked them in completely. They still had time to scurry over to the elevated platform that held the car, but they didn't have long—only a few moments before they would be totally closed off.

Without thought, he turned and grabbed Jason. Dani was holding Laura and he yelled to them all, "Come with me!"

The crowd stopped at the sudden move. Bill stole a glance at Mr. Bright, who appeared more perplexed than perturbed by this anomaly...but one that didn't seem likely to delay the inevitable.

They made a run for it. It was a short distance and as soon as they arrived, Bill helped everyone up onto the platform. With looks of confusion from the group, Bill told them to get into the car, which was met with even more confusion. They all knew that the car hadn't run in years. They cautiously moved on the platform because there was little room left alongside the car. One misstep could easily lead to a three foot fall to the ground.

Jason tried the back door closest to him and it opened with no trouble. He immediately grabbed his sister and dove into the back seat. Kathy followed. Dani shut their door quickly and tried the passenger side front door, which also opened. She quickly got in. Bill remained at the back of the beautiful car, looking at everything surrounding him—his life, his memories, his years of blood, sweat, and tears—all being obliterated before his very eyes. A small voice in the back of his mind spoke up, "A small price to pay for your family." And with that thought, he moved to the driver's side and opened the door. Once inside, he ensured all the doors were locked...not that it would do much good. Eventually, the townspeople would break the windows and pull them out, but he wasn't going to make it easier for them. In some ways, this was Bill's last act of defiance, similar to a man who was losing a fight. He might go down, but he would go down swinging, and continue swinging all the way down, until he couldn't swing anymore.

There was a moment of reprieve in the car, a moment to catch their breath. "What are we going to do now?" Dani asked innocently.

So much for the moment of reprieve, Bill thought to himself. He didn't have an answer to that question. He was exhausted and he was scared. Although he knew he would continue to fight, however that might be, he couldn't help but feel like he just wanted to give up. "Dad, I could really use your help right now," he thought.

He sighed and the words "I don't know" began to form in his mouth. Before they left his lips, something inexplicable happened, but with the week they were having, it was just one more strange thing to occur in a long line of unexplained events. The amber light on the radio dial illuminated and the frequency needle began to move on its own. The staticky sound you hear while searching for a signal sounded lightly from the speakers.

"And welcome back. This is WKHL, playing the greatest, but not the latest. Coming up next is 30 minutes, no interruptions, of oldies you can groove to..."

Bill looked dumbfounded at the radio and then at Dani, whose face mirrored his own. This wasn't possible. Bill had taken the battery out of the car years ago, not to mention that he didn't even have the keys with him...but...the radio was playing. Then the car roared alive; the engine revved and boy, was it strong! The rumble of the muffler shook the back end of the platform, with the engine rattling its front end.

Bill looked out the driver's side window and saw Mr. Bright. He was closer now and though he continued to smile his creepy, unearthly smile, the expression of quiet confidence he had displayed just a moment before, had changed. He looked as if he was seeing something he had never seen before.

Bill looked at everyone else in the car as an idea formed. "It might just work," he thought. "All right everyone...hold on tight! It's going to get bumpy. Kathy, give me your crystal ball!"

Kathy handed it over and he placed it on the dashboard, lodging it between the dash and windshield, directly over the steering wheel. He then stepped on the brake pedal and put the car in gear and for the first time in...well, as far back as he could remember...the car moved. It lurched forward and Bill gunned it, slapping the gas pedal to the floor as fiercely as he could. The ol' gal moved as if she had just come off the assembly line. There was no delay.

"Hold on!" Bill yelled one final time as the car pushed forward and sprang haphazardly off the platform, jarring everyone inside. Thankfully, the wheels caught squarely onto the ground so that the car rolled forward and kept moving. They were free...at least from the platform. They still had thousands of townspeople surrounding them.

Instead of looking directly at the road, Bill focused his gaze on the crystal ball. What he saw was the same as he had seen when Kathy had first brought it out of her tent—there was no sign of the thousands of people crowding around them. It was as if they weren't even there, and strangely enough, as the car raced forward, it met no resistance like his truck had when he slammed into the crowd earlier.

Bill didn't take his eyes off the crystal ball, even for a second, as they seemingly drove through the crowd. They continued to pick up speed and finally met the pavement. Once they hit the black top, the tires dug in more easily and with the increased traction, they were able to gain more momentum. It was evident that they would soon be free and clear of the town crowd.

The storm was still strong, though, and they could feel the wind gusting against the car. They were heading into town now, guided by Bill's memory of the trip into this hellhole just a few short days ago. He was going purely on adrenaline and whim, trusting instinct over thought and letting the car—this beautiful car of his dad's—do the hard work. Their only objective now was to escape without any more casualties.

They shortly found their way back to the two-lane road that brought them to the highway that headed into town and Bill noticed the huge, old oak he had admired a couple of days prior. Just past the tree, the road now seemed to gently turn in on itself into a curve, which would take them back into town. But Bill remembered that there had been a road right beside that tree. Something told him to just go, so, following his gut, that's what he did. He floored it and they were off road again, driving through the dirt and pasture that now occupied the space beside the old tree, going who knows where. The storm had abated to some extent, but fog immediately replaced the rain. It was almost otherworldly; it was just like the fog they had experienced the first night they were open. It was very dense—to the point that he couldn't make out anything beyond the hood of the car. He hoped and prayed that they wouldn't hit any other trees that he couldn't see. The car was moving fast; the speedometer read 65 MPH, though he knew it could move faster. The bumps and grooves of the ground gave way to the crunch of gravel. Bill opened his window to look out. They were now on a gravel roadway.

The fog was still dense, but within a minute of hitting gravel, they came shooting out of the grey shroud and into blinding sunlight. The abrupt change shocked him and caused him to nearly lose control of the car. He fought to maintain control, and as he did, he noticed that the car had lost power and they were now rolling merely due to inertia. This made it easier to regain control, but it wasn't long before they rolled to a complete stop.

Bill was in shock. The silence in the car was deafening as everyone was going through their own astonishment and relief. The crystal ball rolled off the dash and Bill grabbed it with his right hand, then opened the driver's door, shifting the crystal ball into his left hand. He grabbed the staff, got out, and took a couple wobbly steps before going to his knees and vomiting.

When he finished, he looked up to see a wall of fog, not more than 100 feet away. It looked angry; it was seething with different colors—not just grey. Then Bill saw a figure emerge and walk toward him. It was Mr. Bright. Immediately, he got to his feet. It wasn't over yet.

Mr. Bright kept coming closer and when he was about 20 feet away, he said, "Come now...you may think you've escaped, but I'm going to bring you back with me now."

Bill felt a flame ignite in chest, down to the pit of his soul. The anger built and although Mr. Bright was evidently some ancient, powerful being, Bill was determined to win this battle.

"No! You're in my world now!" Bill yelled. He didn't know why he said this, but just like going on instinct with the car and finding the gravel road beyond the tree, it just felt right. So did his next move. He raised his staff like a spear and, using the crystal ball as a scope of sorts, he aimed and threw it with all his might. The staff soared through the air, its color changing from a dull, faded brown to a glowing, pulsating shift through every hue of the spectrum. Bill kept his eyes on the staff through the prism of the crystal ball. Only when the staff struck did Bill direct his gaze at Mr. Bright again.

For the first time since Bill had met him, Mr. Bright's smile morphed into something else entirely—an expression of utter shock and horror. Having impaled him through his chest, the staff came to rest, still embedded in his torso and peeking out of his upper back. Its colors pulsated more rapidly and Bill could see it vibrate in unison with the color changes.

Mr. Bright had clearly been wounded and began to stumble back toward his home, his beloved town, his sanctuary. Bill couldn't allow that to happen, so he took off, sprinting behind him. Once he caught up, he tackled him and took him to the ground. Mr. Bright lunged at him, but there was no power behind the sad attempt to defend himself.

"Let go of me. You have no idea what you've done."

"I don't care! You've put my family and me through Hell and done God knows what with my friends. You will never hurt anyone else again!" Bill shouted in his face.

Mr. Bright stopped struggling, looked at Bill, and cackled. The devious laugh exhibited no humor and chilled Bill to the bone. The laugh continued and melded with the pulsating vibrations of the staff stuck in his chest. What happened next caused Bill to question his sanity and whether this was, in fact, reality. Mr. Bright's face began to crack and disintegrate, like a figure made of ash. Once the process began, it was only a matter of seconds before his entire body had crumbled and was scattered to the wind.

Almost in disbelief over what had just taken place before his eyes, Bill slowly rocked back and sat cross-legged on the ground. The staff remained, and it had returned to its previous dull brown hue; it no longer pulsated and looked to be a run-of-the-mill walking stick. If Bill hadn't seen and experienced this whole turn of events, he wouldn't have believed it. He looked up at the foggy wall of angry, swirling colors and that, too, disappeared, but not in the typical fashion that fog or smoke dissipates. This was more like it quickly phased out; it was there, then it was suddenly gone.

Bill sat there silently in a state of shock for a time. He felt a hand on his shoulder and looked up to see that it was Dani. She knelt down and sat beside him.

She was so beautiful to him.

"I knew you were going to take care of us," she said.

"That's a lie, but I appreciate it. I honestly didn't think we were going to make it," he replied.

A silence followed as both wrestled with the emotions that came with survival... it teetered on the edge of a sharp blade, between the engulfing sorrow of the loss of everything and the joy of living...surviving. They were the kind of thoughts that made a mind numb and fuzzy. But as with all things, life does go on—at least for those who survive, that is.

Breaking the silence. Dani spoke, "What do you want to do now?"

Bill thought about it. He'd been in the traveling show business for most of his life and had a lot of money tied up in it, as well as its resultant debt. He wanted to continue to dwell about all the ones—his carnival family—that didn't make it...but he couldn't focus on that now. That mourning would take place later, along with serious contemplation about what they really were going to do next.

They certainly couldn't file an insurance claim for, well, everything that had been destroyed. No one would believe them, so it wasn't like they could tell anyone without ending up in an asylum.

He looked at his wife and a feeling of comfort washed over him. In that moment, he knew they were going to be okay, even with the recurring nightmares that were sure to come. "I'm not sure, but I don't think I want to do a traveling show anymore," Bill finally said. "These towns are creepy."

ABOUT THE AUTHOR

J.E. Jack can be found reading everything from historical textbooks to young adult mystery/thrillers. Developing a love for adventure and self-learning early in life, Joshua has traveled the world and been fortunate enough to survive. With almost two decades of involvement in the military/law enforcement community, he tries to bring different experiences, emotions, and thoughts to his readers. "Something Wicked Waits" is his fourth novel, and he is now working on the next writing project. He currently lives near the coast of Louisiana with his family.

If you enjoyed the book and want see future books by this author, be sure to join us on Facebook by clicking on

the name and liking the page to follow along at www.fac
ebook.com/AuthorJEJack/

Additional works may be found at amazon.com/auth
or/jejack

Or join the newsletter list to get notified of new releases
and other news immediately by www.subscribepage.com
/authorjejack

Or send an email to authorjejack@gmail.com.

ALSO BY J.E. JACK

Them Bones: Some Memories will haunt you.

Nothing ever happens in the little village of Pittsburg, that is, until it does. For fourteen-year-old Joe Anderson, that was the case during the summer of 1992. The events that unfolded following a childhood game of hide and go seek in the woods changed the face of a small town and left a mark that was forever etched into the recesses of a boy's heart and mind. It was a summer of adventure, friendship, murder, first love, and pain. Them Bones is a coming-of-age, murder mystery novel set in a small, rural village with secrets of its own.

The Hermit: Things Aren't Always What They Seem

It's the last day of the school year in 1994 and for fifteen-year-old Chris, it's going to be another boring summer of staying at his aunt's farm in southern Illinois. At least, that's what he thought until he, along with his brother Brian and cousin Sam, meets the hermit. What follows is a summer of intrigue, suspicion, and fear that has lasting consequences. One thing is for certain though—things aren't always what they seem.

Grave Disturbance: Every City Has Secrets That Should Remain Buried

Detective Robinson is only trying to help his fellow detective by taking her duty weekend, something he had done many times before, and for the most part, had always been routine. That is, until this weekend. What starts off as a normal call for vandalism in a cemetery quickly turns into

something much darker and deadly. As Robinson uncovers secrets from the past, will he be able to stop the threat before something more sinister happens? One thing is for certain, these secrets were better left buried.

"Grave Disturbance," is J.E. Jack's third novel and is a supernatural thriller set in the small coastal city of Pensacola, Florida.

Made in the USA
Monee, IL
21 May 2024

58749926R10204